CONTAINED

A CASEY CORT LEGAL THRILLER

AIME AUSTIN

AIME AUSTIN
www.AimeAustin.com

LOS ANGELES, CALIFORNIA

ALSO BY AIME AUSTIN

Judged

Ransomed

Caged

Disgraced

Unarmed

Kidnapped

Reunited

Poisoned

Abused

CONTAINED

A CASEY CORT LEGAL THRILLER

AIME AUSTIN

Contained
Aime Austin

This edition published by
Moore Digital Media Inc.
1125 N Fairfax Avenue
Unit 46071
West Hollywood, CA 90046
www.*aimeaustin*.com

Cover Designer: Wicked Good Book Covers
Cover Images © Depositphotos, Shutterstock

Contained/Aime Austin. — 2d ed.

*For whosoever shall keep the whole law, and yet
offend in one point, he is guilty of all."*

—James 2:10

1

"What are you doing here?"

That question had come from Neil Walsh, an old-timer narcotics detective. Every year, I expected him to be on the list of those taking retirement. Hadn't happened so far. I think he was a lifer. Actually loved the job even after the "War on Drugs" had proved to be a huge failure.

"I didn't think anyone with the last name Brody worked between Thanksgiving and New Year's," he said.

I was one of a handful of prosecutors who didn't get shit from the cops. My father the presiding judge and my uncle the attorney general had assured a level of deference that I'd be lying if I said I didn't enjoy.

"I could ask you the same," I said. "Some kind of drug killing keeping you at work this close to the holidays? You have the kind of seniority that would get you all of December off."

My last name had gotten me up to major crimes on the fast track. My perfect win rate was keeping me there. I stayed away from drugs and vice. There was no satisfaction in prosecuting crimes where it was like a beaver damning a river—unsuccessfully.

"Not exactly," he said.

Without invitation, he pulled a chair from the empty desk in my office. Except for the prosecuting attorney Lorraine Pope, the rest of us had to share offices. I'd never had an office mate, but the other desk and chairs remained no matter how many requests I put in to maintenance.

It was one of those that Walsh lifted up to move next to instead of across from me and sat a little too close for comfort. What was it about cops and boundaries? They got in suspects' faces for a reason but didn't really pull back for anyone else. Intimidation was the name of the game. I'd learned that leaning back lost me respect points, so I leaned in instead.

"Not exactly?" I parroted back. I wasn't easily intimidated. I could hold my own with these guys. My father and uncle had hardened me early.

"Look. You remember the Container Case?"

I spread my hands wide on the desk. Shifted in my seat. Who didn't remember that case? It was the biggest unsolved crime in Cleveland in the last handful of years.

"The feds took on that one and lost big time." I released my right hand which was gripping my blotter like it was a sponge in need of wringing out. My ex-fiancé's other fiancé had tanked that case single-handedly. I didn't ever like the idea of criminals getting away, but there was a little stab of pleasure in the fact that Casey's new guy had blown that one to smithereens without so much as a single conviction. I'd have nailed the guy to the cross.

"Here's a gift," he said. He rooted around in a beat-up black satchel at his side, then tossed a cell phone sealed in an evidence bag onto my desk. "Picked it up in a drug bust. Computer geeks finally got around cracking this one open. More interesting than your standard burner."

This time when I leaned in, it wasn't a ploy for false communion. He'd suckered me in like he'd probably planned before he'd even walked out of the elevator's ninth floor exit.

"How so?" I asked. The Trojan Horse had been a gift. I was wary of all offerings.

"There were only about twenty calls on the phone. A bunch in the last month from this phone from a guy we call the Iceman."

"Meth?"

"None other. That won't interest you. Meth lab busts are a dime a dozen. Half the stupid fuckers blow themselves up before we get to them anyway. Gotta love the irony of cookers killing themselves before they can collect the profits. Half the cases close themselves."

"The phone?" I asked, pulling him back. I'd heard that Walsh could hold down a bar stool for hours spinning out stories about his time on the job. Things were slow during the holidays, but I still didn't have the time for a yarn.

"Right. There were three calls from two years ago. November 2004. A call to a known Toledo drug dealer. The second was to the Iceman. He didn't have a burner then but a regular cell. So we know that someone else was in business with him. The first call on the phone—that's where the gold is."

And Neil Walsh was going to make me dig for it. I leaned back in my chair. Took a deep breath. First, I steepled my fingers then folded them together, interlacing them like I was a compliant child sitting at a Catholic school desk. Maybe I had a little bit of time to wield a metaphorical pick-axe.

"Who called who?"

"I'm no genius, but I'm sure one of those words should be whom?"

"Whom was called?" I threw out, though that sounded wrong to my own ears.

"Country code was twenty," he offered.

"I'm not a telephone operator," I replied. "Only code I know by heart is 353."

"Ireland." Walsh nodded in confirmation. I'm sure he'd dialed those international digits to his family back in the homeland same as I did. "Twenty is Egypt," he supplied.

I wracked my brain. Came up empty. Asked the question. "Should I know someone from Egypt?"

"In September or October two years ago, this all-points went out for a girl. She'd disappeared from her brother's home in Richmond Heights."

I plumbed my brain again, but not much came up. Sadly, missing children weren't as rare as people might expect.

"How old was she?"

"Sixteen."

"Was she legal?" I asked. America may be the land of huddled masses and all that, but I didn't think the quotas for folks from the Middle East were especially high after 9/11.

"Not in the least bit," Walsh confirmed.

"Foul play?"

"Maybe." He flipped his right palm toward the ceiling. "Maybe not," he said as he turned the same hand toward the floor.

"Did she self-deport? Why was anyone looking for a teenage girl that hard? Don't most of them end up running away with boyfriends or going into prostitution or something along those lines?"

"It was who her brother was...is that's the important part of this story. He's motel owner Hami Emad."

"That name sounds familiar..." This time when I shifted in my seat it wasn't because of residual jealousy over my ex. It was because Walsh was treading too close for comfort. I was ninety-nine percent sure that my nighttime...proclivities were as secret as they could be when others were involved.

What I knew of Walsh didn't suggest he was devious enough to be playing me. Had to watch my steps carefully, though. I nodded, trying to pawn off my pensive look as one of deep thought.

"Go on," I said.

"Emad was a person of interest in the Container Case," Walsh said. He extracted a small notebook from his bag. Flipped through a few pages. Traced a thick finger on something. "Him and his fellow neighbor, one Mostafa Tarik. Emad owned the Sleepy Time. Tarik, the Sunrise. The containers were found behind and between their establishments."

"The call?" I interrupted his walk down evidence memory lane.

"We think it was from Rida Emad to some relatives in Egypt. The call came from Detroit. Somehow she made it from Cleveland to Michigan and managed to get a seat on a flight from there to Cairo. That bit was easy enough to dig up after a few calls. I'm betting her brother didn't give her enough walking around money to buy a one-way ticket to the Middle East."

"Who else do you think bought the ticket? Maybe the pressure of being undocumented got to her. Maybe her family was ready to marry her off or something. Maybe the brother's call was premature, and he didn't want to take it back." I was digging for excuses because I was none too interested in delving too deeply into this girl's disappearance.

"Wasn't no drug dealer. They just kill people who cause problems. Those motherfuckers don't hesitate. Got no remorse." He shook his head as if sociopathy were the worst traits of drug dealers. "The way I see it, the guy who ran that operation kidnapped that girl to keep Emad quiet. Either that or she was the one running things."

"A sixteen-year-old girl?"

"We've seen younger in narcotics. Some of the best street dealers are young. They're scrappy. Don't have a lot to lose. Have better math skills than most adults."

"Then why not kill her?"

"Ninety percent of prostitution cases are misdemeanors. The only felonies are promoting prostitution, kidnapping—if the girls are unwilling—or murder. Most of the pimps stay the hell away from anything that could mean real time. It's one of the reasons it's impossible to shut this shit down."

It's the world's oldest profession for a reason, I thought. I did not say that out loud.

"How does this girl fit in?" I asked instead.

"She ain't no terrorist, so there wouldn't be any money to pursue her once she left the state, much less the country. The Feds don't use their resources like that anymore. It's all about Al-Qaeda and Bin Laden. The way I figure it, they disappeared the witness with all the information, who could tie it all together. Egypt may not be paradise, but it was probably better than death," Walsh summed up.

"This little walk down memory lane has been interesting," I said. "Why are you bringing this to me? You said gift. I don't see any shiny foil paper or a red bow or anything. I like my presents pretty. This ugly baby"—I gingerly fingered the thick plastic evidence bag—"belongs to the fine folks in that pretty new building on East Ninth street."

"The Feds don't deserve all the glory," he started. "Been on the force thirty-plus years. Didn't go to law school or anything, but I'm thinking they've maybe got a Contained problem. Whereas you don't. Would be a feather in your cap to take down an entire criminal operation the feds with their million-dollar needle in a haystack probes couldn't find. This here is your key to the kingdom."

Excitement and dread warred inside me. Every prosecutor wanted those keys. Needed a case that would catapult them to the front of the line for the top deputy job, or even better, the top elected job.

Could use a case that kept them from getting fired. A Teflon case. A case that wouldn't make a certain prosecutor with the last name Brody as beholden to his family as he'd been for the last dozen or more years.

I picked up the bag. Looked at the black plastic object inside. One that had been so innocently produced in China where its future as a tool of crime hadn't yet been determined. Turned it this way and that, watching the cheap buttons gleam in the overhead fluorescent light.

Was there a way, I wondered, to use this to keep my secrets locked up tight while earning the crown of the prosecutor of the decade?

I may not be a savvy sixteen-year-old fresh from high school algebra, but I was doing some calculus in my head, nonetheless. I couldn't see a downside.

"I'm in," I said. "What's the next step?"

2

I hefted the GRE study book into my lap. Thing had to weigh fifty pounds easy. I smiled at my parents then looked at my niece and nephew. Legos and something called Moon Sand were going to be all over the family room floor in a minute. I'd be home before it was time to clean up.

"Hey," I said. "I got you something I think you'll love."

My nine-year-old niece picked up the gift I pointed to and started to tear off the paper without so much as a word.

"Oh, my god. You got me the Digi Makeover! None of my friends have this. I can't wait to do this. Grandma, can I plug this into the TV?"

I looked over at the big projection monitor. Miracle on Thirty-fourth Street was playing on silent.

"Not right now, honey. Let's save it for later," my mother said while shooting daggers in my direction.

"Imma get me one more piece of that seven up cake," I said. I left the graduate school prep book on the couch. It was big enough to claim its own spot. Their little Cocker Spaniel was going to have to find somewhere else to nap this afternoon.

My sister Andretta had proceeded me into the kitchen once she'd opened her own gifts.

"What did they get you?" Retta asked. She had already cut herself a big slice of the cake. I knew Retta wouldn't dare take it outside of this room. At five feet even and three hundred pounds plus, every bite she put into her mouth was subject to my parents' scrutiny and comment.

"It wasn't a gift certificate to Planet Fitness." That had been their gift to her. The other was a book on how it wasn't too late to pursue one's dreams, a not so subtle nudge for her to go back to school and finish her degree. With school, they were like a broken record.

"Of course not. You're thin so you'll never need exercise." Ten years ago, she'd have snapped at me, and we'd have ended up in an argument about who our parents were trying to torture worse. Now, her voice was resigned. There was no bait to take.

"It was a GRE prep book."

"They still want you to get that MBA?" She flicked her eyes at me for a second before turning back to the cake on her plate.

"Undergrad at Dad's alma mater in Atlanta wasn't enough."

"Did you tell him that you don't need to be killing it on Wall Street in order to be happy?"

"How has that gone over?" I asked. We'd both battled it out with our parents over their interference in our lives. My sister had stopped because they gave her money, and these little digs were their strings. They rarely came at me anymore, because the more they nagged me the shorter my visits.

"Why do we come here?" she asked between bites. "We're old enough to do this on our own. You could come to my place. I promise to get you a gift card to the Gap. You get me one to Macy's. We can call it even. I'll cook. You'll eat. The kids will run around like they've lost they minds, and no one will be insulted."

"I'm here for Mama," I said. She'd been diagnosed with Huntington's disease. Medication managed it, but it was Mama's trump card.

"Because she could die any moment, right?" Retta sucked her teeth. "No offense, but she's been dying for twenty years. If she ain't dead yet, then that disease isn't half as aggressive as the doctors think." Despite my sister's words, I knew that she loved our mother as much as I did. But them two had been clashing for as long as I could remember. I figured it was a female thing.

"Maybe she's just Fortunate," I said. Our last name was a big cosmic family joke. Whenever anything good happened, our parents linked it to our name. My sister didn't laugh.

"When you signed up to get that MBA?"

"As soon as hell freezes over. But hey, you gotta cut them some slack. They did say that a master's in education would be okay. Even engineering." My laugh was strained even to my own ears. "Look how much they've broadened their horizons."

"Nothing about law school?"

"Let's not get crazy. You know how much Daddy hates lawyers."

"Ain't that the truth."

"You put your foot in this." I took a second, larger bite of the sweet yet tart cake.

"Real lemon and lime in the cake."

"Damn." I stood. Opened the fridge. Poured me some of the milk from the gallon-size red-topped jug. Took another bite and chased it with the dairy.

"You should take some home."

"It's only me." I shrugged.

"Why is that? You're cute. Dress well even if I think the clothes are too damn big."

I shrugged.

"Can I ask you something?"

"Sure."

"You gay? You rattling around in the closet? You know I wouldn't care either way." Wasn't the first time someone in my family had hinted at that. Didn't have a girl on my arm every minute of the day and people wondered if something was up. I knew guys on the down low. I wasn't one of them.

"Nah. Ain't nothing like that. Looking for the perfect girl is all. Nice. Got no kids. Has friends and stuff to do so that she ain't hounding me day and night," I said. Most of that was true. The other part was that I didn't know how long I could keep my home life and job separate. Wasn't sure what woman wouldn't be nosy and all up in my private business. For now, that business came first. Maybe later when I was older would I worry about the second. Maybe when I went legit. I was only one or two big payouts from being able to quit this gig. Sledge hadn't liked no side hustle, but he was in jail, and I was in charge.

"Sounds like you're avoiding anything that could even be called a relationship."

It was more like the cobbler's kids had no shoes. After all these years working girls, the last thing I wanted was a girl. I couldn't even begin to imagine how I could make it work. Everyone I met wanted a couple of kids, a dog, a picket fence. I had an apartment, a fleet of vans, and fifteen girls who supported all of that, plus Sledge's family besides. Not the stuff happily ever after was made of.

"Can I talk to you about something serious?" I asked, dropping my voice just above a whisper.

Retta put down her fork and cocked her head toward the living room.

"Daddy just started the lecture on the importance of a liberal arts education. They won't be in here for a minute."

I was familiar with that lecture. It lasted about thirty-six minutes. Not saying I've timed it or anything, but I'd have bet all the money I had hidden in a safe in my clothes closet on it being between thirty-five and thirty-seven minutes long tonight.

"Your kids going to sit that long?"

"They already get it. They listen to Daddy, and someday this summer when it's hot as hell, he'll return the favor in ice cream."

Wasn't nothing in this world that wasn't a barter, a deal, or at minimum a tit for tat. Nothing.

"I gotta problem," I said.

"You know I ain't got no money—"

"When have I ever asked you for anything?" It had mostly been the other way around. I didn't point that out.

She'd flat out deny it or get up and leave in a huff, and I still wouldn't have my favor.

"This is serious. I need you to promise what I'm about to say don't go past this room."

"You scaring me. You ain't got cancer or AIDS or something like that?"

"How many times I gotta tell you? I'm not gay. I'm not sick or dying. I got a worse problem than that."

"What?"

"I might be facing jail time. I've gotta make arrangements."

"Jail!" she practically shouted.

"Keep it down! What did I just say?"

"You slinging? You said you wasn't slinging. I never believed that shit you shoveled Mama and Daddy about affiliate marketing. But I figured you was doing online porn or gambling or something mostly legal, but maybe not in Utah or Alabama or some shit."

"I am not slinging. I got caught up with someone who might be. I'm hustling no different than half the brothers out here. But some of these young knuckleheads always ready to make a buck or two more than they working for. Guy got arrested for meth. Put my name in it. Lawyer think I can get out of it. They got no evidence on me, but—"

"I know how it be in Cleveland. They'll only be happy when we're all up under the jail. Don't know who will be left to sweep the streets or drive the buses, but maybe they haven't thought that far."

"I'd either need someone to make sure my rent is paid so I got a place to come back to. Or I may need to get rid of the place. It would depend if I get time and how much I get."

CONTAINED

"This just a drug charge?" Retta probed. She'd cut herself a second fat slice and was working her way through the pale-yellow cake.

"You never know with this kind of thing."

"You got enough money to cover it all?"

"I'd give you the information," I said. "Account with Society."

"Drugs. So even if—"

"Even if you're not slinging, it's too easy to get caught up. I've been careful. But everyone I work with isn't. You remember the lecture Daddy gave us."

"Most drug dealers are earning minimum wage."

"Yup. With a downside. Every guy out here is playing the lottery. Hoping for a big payday if they just do this one thing…. He used a burner for his other business. Then he called me. Now the cops are convinced I'm somehow mixed up. I don't need to do GRE logic puzzles to know that proving a negative is an uphill battle. Jury sees me and will think I'm guilty, so I need to stay the hell out of a courtroom."

"You don't got kids or anything, right? No one who's expecting something of you if you up and go away?"

"Not gay, Retta. No kids. Just a working mofo. Hard to be a black man in Cleveland. For me it just got harder. Better finish up that cake. I hear Daddy winding down. They'll be wondering where we went in a hot minute."

"If you're home this time next year, you gotta promise me something. Holidays at my place from now on."

"Holidays at your place," I promised.

"If Mama asks where the cake went, tell her you packed some for yourself. Please?"

"I took the cake," I said, confirming the story she was going to tell.

3

"A new 2007 car is not what we talked about," I whispered to my dad, trying to keep my voice low enough so that the retreating salesman couldn't hear us. I wasn't well versed in the car buying process, but I figured the first rule was keeping the salesman out of our conversation.

"The cost difference between this and a certified used car isn't that big," my father said. He lifted his wool cap, smoothed back the curly flyaway hair that was a lot like my own, and fitted it back on his head.

"That few thousand is big to me. That's a sixty-dollar difference in the monthly payment." I wouldn't mention it to my father, but I'd run all the amortization numbers at home before he'd picked me up. Even with my parents' generous offer of help with a new car, my monthly budget remained tight. I should have saved the Hudson money instead of blowing it on new furniture and clothes. But none of that stuff was returnable nor could I turn back the clock. All I could do was to be as careful with this purchase as I should have been with the others.

"What if you had no monthly payment?"

"Even with your help, and if I get anything selling the Honda, I don't have the money to pay for a new car outright."

"But I do," he said.

I turned to look my dad directly in the eye. With all the trucks rumbling down the street of dealerships, I wasn't sure I'd heard him correctly.

"Dad, this isn't at all what we talked about. This isn't what I was asking from you."

"I know, dear one, but I'm giving it willingly. I've learned a lot over the past few months. One thing I've learned for sure is that I can't take the money with me. Your mother and I are comfortable in our retirement. You've struggled a lot over the last years. Is it too much to ask to let me ease some of that burden?"

"Would Mama agree?" I asked. I knew that in some ways I was a daddy's girl. That my mother thought I should stand up on my own two feet. That my mother felt like I'd been the architect of my own misery over the last decade.

"Wholeheartedly. We both had the same idea this morning."

"Do you talk to each other in German?" I asked. I wondered if that's how he wooed her, convinced her to compromise, by whispering to her in her native tongue. Since ending my engagement to Miles, I'd started to pay more attention to my parents and other couples and how they worked. I was starting to realize that not only didn't I know a lot about the inner workings of my own failed relationships, I had zero idea how my parents had done it over decades.

"Sometimes at night. If we're tired. Or if it's too hard to think of the right thing to say in English," he answered. It wasn't what I wanted to know, but it was what I'd asked.

"It's hard feeling like I never knew who you really were. It's like you didn't trust me with your secrets or something."

"I didn't trust me. I didn't trust my own memories which often betrayed me. I didn't trust that probing for the truth wouldn't make me fall apart."

"I'm sorry. I wasn't trying to make this an 'about me' thing"—I air quoted—"it's just hard trying to integrate the knowledge from the trip into what I've always known about you."

"I'm sorry—"

"You don't have to apologize." I held up my hand. "Nazi Germany was an evil place and time that gave rise to all sorts of crimes against humanity. I don't know how long it will be before the repercussions stop rippling across the world."

If the salesman heard us talking about World War II, he ignored that. Instead, with a wide smile plastered on his face, he pulled us into a three-person huddle.

"So, can we make you a deal today? The Subaru Forrester is a great car." He patted the steaming hood of the one we'd just test driven. "The brand is well-known and loved because they all have four-wheel drive. Which is a must with all of our winter weather and lake-effect snow. The cold weather could descend at any moment—there were even a few flurries this morning. When a Canadian breeze comes across the lake, you'll be happy that you're safely tucked into the heated seats. Did I show you how to turn those on?"

"You did," I interjected before he ran out of breath extolling the car's features.

"Let's make a deal," my dad said.

"Good. Great. End of the year prices are insane. Let's go to my desk to see what incentives you qualify for." The salesman walked briskly through the glass doors with a pep in his step that hadn't been there earlier.

"Are you sure?" I did not want to be one of those kids who would happily bankrupt their parents' retirement for their own immediate gratification.

"Very. Let's get you a safe, new car."

While my father and the sales manager—a new player who'd appeared on stage in the car buying drama—were haggling over price, my phone rang. I pulled the small gadget from the messenger bag I was using as a purse today and used my thumb to move up the slider. I fumbled with it and didn't have a chance to look at the number to see who was calling. I tried to avoid clients' non-emergency calls around the holiday season when emotions were heightened but little could be done for them while the wheels of justice nearly ground to a halt between Christmas and New Year's.

"Casey Cort." I spoke formally, in case this was truthfully a client emergency. My clients seemed to only have emergencies when it was least likely I could actually address them.

"Casey, it's Ron Pinheiro..." the unfamiliar voice said through the phone. When I didn't reply right away, he added, "From Dalton Lacey."

My mind raced as I tried to figure out why one of my best friend Lulu's colleagues would be calling me on the day after Christmas of all days.

"Is there some kind of issue with Hudson?" I blurted out. Landing the adoption agency's clients had been a major feather in my cap until I'd learned their baby sourcing may not have been on the up and up. I'd pulled back quietly but hadn't really had that hard conversation with anyone at Dalton. It had been Ronaldo who had facilitated the referral.

I waved to get the attention of my dad and the sales manager, pointed to the phone, pulled my coat together as best I could one-handed, and walked back into the cold as I started rehearsing an answer to potentially sticky client questions.

"No, this isn't about Hudson," he was saying when I tuned him back in. "I wanted to talk to you about something else. Do you have a minute?"

"Sure," I said, eyeing the traffic on busy Broadway Avenue in Bedford. We'd picked this area because it was the strip of auto dealers closest to my house. The Mercedes dealership across the street was doing a pretty brisk business as was the Volvo one next to me. "How can I help you?" I asked. Just because the Hudson relationship had gone belly-up didn't mean that I wouldn't take another referral. I just hoped I hadn't somehow been tarred in the meantime and this call wasn't about my ban from firm referrals.

"It's not a work thing," he said.

"Okay…" My mind raced. Did he know about the supposedly secret relationship between my best friend and one of the firm's partners? I most certainly did not want to get in the middle of that.

Ron's "It's about New Year's Eve," halted my speeding thoughts. I shifted in my leather boots and focused all my attention on the words coming through the phone.

"Okay…" was my repeated response. I didn't have anything else in my arsenal.

"There's this party at the club—the Shaker Heights Country Club—on New Year's Eve. I was hoping that you'd join me." I couldn't have been more surprised if he'd asked me to join him on a rocket headed for the International Space Station.

"On a date?" I blurted out, then immediately regretted. Of course he wasn't asking me on a date date. He probably needed someone to have on his arm and he thought I'd be available. Because everyone who had half a brain knew a woman like me was almost always available.

"Yes," came back unpredictably.

"Um. What day is it?" Cause of course there were so many New Year's Eves. I wanted to snap the phone shut and start again, this time with my smart, cool girl persona answering instead.

I could hear the sound of him walking. "Sunday night. It would start at nine…until after midnight, of course. If you're busy, I understand."

"I'm not busy," I answered plainly, honestly.

"Does that mean you'll come?"

"Sure. Yes. Thank you. I'd be happy to come."

"I…um…have your information from the firm's files. Can I pick you up around nine, then?"

"Yes. Thanks. I'm looking forward to it." I could hear the stiff formality in my own reply, but I didn't know how else to be now that I knew it may be a real date.

"See you then," he said before ringing off.

I held the phone away from my ear and looked at the plastic and metal gadget. If someone had asked me to make a list of all the things that would happen today, this would not have been one. I had a date for New Year's Eve, I practically crowed to myself. Until this moment, I hadn't realized how much I'd wanted exactly that.

"Everything okay?" Dad asked when I walked back into the dealership. He was sitting alone at a desk.

"What happened to everyone?"

"They're in the back pretending to make magic happen. I don't know. I gave them my all-cash bottom line, and now we'll see if they can 'make it work.'"

"All cash?" I made an effort to close my fallen jaw.

"This is our gift. You don't need any more debt. Your mom and I truly regret recommending you finance graduate school. The loan situation was so much worse than we could have known."

"It's too much."

"Nothing is too much. We've paid off the house, Casey. We don't have much in the way of expenses. Please let us do this for you."

"Thank you?"

"That's the spirit. Do you have to run to the jail?"

"Jail?"

"The phone call."

"Oh gosh no. Guess what, Dad? I have a date for New Year's Eve."

"Who's going to be your date?" Dad's face held cautious optimism.

"A lawyer at Lulu's firm. His name is Ron. He's a senior associate over there. I worked with him on some pro bono stuff."

His shoulders came down. I wondered if he'd thought I was backsliding with Miles or Tom. I did have the annoying habit of going back to inappropriate guys who'd dumped me at least once.

"Do you like him?" Dad asked, as if that were the most important thing.

"I don't even know him, Dad. Not that well at least."

"Where is this party?"

"At the Shaker Heights Country Club. Probably a firm thing, or maybe he's a member there. I have no idea. I'll have to dress up, though. I'm not even sure I have something to wear."

"Why don't you ask your mother or Lulu to take you shopping."

"I can shop for my own dress, Dad."

He looked me up and down like he had doubts about that but held his tongue.

"Yes, of course." He coughed into his hand. "I miss the days you were at home and your dates would pick you up there. Now that you're in Shaker Square, I can't grill them. Make them promise to treat you well."

"Promise?"

"When you were getting your coat or talking to your mom, I may have pulled them aside to give them a little talking to."

"No one ever said a thing to me."

"That's because it was a man-to-man thing."

Before I could ask more about this macho, protective side of my dad I'd never seen, the sales team hustled back toward the desk, stacks of papers in hand.

"We ran the numbers, and even though we'll make zero profit on this, we can meet your price if you'll take a car off the lot today."

"Do you want the red one?" Dad asked. I'd been eyeing the new top-of-the-line model while taking the year-old bare bones one for a test drive.

I nodded obediently. I very much wanted the red one.

"We'll take the red one, then. Let's get this done as soon as we can so my daughter can drive it home before it gets dark."

4

Even though the Cuyahoga River was only four thousand feet wide, it may as well have been twenty-five miles. That was the distance between my home club—my parents' country club in Westlake—and this one I was driving up to in Shaker Heights.

I would have been satisfied to lift a glass with my dad and uncles, comfortable in the hazy confines of the smoking lounge in my own club. But I was here at the insistence of my boss, one Lorraine Pope.

Each side of Cleveland had their own United States Congressman, their own local city council representatives. But on the county level, each side had equal voting rights to a single prosecutor.

Since the Westsiders already knew me and my family, Pope had wanted me glad-handing on this side of the river.

She'd offered to excuse me if I had plans. But since I'd broken up with Casey, I hadn't found another girl to take her place. I needed someone on my arm for events like these, but the few girls I'd dated asked too many damned questions about my free time without them.

I envied my father and grandfather growing up and marrying in an era when wives didn't ask questions. The women had kids, volunteered at school, summered on one of a thousand Michigan lakes, and did not involve themselves in the world of men.

With all these girls going to college and graduate school, though, they were looking for a marriage of equals. My pedigree and influence didn't go as far these days. It was like there was a certain level of education inflation. As everyone else got some, what I had became less impressive. If I'd known it was going to go this way, I'd have maybe leveled up to Case Western, the top school in town, and not attended the bottom one. It was all water under the Innerbelt Bridge, though. I peered through the windshield to gauge how much longer I was going to have to cool my jets. From the brake lights in front of me, I had a couple of minutes.

As I hit the brake, I glanced at the car dashboard. It was ten. I'd walk around, shake hands, then do an Irish goodbye long before the clock struck midnight. Now that I was on the Eastside, I had some definite ideas of how I'd like to ring in 2007.

Inching up the valet line, I took a second glance at the Lexus in front of me. The personalized plate read RIPESQ. Another freaking lawyer. There were almost as many in town as doctors. If someone got sick or were in trouble, northeast Ohio would be the right place to go down.

A man, overcoat over tuxedo, stepped out when the valet opened the door. My eyes immediately strayed to the passenger side door. Just because I didn't have one on my own arm, didn't mean I couldn't appreciate a good-looking woman. I especially loved a good high heel. Unfortunately, the leg that extended from the passenger side was strapped into a velvet wedge. Not my favorite. With nothing better to do than wait my turn, I kept watch anyway. A woman with a dark-colored dress stepped out. The lawyer came around and immediately wrapped a thick shawl around the woman's shoulders. She looked up to thank him and the light caught her features.

Casey?

What in the heck was my ex doing here? One of the things I'd liked about her was that she operated well outside of Cleveland's toniest circles. Her blue-collar roots had been refreshing at events we'd attended with the same people I'd known and spent time with for all my life.

The RIPESQ guy leaned in and whispered something. Casey threw her head back, laughing hard at what was probably an unfunny joke. I'd never met Mister personalized plate, but I could tell you that I was funnier. I was Irish. It came naturally. The moment they stepped away from the car, I blared my horn. Someone needed to speed up the line. I wasn't here to take in public displays of affection.

Once I got inside the club, I made a beeline for the bar. A stiff whisky would go a long way towards smoothing out the uneasy feeling coursing its way through my body. I'd been fine when I'd left my apartment. A little bit annoyed at Lori Pope, and a little chilled after the long, cold drive across the river, but fine.

Two fingers of eighteen-year-old Macallan in hand, I was about to pivot right when a meaty hand came around my neck.

"Tom Brody, as I live and breathe. I didn't know you knew where the Eastside was."

I shifted so his hand fell. "Tobias Whelchel, long time no see."

"I never know if I should be kissing your ring or opening an investigation when I see you."

For a moment my heart stopped beating. Literally went still in my chest. Then I caught the slight uptick at the side of Whelchel's mouth and realized he was kidding. With my family, it was hard to know where law enforcement came down. There were more than a few people who I think would be very happy to see the Brodys go away to jail or pasture so they could begin their own political dominance. They may couch it in rooting out corruption, but believe you me, they'd do exactly the same things that my family has done while on top. It's the nature of power.

I stuck out my hand with its gold class ring facing the ceiling. The lighting was angled in such a way that it gleamed.

"Anytime."

"Ha. You keep your nose clean and the only place we'll cross paths is the men's room."

"As long as it's paths and not swords."

"I keep mine in its holster. That's the way my wife likes it."

"Single is the only way to roll. Speaking of which, there are a lot of single ladies in the room. Gotta mingle."

"One of the tri-county's most eligible bachelors must. Enjoy yourself. Too bad most of the ladies here aren't to your taste."

I hesitated again, just slightly. Slowly, I turned, making sure to keep my face as impassive as possible.

"How so?"

"I heard that you like them younger. The senior citizen brigade isn't exactly your cohort. At least that's what I hear through the grapevine."

"In vino veritas is a lie. Nice talking," I said. Then I moved away as quickly as possible. I gulped at whisky that should have been sipped. The warmth that flooded me was my reward, though.

Like an owl stalking its prey, I took in the room. Whelchel was right. There were a fair number of dowagers. Widows of long-dead politicians and other county power brokers. Those women could crown a prince with a few carefully placed words. My eyes didn't linger on the power brokers but scanned the room with laser-like focus. In less than a minute, I spotted my ex. I finished my drink and plopped the empty cut crystal tumbler on a passing waiter's tray.

"Casey Cort. Long time no see," I said, after I'd approached her and her date whom I topped by at least four inches. I smacked both of her rouged cheeks loudly with my lips. "The last time had to be when you were in my apartment getting your birth certificate. Did you find what you were looking for in...Poland, was it?"

"Ron Pinheiro," Casey's date said as he extended his hand. "I don't believe we've met. I'm at Dalton Lacey."

"Tom Brody. With the prosecutor's major crimes unit. Casey and I were engaged, but she broke it off. Broke my heart."

"Tom!" Her rebuke was a whispered shout.

"What? It's true. I've been single since. There's not another woman like you."

"I'm discovering that," Pinheiro said. His face softened as he looked at Casey.

"Is he your date?" I asked. "What happened to your other fiancé?"

"Tom Brody!" Casey took my upper arm in hand and pulled me to a corner, but not before throwing an "excuse me" over her shoulder toward her date.

"Got you where I wanted you." I admitted. "Finally."

"Are you drunk?"

"Just a single drink, Casey."

"Why are you acting this way? I thought we'd agreed that we didn't need to talk. I keep my mouth shut. That was a two-way street, no?"

"Why am I not allowed to miss you, Casey?"

"Because you never loved me to begin with."

"That's not true." For a long moment, my edges blurred by the Macallan, I thought there may be some truth to what I'd just said. I mean, I know I didn't love her in that romance novel or movie type way. But I'd never loved any woman that way.

Even the woman I was engaged to before Casey—who was arguably prettier and skinnier and in my league— wasn't a love match. I wasn't sure such a thing existed. If I could have convinced Casey of that, we'd be here together. Not me single and Ron, Esquire on her arm.

"Jesus H. Christ," Casey said, interrupting my less than charitable thoughts. "I don't have time for revisionist history. Why are you here anyway? Shouldn't you be in Lakewood or Westlake or wherever the Westside rich gather?"

"My boss thinks that I need to socialize more. Meet some Eastside...donors...I mean...voters."

"I'm as broke as ever, so you may want to cross me off your list."

"Mr. Dalton Lacey over there is wearing a Rolex. Surely he's got some coin to spare."

"After your little performance, his purse strings may be pulled tighter than a nun's asshole. Why are you trying to ruin my date, Tom? This thing that's happening now? We don't do this. Life is not a sitcom. There's no laugh track under this little farcical walk down memory lane."

"I'm not trying to ruin anything. I just have to wonder why you're ping ponging between men. Leaving a string of broken hearts across the city."

I did truly wonder what had happened with the black guy who'd come after me. She'd been wearing his ring during that visit to my apartment, but she'd been just as cagey with facts back then.

"No one's heart has been broken, Tom. Least of all yours. Now if you'll excuse me, I want to get back to this date. He doesn't have an agenda. Doesn't want me as a beard or to act as a stand-in for his mom. He likes me for me, apparently. I did not cinch myself into all this"—she gestured to the red velvet dress that hugged her boobs and left one of her shoulders bare—"to be visited by ghosts of Christmas past, okay?"

I threw up my hands like a criminal about to be arrested. "Just schmoozing."

"Hey, I just saw Vernon Dinwiddie walk in. You must have half your client roster in common. Maybe you can do a little work making deals on a few cases and hit him up for a little money to boot."

"Back to your boy toy, then," I said backing away, my hands still raised in supplication. She was right about Dinwiddie. I could close at least three cases if he was ready to deal. Plus he was always good for a donation. A man with that many cases against us was always good for a few hundred dollars.

"Good night, Tom."

She stalked as well as she could in heels back to her date. I watched her lips move, her shoulders shrug, her palms turn up to the ceiling as she tried to smooth out the wrinkles I'd thrown into her night.

I snagged a second drink from a server, downed it, and fished my valet ticket out of my pocket. I was done with this. Dinwiddie and I could hash it out another day. Lori Pope could do her own trolling for money. Whether she was reelected or defeated in November, I'd keep my job, office, and title either way. As one of my dates used to say, "Don't make me no nevermind."

I evened out my silk scarf and took my leave. Tapped my foot at the top of the circular drive until the valet ran up to me.

"Sir?"

"Blue 2004 Acura." I handed him a twenty along with my claim ticket. "The quicker the better. I have somewhere else to be."

"Yes, sir," he said. He'd mastered obsequious. That was better. He was suitably humble and grateful for the work and my generous tip. Not like Casey. I'd just about single-handedly made her career, and here she was cozying up to another lawyer. Maybe she thought she could sleep her way into Dalton Lacey. If I'd been nicer, I'd have told her the white shoe pedigree wouldn't make any difference. We all were a product of where we came from. She was a working-class, Westside Catholic girl. Nothing more. Nothing less.

Keys jangled in front of me grabbing my attention. "Sir, you okay to drive?"

"Fine. Good looking out," I said, then jumped into the low-slung car and peeled away. There was little traffic this close to midnight, so I was able to get to the bar in less than twenty minutes. Seventy-second and St. Clair Avenue wasn't the kind of neighborhood to have a valet. I parked as close to the turn of the last century building as I could and sent up a quick prayer to god that any vandals who might do damage to my car had their lips firmly around noisemakers and forties.

"Got ID?" the bouncer said while rubbing his hands together. The earlier near sixty-degree weather had dissipated, leaving near freezing weather in its wake.

I opened my wallet. Instead of handing over my driver's license, I gave him a card I'd gotten from Carter back before he'd been sent up to the penitentiary. He'd been a planner, so I assumed it would be honored same as it used to be.

"Hammer been gone for a minute. Grand running things now. He said anyone come in with an old card gets VIP treatment. Take the steps in the back."

"Been here before. Got it," I said as I snatched the card back and slipped it into my wallet, tucking it behind my club's card glossy with greens.

"Have a good time. Happy new year and all that," he said before turning back to the tiny phone in his hand where he was pressing hard on the tiny plastic keys like his life depended on it.

When I got inside, Dick Clark looked about forty on the big screen in the corner. I'd buy a youth serum if he were selling. Weren't too many people in the bar. Was kind of a family holiday, I guessed. My family was no doubt holding down their table at the club as people not so subtly tried to curry favor. I didn't miss it one bit. All that largesse could be exhausting.

As I pushed my way through the red velvet curtain that separated back from front, Casey floated into my mind. Her dress had been this exact color. Don't know why she was bothering me all of a sudden. We'd wanted different things, and she hadn't been willing to make any kind of compromise to keep us together.

I sent up a wish for good luck to the heavens that she found what she was looking for. As far as I was concerned, neither true love nor anything like it existed. Not in any universe that I'd ever visited. I just needed to find another girl who was willing to be arm candy in exchange for a big house and never having to work. As one of the tri-county's most eligible bachelors, she shouldn't be too hard to find once I put my mind to it. Maybe I'd add it to my resolutions list. My mother would be happy to hear that I was back on the hunt.

"Tom." A short black guy with braids shook my hand.

"Have we met?"

"Coupla years back when Sledge was running the place. Grand. I'm in charge now."

"Anything changed?"

"Some of the girls. Not much else. Got a couple that you'll like just fine, though."

I stepped to go through another curtain past the single dancer on the tiny stage to the back steps leading up to the rooms above the bar.

"Hold up."

I stopped, then turned slowly. "What?"

"Sledge said you gave him advice once." The guy, Grand, I guess, was a little cocky for my taste. He continued without any prompting from me. "I gotta problem I think you could help me out with."

"What kind of problem?"

"Legal."

"I work for the county, you know." I hated that people saw lawyers as one massive lump of people who were placed on earth to solve their problems. The fact that I worked for the office that could prosecute him in a heartbeat didn't seem to register.

"Got my own lawyer," he replied. I took pains to hide my surprise. "Don't need no help with that. Need to give her a little guidance is all."

I loosened my cuff links, shoved them deep in my pocket. Wished I'd worn a traditional shirt and not French cuffs. The one-of-a-kind clasps had been a gift from my father after I'd passed the bar. Didn't want to lose them. Not in a place like this where I'd never get them back.

"How can I help?" This was the trade-off. Life was all trade-offs. They kept me in hot and cold running girls, and I helped out when I could. It was one of the first lessons I'd learned at my father's knee and the most true.

"I think the police may be tipped off to what I got going on here." Grand's statement was blunt, but not angry that I could tell.

"How did it happen?" I asked. Sledge had run a tight operation and it was only an overzealous health inspector who had gotten the cops and subsequently my office involved the first time. He'd done good. I'd offered up Casey Cort to him and he'd taken the bait. Then I'd finagled the assignment of Nicole Long to the case. Long had an on again, on again problem with alcohol that any defense attorney worth their salt, and even Casey, could handle with ease.

The thing I had to admire in Sledge, beyond his taste in girls, was his ability to handle a situation when given a leg up. I wasn't sure this deputy of his, who looked all of fifteen, though I knew he had to be older, had the same ability. Wish I could figure out a way to suss that out before I listened to his tale of woe.

"I can't do everything, bro. I have to contract out. One of my workers didn't understand the limitations of our operation. Doing a little side hustle in meth, got the cops sniffing around."

"He gonna talk?"

"Can't rule it out. But I put the chances at under ten percent."

"So an isolated guy got caught with some drugs. How is that your problem?"

"The problem was his phone. We give them burners. Take them back after a month, toss them. Learned that shit from The Wire. When Sledge got arrested, the phone got kept by mistake. Guy held onto it longer than he should have. Could tie him back to us even if he don't talk."

"Look, Cuyahoga County isn't the FBI," I started. I was starting to get itchy and needed to get my libido scratched by one of my preferred girls. Discussing the finer points of

Cleveland police investigation procedures was not a turn on. I laid it out plainly and quickly. "It's not even an episode of CSI or Law and Order. If someone looks like they're going to plead guilty, we don't run DNA, or even regular serology. No pulling phone records. All that costs money and we're on a budget like every government office."

"He refuses to plea. Says he's going to take it to trial. Been in jail for two months, so it's coming down to the wire."

For all the county court's flaws, my dad did not allow the common pleas judges under him to play fast and loose with a defendant's speedy trial rights. If a perp was in jail, he was entitled to a trial ninety days from the time of his arrest or indictment, whichever came first.

"If you bail him out, it would slow down the three-for-one trial clock. Turn your last thirty into ninety. Maybe I can put in a few calls. What's his name? Cop? And what in the hell is on this phone anyway?"

"His name Derek Waters. Cop is some guy named Neil Walsh. The phone? Got a call from a girl we...uh...helped leave Cleveland. Rida Emad."

"Got it," I said. I hoped my head hadn't spun Exorcist style on my neck when my brain put two and two together.

Grand's "You don't need to write that shit down?" brought me right back to the present.

"Keeping records is the kind of thing that gets people into trouble," I threw back at him.

"You right. Ready to go upstairs?"

"Very."

"Busy night. Only have Shonna here."

I tried not to show my disappointment. I liked black girls, and Shonna was some mix that in the dark looked nearly white.

"It's New Year's Eve. Girls are booked remotely. Couldn't get anyone back in time. Made a couple of calls when you first came in." Which meant I needed to be grateful anyone was here at all. I heard the message loud and clear.

"Fine. I'll be in the back room. Send her in."

I took myself up the stairs and tried to curb my disappointment. Sex was sex, though. I didn't need to have everything every time. Something my father once said came to mind.

All cats are gray in the dark.

I pulled off my tuxedo jacket and bowtie and hung both up on a coatrack in the corner. Moved the cufflinks from my trousers to my breast pocket.

After I'd laid down on the bed with my head propped on the pillows, the doorknob turned and clicked open. The girl who walked in was prettier than I remembered, so that was a start. Maybe five foot four, lots of curly brown hair, long thin limbs.

"Hey there, hon. I'm Shonna. What you like?"

"Tom," I said, holding out my hand.

She ignored my hand but took the gesture as an invitation to lay down next to me. Prop her own head on the pillows.

"Straight, or blow job, or in the butt?"

"Shh. Give me a minute," I said. I hated this part. The girl that used to be my regular up and quit a couple of years ago and it hadn't been quite the same. She knew just how I liked it. Didn't ask any questions. She would slip out of her clothes and drop right to her knees. Once her soft hand and even softer lips were wrapped around me, the rest took care of itself. At the memory, I started to feel myself stir in my pants.

"Did you know a girl named Destiny?"

"Destiny. Damn. She long gone. Slipped right out. Sledge was mad as hell that night. But she was getting old anyway."

"Slipped right out of where?"

"You know what? I ain't supposed to be talking." Shonna stood up then and slipped out of the cheap sequined dress she was wearing. Underneath was a lacy bra that did nothing to hide her dark nipples and a thong which exposed nearly everything else.

"Heels on or off?"

"Off," I commanded. This girl's near nudity, coupled with my memories of Destiny, did what it was designed to do, took my brain offline. I stopped wondering what happened to Destiny or caring about Grand's problems with the cops. "I want it straight," I said. Then got on with it.

On my way back downstairs, Grand appeared. So much for my second Irish goodbye of the night.

"Kept an eye on your car, man. It's all good. Have a happy new year." He thrust his hand out for a shake.

I shoved my own in my pocket. "Good looking out," I replied. It was an imitation of what I'd heard all these guys say to each other time and again.

It was only when I was driving over the river, putting myself back together, that I realized I was a single cufflink short.

Damn.

5

"Thanks again, man, for bailing me out." Derek Waters pulled his bare hand from the pocket of his puffy coat and attempted to go for a handshake. I wasn't in the mood for all that and kept my own in my pocket even though it was warm for January.

"What's the indictment say, Ice?" We'd been friendly, if not friends, for years. Shared the secret of our little whore network. I made my voice as cold as his name.

This nigger was threatening my livelihood and that of the women who worked for me, not to mention Sledge who still got points off the top. That was a lot of people who could be put out of work if Ice didn't man up and keep quiet.

Waters fished the creased white paper from the pocket of his oversized black coat. He squinted at the black type.

"Says here…meth…methamphetamine possession and aggravated drug trafficking."

"Maybe you shouldn't sell something you can't pronounce." I jabbed at my temples. I'd have a headache in twenty minutes from the stress if I didn't pop a couple of aspirin soon. I fished in my pocket where I kept a bottle sometimes. But I came up empty.

"Give me a break, Grand. You didn't hire me for my book knowledge."

"I didn't hire you to sell meth either."

"You knew I had a side hustle. Kept quiet when it all went down for Sledge."

I tried not to squirm in my jacket. I had known. Turned a side-eye. Let my boss go to prison for something he didn't really do.

"It wasn't my business until it affected my business," I said.

"How much time am I looking at?" Waters asked.

"Do I look like your lawyer?" I squinted at him in the sun. "You hired someone, right?"

"I ain't got no money for that."

"You get paid every week for driving the girls around. What you mean you broke?"

"That's why I was dealing ice."

"You was never called the Iceman because you wore diamonds," I said. I fingered my own diamond, the one I wore in my left ear. It was my marker of success. I didn't go for flashy cars or a nicer living situation. The more I made, the bigger my stud got.

"Nah, man. Look, that was a little white lie I told Sledge. You know he wouldn'ta hired me if he knew I had a side hustle. He was strict on shit like that."

"He was strict because we can't have shit like this happening."

"I'm sorry."

"Sorry ain't going to roll this back. We gotta talk about the phone."

"I shoulda tossed it. But I sometimes keep a burner in the drawer in case."

"In case what?" I asked, though I already knew the answer was going to be some version of laziness.

"Dropped my phone in a puddle around Thanksgiving. So had to swap something in. The store I usually go to was closed up and shit." Yup, laziness. He did not disappoint.

"Were you dealing out the van?" Waters' face said he did not want to answer that question. That was my answer right there, but I wanted to hear him say it. "Answer me." I was much nicer than Sledge. Way less scary. Up until this moment, I'd thought that was an asset. In the good cop/bad cop game, I was the good cop. Being nice, I thought, would get me loyalty. Maybe I needed to be a little bit more like Sledge. Folks may not have been as loyal, but they was certainly scared to cross him.

"Not all the time," Waters hedged. "But two jobs was hard. People want their girls and people want their drugs. If I could do them together, sometimes I did. Weren't no problem for over a year."

He sounded like my sister. A slice of cake here and there wasn't a problem until she was well past the end of the scale.

"Until it was," I said.

"Yeah, well."

"Look. Here's my problem as I see it. You are in the position to trade information. I know you don't want to go to jail. Nobody do. But I can't let you take this operation down. It can't go like that."

"What you saying?" Waters looked me in the eye for the first time.

"We going to make a deal," I explained.

"Why it sound like I got no choice?"

"Because you don't. Here's how this gonna go. You alone is going down for the meth. Anyone ask you anything about that phone, you got nothing to say. No matter they threaten to lock you up for life and put a needle in your arm, you got nothing to say. What I'm gonna do for you is this. I'm gonna hire you a lawyer. Second, I'm going to explain the concept of insurance."

"Insurance. Like for your car?"

"No. Insurance for me. Me and Sledge. Remember Dashanique?"

"Jesus, man. Nobody want to think about that."

"Tucked away someplace no one know but me and Sledge is video from that night." It had been one of Sledge's smartest moves. Nobody went away for seeing prostitutes. Even when they were underage, it was still treated like a nuisance crime. Sometimes with some kind of diversion class thrown in. Nothing too serious, though. But a video of guys fucking an underage girl to death would force a prosecutor's hand.

Especially if that video got out, went viral. They'd throw the book at every guy in that room. Sometimes we let the guys who work for us take a turn. Waters always took us up on it. He had been the person who was in charge of keeping the new girl gang bangs under control. He'd failed that night.

Dashanique had been easily replaced, so that was no matter. We'd kept Waters on because he was otherwise real good at his job. Didn't mean we hadn't kept a little something in our back pockets.

"Motherfucker." He shook his head, looking somewhat defeated.

"Drug possession ain't murder. Aggravated murder will put a needle in your arm. You feel me."

"I hear you."

"I want to make one hundred percent sure you understand before I drive you over to the lawyer's office."

"Will he get me off?"

"I don't know." I shrugged. "Depend on how guilty you are, I guess. You'll need to talk to him about that. You ready?"

"Yeah. Whatever."

"Don't whatever me. I need to know we got a deal." I held out my hand. Waters looked around a minute before he took it and shook hard. I let that pass. My bones only hurt for a second. He may be hurting up to eleven years.

I turned right from Ontario onto Public Square and pulled the door open into the lobby of number seventy-five.

Checked the directory and pressed the elevator button. Got on and pressed number six. I didn't check to make sure Waters was following me.

"Who this guy?" he asked.

"You'll know in a minute." I strode toward the suite door and twisted the knob.

"Dion Fortune here for Justin McPhee. Got a ten-thirty appointment."

"Have a seat. I'll let him know you're here." An older woman gestured toward some chairs then lifted the phone receiver. After whispering something into it, she hung up.

In less than a minute, a bland white guy came to greet us. This lawyer, I thought, could be a serial killer. Weren't they always white guys that no one really noticed? Yet I knew if some cops had to choose between the two of us when looking for a suspect, they'd choose me every single time.

"Dion?" The lawyer's eyebrows rose in question.

I stood and extended my hand. "I'm Dion Fortune. This here my...associate...Derek Waters."

"Let's go to my office."

I followed behind him while Derek shuffled behind me. McPhee pushed open a door with his name on a little brass plaque by it. I didn't wait for an invitation to take a seat in one of the chairs. Derek took the other. The lawyer sat behind his desk, pulled out a pad, clicked his pen tip in place, and finally looked from me to Derek.

"Mr. Fortune. Mr. Waters, was it?" Ice nodded in confirmation. "How can I help you guys?"

"I...Derek...Mr. Waters here has been charged with possession and trafficking of methamphetamine," I answered.

"You got the indictment?"

I gave Waters a pointed look. He fished the now wrinkled paper from his pocket and handed it over.

McPhee turned his head towards me. "What's your connection? You a co-defendant? Been indicted also?"

I wanted to answer that I wasn't that stupid then thought better of it. "He broke," I started. "I'm paying your fee. What is it gonna cost anyway?"

"I usually don't jump to the money right away." The lawyer shifted in his seat, looking uncomfortable.

"Today, for me, take the leap."

"For a case like this? Seventy-five hundred."

If I didn't know better, I'd have said he came up with that number out of the blue. Wondered for a minute if it included the black tax. Maybe white meth defendants got five thousand and we'd just gotten up-charged. My own lawyer had made the referral though, so I had to trust this guy was on the up-and-up. I didn't really have the time to shop around.

"Fine." I'd taken a page from Sledge's playbook. Started carrying a black leather messenger bag with all the stuff necessary to run Intraport. I pulled out a manila envelope, bent open the wires, and extracted a thick wad of cash. Took a couple of minutes to count and recount a stack of twenties and hundreds...enough to come to seventy-five hundred dollars.

"Let me get some paperwork," McPhee said. "I'll be right back."

Despite his maroon sweater vest over a plaid button-down, he wasn't any different than anyone else. Cash money always got people to do what you needed.

He came back with a narrow spiral notebook. Wrote out a receipt for the cash. Had both me and him sign it. Then he handed over three copies of a five-page retainer agreement.

I'd seen Casey Cort's, and this wasn't much different. In the space regarding who was paying, I didn't put my name, though. Instead, I penned in Intraport Incorporated, signing as its vice president.

I nudged Waters, handing him the pen and pointing to the line that said client. Then I pushed the papers back toward McPhee. He counter-signed and handed a copy to each of us. I folded it up over the pale-yellow carbon receipt and shoved both into my black leather bag.

"If you don't mind waiting in the reception area while I talk to Mr. Waters," McPhee said to me. I took the hint and rose. Stepped out the door and pulled it not quite closed. I pressed my head against the wood while my hand on the knob kept the door steady.

"No matter who pays to represent you," McPhee was saying to Ice, "I'm only here for you. Not Mr. Fortune. Not anyone else. Do you understand?"

"I do."

"You don't owe him any loyalty. You only need to be responsible for yourself."

"I'm just a one-man operation," Waters lied. "Needed some help with the money is all."

"Alrighty then. Let's get started on your defense. Tell me what you were doing right before your arrest."

"I run a small delivery business. Just drop stuff off for people off the books."

Satisfied that the Iceman had gotten my message loud and clear, I stepped away from the door and silently pulled it closed.

6

My phone buzzed. I stopped in my tracks only steps from the vestibule of Justin's office building next door to my own. The text tone notification of my cell had me responding just like Pavlov's dog.

I lifted the gadget from my pocket.

Ron: I wish I could be with you tonight. I'd much rather look at your beautiful face than this brief that's due on Monday. Again, I'm sorry to cancel.

Me: Work. I get it. Hopefully, you'll get some sleep this weekend.

Ron: I wish I were sleeping next to you. Instead, I may be camped out on some partner's couch while he double-checks everything I've written.

Me: LOL. I'm sure he'll keep you warm. Thanks again for inviting me to the club for New Year's. It was one of the best nights I've had in a long time.
Ron: Same here.

Since I wasn't an expert at communication in one hundred forty characters or less, I decided to leave it there and carried the warm feeling Ron had evoked with me through the doors to meet Justin.

"Oh, I didn't expect to see you in the lobby." Justin McPhee was standing a few feet back from the door I'd just entered, coat, briefcase, and umbrella in hand. I'd invited him out because not only was I suddenly free and not in any hurry to go home to my cold apartment and my cat, but I also needed advice. As a solo practitioner, I had to cultivate my own mentors. "Are we still on?" I hadn't exactly run the whole "mentor" idea past him. I'd proposed a collegial get together. I'd planned to save picking his brain until after I'd bought him a drink.

"It's past six. Thought maybe we could grab dinner while we talk."

"Um...sure." I hesitated only a moment while I recalibrated. "Why not? What place has big enough tables that I can lay out a file?"

"How about Red? It's warm out, so the walk shouldn't be too bad."

Red, the Steakhouse was its pretentious name. It had opened a couple of years ago. I'd never been. The menu was far too rich for my thighs and my pocketbook. I was thinking of a way to say that, albeit tactfully, when Justin beat me to the punch.

"Dinner's on me. I haven't been in a couple of months. Probably not since Thanksgiving. One of my favorites downtown, though," he said.

I wanted to do that dance where I push back and offer to split the bill. But I didn't have "split it" money. My parents' generous gift of the Subaru had solved the problem of unreliable transportation. But I hadn't had a car payment before, and not having one now hadn't made any difference in the bottom line. Not that I wasn't grateful for their generous gift. Every time I got into the heated leather seat, every time I turned the key and the engine purred instead of stuttered, I sent up a prayer of thanks.

"Let's go, then," I said, assured my card wouldn't be declined after a decadent meal or even happy hour specials.

The rain that had abated earlier started in earnest again. Justin had his golf umbrella open before I could fish my Totes from my leather bag.

"We can share." He sidled closer to me. He smelled like Irish Spring. "Easier that way."

Again, I acquiesced. Sometimes it was easier that way—giving in. I spent half my day fighting and didn't want my usual daytime antagonism to bleed over into my evening.

During the five-minute walk over we mused about the warm winter weather being a tease of the spring that was still months away. It was nearly fifty degrees now, and it was only a matter of time before the other shoe dropped. In Cleveland, that shoe was full of Arctic breezes that only got colder on their way south from Canada over Lake Erie and into the city, and snow. We talked about snow. Mountains of it would come sooner or later. It always did.

"Reservation for two. Justin McPhee," McPhee said when the hostess greeted us.

"You made a reservation?" I asked inartfully.

I wasn't sure if it was the reflection of the fire engine red walls or if a blush tinged Justin's cheeks. I looked down at my sensible shoes and for the first time wondered if he'd thought I'd asked him on a date. I felt my hair brush my cheeks and knew I must have shaken my head. I hoped Justin hadn't noticed, but of course he had.

"You still okay with dinner?"

"Yes, fine." My tone was brusque to hide my own embarrassment. "Where's the coat check?" I asked the hostess. I was already hot in my gray London Fog raincoat. Though it had been unseasonably warm since New Year's, I hadn't taken the thick lining from my coat because I didn't want to be caught standing outside waiting for the Rapid when the Arctic winds finally did come down from Canada. I took the trench off before I got to the coat check window. The last thing I wanted to do was drip sweat in a swanky place like this.

After my coat and accessories were traded for a quarter-size claim chip, the hostess seated us in a back-corner U-shaped booth a stone's throw from a clear glass wine cellar.

I tucked my bag toward the outside of the booth and slid closer to the corner. Justin mirrored me and did the same. Instead of sitting across from each other, we were nearly elbow to elbow. While he busied himself with the wine and drink menu, I surreptitiously took him in. He looked different somehow.

Instead of his usual sweater vest, he was wearing a dark gray button-down shirt and black slacks. It was like he was channeling Regis Philbin from Millionaire. His hair wasn't shorter so much as it was shinier and more groomed. And he smelled surprisingly good. I shifted in my seat, moving myself a millimeter away from him. I was getting that but-terfly feeling low in my belly and I didn't want it at all. I wanted to save that for Ron Pinheiro.

Each day since our date on Sunday night, I'd woken up to a good-morning text and went to bed to a good-night text. I was loving the idea that he was thinking about me every day. Tom had had his prostitutes. Miles, his job. Ron was the first guy I'd dated who genuinely had an interest in me. He'd promised a date this weekend after cancelling to-night's, and I couldn't wait to spend time with him. I won-dered if I needed to tell Justin he was barking up the wrong tree. Or maybe I was blowing this all out of proportion. Staying quiet before I firmly planted a foot in my mouth was probably a good idea.

"You still take the Rapid to work every day?" McPhee asked, his eyes continuing to peruse the wine list.

"You remember that?" No matter how many times I told people I didn't drive to work, most asked me where I parked on the regular. "Sure, I take light rail. Got a new car, but still don't drive downtown."

"New car, huh? What did you get?"

"Subaru Forrester. L.L. Bean edition," I said proudly be-fore I realized that maybe it was tacky to have made that announcement.

"Cool car. Can't beat four-wheel drive when the snow's here. You good with red?"

"They call it 'garnet red pearl.' How'd you guess? I don't remember saying anything about the color, but I've kind of always wanted a red car even if I'm more likely to get a ticket."

"I'm not that good of a mind reader." Justin flipped the wine list over, leather side up. I realized then he'd probably been talking about wine, not my car's paint. "Do you think they call it a clutch of cars?" he asked. "That would be appropriate."

The loud bark of laughter that escaped my mouth was unexpected. I didn't have a clue why he made me laugh so easily.

"Oh god, I'm so clueless sometimes. Did you mean the wine or the car?"

Justin's smile transformed his face. "Either. Seriously, wine. There's a great Clare Valley Australian Malbec on the list."

"That's fine," I said. Before I could insist that he order only a glass for me, he was conferring with our waiter who in no time brought back an entire bottle from the huge Plexiglas-wrapped storage cube next to us.

Justin and the waiter did the whole wine tasting ritual. After my non-date nodded, the waiter poured us both generous glasses.

"I'll be back in a moment to take your order."

I took that as a hint to look at the menu. Once I did, I tried not to gasp out loud. These prices were high, especially for Cleveland. There wasn't an appetizer under fifteen or an entrée under thirty. I didn't want to think about how much the markup had been on the wine I was enjoying.

"You like calamari?" Justin turned toward me. "The chili calamari here is pretty good."

"What do you recommend for dinner, since you've been here before?" I asked, so I could gauge the price ballpark he was in.

"The lobster pasta, if you like that kind of thing. For steak, definitely the rib eye or the New York strip. Both juicy cuts and they do cook it right here."

I looked down at the menu. The only thing more expensive than those cuts was the fifty-dollar filet mignon.

"Sure, splitting the fried squid sounds great," I said, mentally cutting the appetizer cost in half.

"Want to share creamed spinach? My mom wasn't so much of a cook of American classics. More potatoes and perogies. Less mac and cheese."

"Same here. Want to split both?"

"Good choice. Which steak? That is, if you're having steak. Didn't mean to assume."

"No worries. I'll go with the rib eye. Probably can't go wrong there."

When the waiter returned, Justin put in the order for both of us. His delivery was shockingly smooth. It wasn't what I'd expected from him. Not high-end steakhouse for sure. He was perogies and brisket like I was strudel and wurst. I blinked slowly and took in the room again with a glossy red accent wall that reflected not only the patrons but the restaurant's name, and starched white tablecloths. Suddenly self-conscious, I took my napkin, unrolled the heavy silverware from it, and placed the starched fabric in my lap. I needed to get back to my original reason for this meeting before it veered any more into friend or date territory.

"I wanted to talk to you about a couple of things. Bounce a couple of ideas off you, if that's okay. You know how hard it can be going solo."

He nodded, then folded his hands in his lap. "Thanks for that referral by the way."

I tilted my head like I didn't remember any referrals while my heart went wild. When Dion Fortune had come to me with his problem, I'd agreed to help him out. Part of me felt that it was the least I could do given my inability to keep his boss out of jail the second time 'round. But when he'd called and indicated the guy who could bring their whole operation down had gotten popped, I'd recognized that potential conflict of interest right away and shoved that one straight off my proverbial plate and onto Justin's.

"Sure. No problem."

"Why didn't you take it?" he asked. "You're back doing criminal, at least felonies, right?"

"Absolutely. Back to taking what comes in the door," I admitted. I deflected the other. Using the term conflict of interest would flag my client's and his client's potential co-defendant status and possibly breach the confidentiality I'd been so careful to keep—especially considering the explosive nature of the bigger operation they had going on.

The waiter chose that perfect moment to swoop into our little corner with a bowl brimming with breaded and deep-fried rings and tentacles. He then produced mayonnaise flecked with red and green.

"You look great tonight, Casey," McPhee said matter-of-factly.

"Thanks." I tried not to squirm under his obvious scrutiny. "Um, so this looks really good. Dig in. Don't hold back on my account," I said. I pulled my water glass toward me and took a big and silent gulp.

"So the guy you referred. He wants to plea. Some other guy came in to pay the whole retainer. So I'm thinking this is a definite one to go to trial. I just sat back in my chair waiting to hear the whole story. Waiting to hear how he wants an OJ defense–"

"Oh god, don't they all. That was the worst case to ever happen to defense lawyers. Every client now wants a million-dollar defense for only a few thousand."

"You're telling me. So like I was saying, I'm expecting this long winding tale of innocence and entrapment if not police brutality. But he doesn't do any of that. Says he wants the best plea deal he can get."

"What was the charge again?" I tried to fill my voice with mild disinterest.

"Meth possession and trafficking. He had a lot on him. Doesn't look like a cooker, but definitely had a brisk dealing business."

"What's the problem?" I pressed. "Aren't these the cases everyone wants? He doesn't want OJ. Guy is ready to plea. You take home the fee and pay rent or buy yourself something nice."

"You've known me for a while, Casey. If you don't already know, then I need to tell you that I'm not that kind of attorney. Not here just for the money. Not taking short cuts. I actually care. Maybe a little too much."

I liked the fact that Justin had a conscience. Right now, I didn't want him to focus so much on that as grind the Iceman through the legal mill the justice system was. "I know you're older than me. But you have to know better than to care too much. That way lies madness," I said.

"Are you saying I should follow my client's lead and just plea it down?" His tone bordered on incredulous.

I didn't want him to think I was one of those callous lawyers we both knew all too well, because I wasn't one either. But I also didn't want to clue him in on the fact that I, by way of my client, had my own agenda here.

"Has he been to jail? I think some of these guys don't mind jail. The routine. Meals. Healthcare. Not having to make decisions, especially as so many of them have made a bunch of bad ones."

"I think the guy who came in and paid the bill is pressuring him."

"You explained that the person who pays doesn't get to make the rules, right?"

"Of course. That's my duty. But it's not sitting right. A guy who's not a user, kind of a businessman, actually, walking himself into jail. Into at least a two, if not eight-year stint."

"It could be a business decision. Sometimes defendants weigh out different factors and make a choice. I had a guy do it a couple of years back. He was smart, savvy. I got him out of a jam during a trial. Then he got jammed up in Lucas County. Similar charge, actually, to your guy. He's in for three. A plea was better than an investigation into his...operation."

I took a big bite of calamari. Took a second ring and dipped it in the fancied-up mayonnaise¬—aioli it had said on the menu. It was good. I savored it while my mind raced. I was pretty sure Justin was right. Dion Fortune had turned the screws on Derek Waters. Waters probably knew enough to bring down their trafficking operation. If I knew anything about Sledge, if not Grand, it was that they weren't planning on going down like that. I shut down that train of thought, because I didn't want to think about what the consequences would be if Waters decided to talk...to trade information for freedom.

"I need to let it go, huh?"

Slowly but surely Justin was coming around. I hated myself for the manipulation, but my own client's interests were paramount. Waters came a distant second.

"Probably. Just, you know, CYA. Have him sign something acknowledging that he could make a different, possibly better choice and let him do his thing. If it's life or death or something, he may be choosing life. And that's a valid choice."

"You're probably right."

I nearly sighed in relief, pushing away any guilt about my part in what was happening. Then my phone rang, the bleat sounding distant, but loud enough that several other dinner patrons were giving me the side-eye.

"I'm sorry," I said. I leaned sideways and frantically felt around in my bag until I could lay my hands on the little gadget. I thumbed the screen up and pressed it to my ear when I couldn't figure out how to turn off the ringing. I cupped the receiver with my other hand.

"Casey Cort."

"Can you come over?" Lulu's voice was unusually quiet or hoarse or just different than her usual brash self.

"Lulu? What's up? Are you crying?" I cupped my hand tighter over the receiver and glanced at Justin as I slid along the booth toward the opening. "I need to step out a moment," I whispered.

The air outside was cool, not cold. Mist coated my hair.

"Casey, what are you doing right now?"

"I'm in the middle of dinner. Downtown. In a steakhouse. With Justin McPhee." I stopped when I realized I was oversharing. "What's up? Is this an emergency?"

"No. No. Sorry to interrupt. It's just that Sinclair and I had a fight. I needed someone to talk to. He just stormed out of here. I don't know where he is. When he'll be back."

I didn't say what I was thinking: I hoped he didn't come back. I hoped that he'd go home to his wife and leave my best friend to find someone more suitable, less...married.

"Did you call him?" I asked instead.

"He's not answering his cell phone." Lulu took a big sniff.

"What was the fight about? You need me to get a doggy bag?" After I asked the question, I realized I wouldn't mind the excuse to leave. I'd gotten what I wanted out of Justin—his promise to let Derek Waters drive the case. Lulu's crisis would be an excellent way to avoid the potential date part of the night.

"No. Wait. I hear a key. He's back. Sorry to have bothered you."

My "I'll call you tomorrow" fell on deaf ears. When I realized she was gone, back to Sinclair-land, I closed the phone and went back inside.

"Everything okay?" Justin asked when I came back to the table.

"Probably. I'll turn this off now," I said. I flicked the switch so the phone wouldn't disturb dinner again.

"Is your Lulu the same as the 'Lulu' from Dalton Lacey?"

"Yes, there can't be too many Tallulah's in Cleveland. Have you met her?"

"Ran into her one day when I was there with Ron."

"Right, you and Ron went to Case together. Same class. Same section."

"You remembered that?"

"Small city. I remember a lot." I left out that my memory was supplemented by the fact that I was hoping I'd get to use my knowledge the next time I was on a date with Ron.

"So, Lulu?" he asked.

"Can I pick your brain?" I decided to take the opportunity to check my own biases.

"What's up?"

"This is totally confidential, stranger on a plane type stuff."

"Stranger on a plane?"

"You don't know the people, so I trust that you could give a totally objective opinion. I'm trying to work out some stuff, but it's hard. Maybe I'm too close. Maybe I'm not seeing it the right way."

When the waiter came back, he whipped out one of those tray holders that looked like a hotel suitcase stand. He took the empty calamari bowl from the table, used a scraper on the tablecloth, then placed our steaks and sides on the table along with all the appropriate cutlery.

"Another bottle of wine?"

Before I could protest, Justin nodded. In a moment, another person was back with a new bottle, and our wine glasses were replaced and replenished.

"So, Lulu?" he asked again.

"I should start by saying I probably have a bias."

"We all have a bias. If you know that, then you're more objective than most."

"Okay. Maybe. I don't like her boyfriend. He used to be one of our professors, Civil Procedure, in law school. When I had some problems there, he promised to help me and dropped the ball. So there's that. The other is that he's married and he's older."

"Married?"

"Supposedly, a couple of months back, he left his wife. Wait—that's not fair. I know that he did leave, because he moved out of his family home and into my friend's apartment. Turned her second bedroom into his home office."

"If he told his wife, at least he's on the up-and-up about that."

"Who knows how many months too late. On the surface, there's nothing wrong. They're star-crossed lovers or soul mates or some such who just met at the wrong place and time and are now fixing that."

"You don't sound convinced."

"It's just that he's weird. Like he expects everything to be his way. He announced that he was going to move in. He didn't ask her. He expected me to handle his divorce because that would be payback for the shitty favor he did for me ten-plus years back. He changed the way my friend has dressed, the way she acts. I mean, I know that she had a persona that was…well…a kind of over-the-top persona. But it was uniquely hers. Now she's some Stepford wife, it's now twinsets and wool skirts."

"She growing up? Making partner in those white shoe places requires a certain amount of compromise."

"I want it to be that, but I don't know. I'm not explaining it right."

"You're fine." Our eyes met. His were warm and brown and didn't look away. I broke the stare. "I…I'm not sure you could do anything wrong." He sounded sincere.

"Ha, ha. You're funny. The last decade has been nothing but me making mistakes."

"Hey, I've got one for you."

"One what?"

"I don't know what you call it. But I saw it somewhere and wrote it down. Give me a sec."

He lifted slightly, pulled his wallet from his pants, and opened it. Justin extracted a small piece of lined paper. He put back the wallet, then unfolded the paper.

"Okay here goes. A shrewdness of apes."

His callback to a joke we'd shared ages ago caught me by surprise. That coupled with more glasses of wine than I could count sent me into a spasm of laughter. Once again like last time, the room of stuffy patrons turned our way. When had laughter become gauche?

"Oh my god, they're staring," I gasped.

"Let them look at a pretty woman laughing." I sobered up instantly at the compliment. He continued scanning his wrinkled paper. "I have one more."

"Okay?"

"Claw of panthers."

"Oh my god. These are the best."

He tapped the paper. "I remember now, it's called venery."

"Venery?"

"From the Book of Saint Albans. Published in 1486. Kind of an English gentlemen's guide to hunting."

"What? The fourteen-hundreds? Oh my god, you're a not-so closeted nerd."

"Not-so closeted?" He tried unsuccessfully to look aggrieved.

"Um, you own sweater vests. That was a sign."

"I'm not wearing one tonight."

"I noticed." My voice was nearly as husky as Lulu's had been. Too much damn wine was making Justin sexy in a nerdy kind of way.

"Let's get out of here."

"Where to?" I asked, even though I damn well knew where. I was buzzed, but not drunk enough that my reasoning was that impaired.

"We can finish this wine at my place." He gestured to the second bottle.

"They let you take the bottle?"

"What they don't know won't hurt them."

In a moment, he'd had everything wrapped to go. After he paid the bill, he lifted the cork, pushed it into the wine, then stuck it under one arm. When we got outside, he raised his other arm, and a cab came to a stop in front of the restaurant.

"Twenty-five sixty-four West Tenth." He'd given the cabbie an address only ten blocks west of the restaurant.

"You live in Tremont?" It was as up-and-coming and as hipster as Cleveland could be, which wasn't very much.

"Yup."

It wasn't more than five minutes before we were on a street of two-story two-family clapboard and brick houses. The taxi stopped in front of one that was probably beige in the daylight. Justin passed over a few bills. "Keep the change."

The cyclone fence surrounding the building had a "Beware of dog" sign affixed to the front.

"You have a dog?" My cat, Simba, could be left home alone for long periods of time. A dog seemed like a real commitment.

"Yes, though that's not my sign. Mine's a marshmallow. Former tenants probably."

"What's his name? Or is it a she?"

"It's a he. Morro."

I followed him up the front steps over the rough floor-boards of a building-wide porch and through a front door. He took the steps on the right, wine bottle in hand. I took up the rear with the bulging doggy bag of leftovers.

"Morro?"

"He was a stray I found on Morro Bay a few years back. Some friends and I drove up the coast for vacation."

"California, right?" I was embarrassed that I wasn't sure. I'd traveled so little in my life. My parents had defined "staycation" before that was a thing.

"Beautiful state once you get out of Los Angeles."

"I've never been," I said to his back.

He opened a door at the top of the landing. "Welcome to Casa McPhee. Make yourself at home."

Before I could do more than take in the white kitchen cabinets or the speckled granite countertops or the fact that it looked like Justin knew his way around a kitchen—if the knives on the magnet strip and all the pots stored above the cabinets were any indication—Morro ran into the room then came to a skidding halt in front of me.

"Why did he stop like a car trying to avoid an accident?"

"He's not allowed to jump on guests. I think he forgets every single time until the last moment. It's kind of hilari-ous."

I bent my head and looked the dog in the eye.

"Hello, Morro."

The black and white square faced mutt sniffed at the bag in my hand.

"Morro. Come." The dog immediately went to Justin's side. "I have to let him out. I'll be right back."

Then there was one.

Me.

Alone. In Justin McPhee's apartment. It was odd, really, entering someone's living space. It told you more about them than did their office or car or even clothes. I hung my raincoat on a rack by the door that already held a barn jacket and puffy coat.

I brushed my hands along the sleeves of my black turtle-neck trying to keep back a chill then really took in his apartment. The kitchen opened onto a living room. One leather couch and a huge flat screen TV took up most of that space. I looked left and there was his bedroom which had no door but a double-wide archway leading to it. A soft-looking brown comforter covered the bed.

My eyes ping ponged from there to another smaller room. I poked my head in below a chin-up bar to see a lone desk, computer, and chair. A few free weights lay sadly in a corner. All the walls were some beigey-gray color that was neutral and non-offensive all at the same time.

His bathroom was clean enough. I shut the door and took a quick pee. Flushed and washed my hands. Dried them on the cleanest looking towel. I went back into the kitchen and took a seat on one of the cushy white bar stools.

Morro ran back in well ahead of Justin and sniffed at my knees. I petted his head tentatively. Next thing I knew, the dog flopped on the floor and rolled onto his back, exposing his pinkish white underside which stood in sharp contrast to his glossy black and white coat. I may not be a dog person, but the invitation couldn't have been more blatant. I wasn't going to take Morro up on it. Not tonight, not in my dry clean only skirt.

"Stopped raining," Justin said, hanging his dry coat over my own.

"Only temporary," I responded. In a flash, as Justin walked toward the other side of the counter, my belly flip-flopped. I pressed on with generic weather and geography talk. "It's January. There's a lot more of that to come. Did you like California?"

"It was nice. Land of perpetual summer."

Justin opened a cabinet, got out two wine glasses, and put them on the counter. He'd poured each of us a glass before asking. "Wine?"

I lifted the Malbec to my lips and drank deeply. Got down off my stool, wandered over to the windows, and looked out on the dark and quiet street.

"How long have you lived here?" I asked without looking at him. I closed my eyes for a long moment. Swayed a bit, maybe. I didn't usually have this much wine in such a short period of time.

"Five years. Maybe six."

I wanted to ask him about Ron Pinheiro just then. I hadn't really seen Ron since the New Year's party. That had been a magical night. Not too cold, so I wasn't shivering the entire night in a room heated for men in winter wool and not women in strapless gowns.

When the clock had struck midnight, he'd drained his champagne, laid the flute on the tray of a passing waiter, and turned to me. His eyes locked with mine while I tried not to squirm. Ron tucked my hair behind my ears, flattened his hands against my jaw, leaned forward and kissed me. Right there in front of the entire Eastside country club crowd. It felt like I was in a movie with the lights having gone to a hazy blur.

Other than "Happy new year," he didn't say a thing. We didn't stay long after that. He got the car, drove me home, and gave me a kiss in the car. There was a long pause when I think he expected me to invite him up. I wanted to invite him up, more than anything at that moment. In an instant, I decided against it because I wanted to see him again and didn't think it was a good idea to move too fast. The hard part was that it felt like Ron was moving too slow. We were both busy, but it felt like he was too busy to squeeze in time for me. Fantasies of what we'd do once we had some time together were crowding my reality.

Ron and Justin had been in the same class, the same section. I think they may have been more than acquaintances. The nearly-formed question about Ron died on my lips because something in the room shifted. I couldn't put my finger on exactly what it was. But the air had changed.

It was almost palpable, the wave of longing that rolled off Justin. Before I could put two and two together in the thinking part of my brain, he'd leaned in and kissed me. I held my wine awkwardly at my side as I took in the unexpected touch.

"Do you want to go to my bedroom?"

I put the wine glass down on the windowsill. Nodded. Followed him to the bedroom.

I have zero idea what prompted me to say yes, but I did. I was still questioning myself minutes later when I turned to find Justin standing on the other side of the bed, completely naked. There was something so vulnerable about him at that very moment that kept me from changing my mind and figuring out how to get home.

Instead I sat on the bed, unrolled my tights, then stood and kissed him. The chemistry that we had while talking translated straight to that kiss. My reservations fell away as quickly as my clothes. For the next hour, I had no thoughts about Dion Fortune or Derek Waters or Ron Pinheiro.

It was only me and Justin.

"So are you dating anyone?" I asked from my side of his bed while my breathing returned to normal. He lay on the other side, his head propped on his right arm. I wanted to take back my words the minute I heard myself say them. It was the stupidest question, and I had no idea why I'd asked it.

"Sorry, that's none of my business," I retracted.

His blink was slow, thoughtful.

"Not in a while. Everyone I grew up with is already paired off and married."

"Do you want to be...paired off...married?"

"Someday probably. I think so. It would certainly make my parents happy. How about you?" When I hesitated, he waved a hand in the air. "It's fine, you can tell me."

"I went on a date with Ron for New Year's."

"Pinheiro. Dalton Lacey. That Ron?"

"One and the same. We met because of the pro bono program. Then of course, the Hudson referral."

"I like Ron. He's a nice guy. I'd keep an eye on him, though."

"Okay..." My mind raced. Did that mean we weren't dating? No, of course not. I was mistaking casual sex for something more. Stupid, stupid me. I don't know why I minded. I didn't want to date Justin. Ron was on the front burner. That said, I probably needed to take anything Justin said with a grain of salt. Just because we weren't dating, didn't mean that the green-eyed monster wasn't talking.

"I think that he's on a wobbly line, morally," Justin continued.

"Are you saying this because he's an atheist?" Thinking of Miles, I said, "Free thinkers are often the least morally bankrupt among us."

"Just be careful. That's all I'm going to say."

"I hear you." For a moment, I worried about my own morality. I had to believe that my presence in his bed had nothing to do with my representation of Fortune. My hope that Justin would get Waters to plea, leaving the coast clear for my client to continue his criminal enterprise exploiting women, maybe even trafficking them.

He trailed a hand down my side, clouding my judgment, raising goose bumps.

"Want to go again?"

In for a penny, in for a pound.

"Why not?"

7

I watched the first few flurries of snow fall on the hood of my car. Each melted as soon as it made contact. I looked at the trip meter on my odometer. I was halfway through the eighty-mile trek and wasn't going to turn back for a few flakes. Forty miles and forty-five minutes later, I regretted that decision. But I was already at the Conneaut facility by the time I realized this was more than a few flakes of lake effect snow.

"Tom Brody here for an attorney visit," I announced to the guard once I'd stepped through the heavy metal doors.

"Do you have your bar card and letter from the warden?" he asked. The tone wasn't friendly but wasn't quite on the hostile side either. It was time to clear him of the notion that I wasn't one of the good guys.

"It's not that kind of visit," I said. "I'm not a defense attorney. I'm with the Cuyahoga County prosecutor's office out of Cleveland. I need to speak with Jarrod Carter in regards to an ongoing investigation of a case."

Along with my bar card, I handed over my business card embossed with our gold badge seal.

"Right. Sorry. I'll get a room for you and bring the inmate down."

He escorted me around the metal detector/scanner that would have been at home in any post-9/11 airport. Then he pressed a buzzer in a little control room that had more buttons and levers than a jet's cockpit.

"Third room on the right. It's the warmest. He'll be down in the next fifteen minutes. You need this recorded?"

"Nope. He's not a suspect," I said. I lifted my hand in thanks and walked down the hall to take a seat on the metal chair in the sterile room. It was warm. Too warm. I wondered if it was some kind of tactic to keep visits short. I took off my car-length down coat and hung it on the back of the chair. Before I could sit down, keys jingled and the door opened.

A guard stepped in behind Carter and pulled out the only other empty chair for the prisoner. It struck me as a dick move, not courtesy.

Two dicks were enough for any one room. "You can go," I said to the guard. "Need privacy for this one."

The guard, who'd never taken his hand from his belt or gun, looked between us, his eyes narrowing in suspicion.

"I'm a senior prosecutor in Cleveland. It's fine."

He glanced between us one last time before giving me a two-fingered salute and leaving us to it, closing the door behind him.

"Tom Fucking Brody. You're the last person I expected to see here today. When they said attorney, I thought you were Casey Cort."

Prison hadn't changed Carter's physique in any way. He was still tall, and fully jacked. We were probably the same height, but he outweighed me by a good forty pounds of muscle. I made an effort to hide the uncomfortable feelings that would have a white woman clutching her purse and crossing the street at his approach.

"Nope. Casey's safely tucked away in Cleveland."

Carter gave me a funny look but didn't say anything else about my ex-fiancé.

"So why you here? We not exactly friends like that."

I tried not to shift in my seat. His question was perfectly reasonable considering the unorthodox nature of my visit. I could count on a single hand the number of defendants I'd talked to directly in my nine-plus years in this office. By the time I got a case, defendants were all lawyered up. Any talking would have happened when the cops still had the case. I took a deep breath of the dank air and ploughed forward with my agenda.

"You're supposed to be released—"

"July eighteenth with good time," Carter interrupted. "Six months from now."

"You want to get out early?"

"Christmas done passed."

"Early birthday present. Don't want you to have to spend your thirty-fourth birthday in jail."

I'd done some research before I'd driven all this way. He didn't look surprised that I knew any of it, though.

"That's nice and all, but I'm not interested in making any kind of deal. You gotta know that about me by now."

"You ever heard of the prisoner's dilemma?"

"Ain't no dilemma that I can see. As long as everyone keep they mouth shut, then ain't no problems."

Fat flakes floated by the wire reinforced windowpanes. I didn't have time to beat around the bush and make it back to Lakewood before the roads were clogged with snow and slush—and far more dangerous black ice.

"Rida Emad's phone turned up."

"Turned up where?" His question admitted nothing. Not that I expected anything different.

"Right now it's in evidence lockup. Last week, it was on my desk."

The idea of that phone being found would have scared the shit out of most criminals. Carter barely blinked. If he hadn't been less than four feet from me, I wouldn't even have been sure he'd heard a thing I said. Nerves of steel he had. I could learn something from him. I hadn't had a good night's sleep since that phone had turned up.

"Interesting you keeping track of phones and the like. I personally keep track of videotapes."

My stomach dropped to my knees. I rubbed my palms on my slacks, leaned forward to make sure I'd heard him right.

"Videotapes?"

"Maybe 'keepsake' is the right thing to say. Seems like the kind of word you'd like."

Somehow this meeting had turned inside out. My plan had been to get Carter home so he could take charge of his operation. Make sure Waters kept his other job duties to himself.

"What kind of keepsakes?"

"The kind that helps me remember the first time I meet anyone. Not so good with faces, but pictures help. Do you have a hard time with faces? I heard that people get face blindness when they gotta remember someone from a different race. So that 'all of us look alike' isn't entirely bogus."

"I...I remember the faces of girls...of women like Destiny." I stopped after I'd uttered that girl's name. It was a stupid move, but I was losing control of this meeting and my favorite girl's name had slipped out. I did remember her. I'd been unable to forget her unique combination of sass and vulnerability.

"Seems important. But if, say, you had to pick me out of a line-up, could you?"

"Don't know," I answered honestly. I had no idea what he was talking about. "I'd hope so," I said to placate him.

"No matter. Just know that I don't make mistakes like that. I'm not going to walk up and call you Chad, when I know you're Tom. Tom likes them dark, likes them young, and likes to keep his job. Met your dad last year. Nice guy."

"What do you think I should do with the phone? Guy named Derek Waters had it. Just got out on bail." I didn't give a shit that I'd probably signed Waters' death warrant. I was more interested in saving my own skin.

"Derek understand the dilemma better than you. He got more on the line than any of us right now. Facing first or second degree. A little birdie tells me he gonna plea it down. That he gonna take the time like a man. Least he could do for fucking up a good thing by drug dealing. Second time he fucked up. He know that I like to keep it clean. I'm in here because of him. Now he gotta do the same. He go away. The phone disappears into some basement storage. Problem go away."

"You seem so sure." I was a little bit in awe of his self-assuredness. I was more insulated than most guys, but that didn't mean I wasn't always looking over my shoulder worried that someone would drop a dime on me. Someone like

Tobias Whelchel who could probably smell a corruption scandal five miles away. I was ninety percent sure I could get out of any trouble that came my way. That last ten percent, though…that last ten could keep a man up at night.

"Always, always got insurance. A lotta folks I grew up with say that insurance is stupid. Premiums are a waste of money. That blacks always make payments, but never get paid. I see it differently."

"I'm here to cut you a check then. One that says freedom. I can have you out by the end of next week."

"Nobody do nothing out the goodness of they heart. Maybe mothers, but no one else. I don't have anything to trade for those extra six months."

His dead eye stare told me that six more months in here wouldn't be any skin off his nose. That he would take those days like they were one and come out strong and sane. Carter must have nerves of steel. Jail had done in plenty of hardened criminals. He made it look like a walk through the back nine of the country club.

"But you do," I asserted. "A plea is always easier. Saves taxpayer dollars. Keeps up my win record." I hesitated, but then decided to go for broke. There wasn't no way to get what I wanted, but by asking. "I'd also like to see Destiny again."

"On that first one I can guarantee that I'll keep it under control. On the second I can't help you. She outta the life now."

"Last week's didn't work for me. Well it worked, but you know what I mean." I didn't want him to think that my equipment didn't work. I looked him up and down. Probably didn't compare to whatever he had going on, but I wasn't exactly a slouch either.

"Other people put in their requests early for the holiday. I'll make sure you get what you need going forward. Just need a little notice is all."

Of course he'd have someone like Destiny. I shifted in my seat again, this time to quell my excitement over that future encounter. It was time to close this one up.

"Gotta get going ahead of this storm," I said. "You should be home next week."

"Safe drive back. Cleveland nice this time of year. My mother will be happy to see me."

I slipped on my coat, gathered up my briefcase, and knocked on the door. I didn't say a thing to the deputy, just walked right toward the first locked door.

The other deputy, considerably warmer now, gave me a small smile before buzzing open the lock.

"It's hairy out there. Safe drive back to Cleveland."

"Thanks."

I used my arm to brush the snow off my back window. The wipers would have to take care of the windshield. Carefully, I backed out of the space and pulled out of the parking lot. I was a good slow and slippery six miles in before it dawned on me. That show he'd made of keepsakes and videotapes wasn't about Waters or anyone else, it was about me.

He had a videotape of me fucking some girl.

A car nearly collided with me, bringing me back to the present. Sweat trickled under my arms, down my back, prickled along my upper lip. Adrenaline coursed through my veins.

If I put one foot the wrong way, everything could go wrong for me. Denying charges in some kind of john sweep was one thing. Video could go viral in today's interconnected world. That would embarrass the hell out of my family—and end my career for sure.

Prisoner's dilemma my ass.

My one and only job here was to keep Jarrod Carter—the Sledge Hammer—as quiet as a church mouse.

8

I didn't know why I was nervous, but Sledge Hammer was back. I parked down the street from his mama's house, zipped up my parka and walked the half block down Scarborough Road. Each of the two-story wood framed houses sat on their own lot far apart from one another.

Unless you had some kind of binoculars, you couldn't really see what was going on in someone else's house. When the girls' containers were found, I'd thought Sledge was rash in his decision to relocate them here and start moving them around by van like they were ready-to-order takeout.

When I'd had Alisha hire contractors to pour an extra pad in the back to park some of the vans, that had raised the brows of a few neighbors. When I'd explained that I worked for Jarrod Carter and that he was expanding into subcontracted delivery, it hadn't raised too many eyebrows. The white neighbor on the one side nodded and had skipped tree trimming that year. The black neighbor on the other had also nodded, mumbled about how a black man had to hustle, asked after Sledge's mom, then had also let his bushes grow. I'd followed their lead and had demoted the gardener to lawn care only.

Even with Sledge in jail, things had gone smoothly, me moving the girls in and out of the van under cover of darkness and foliage. Now that the boss was back, I wasn't sure how our relationship would work. I might even need to get another job, start my own thing. I wasn't sure I was ready to be the second-in-command again. At the back door now, I took a deep breath and knocked.

Instead of his niece Alisha, Sledge opened the door, and I let him pull me into a hug. Not a half hug and hand grip, but a full-blown hug, like he was my mother or sister or something. I tried not to look like I was pulling away, while I was in fact, trying to pull away. I hoped that prison hadn't made him gay or anything. Wasn't going to ask him that out loud, though. I'd just keep my distance until I could assess where he was coming from.

Instead, I said, "Who you want for your reunion? I'll make sure she down at the club."

"Shonna, for sure."

Shonna was popular. Dark enough for Westside men's fantasies, light enough for Eastsiders'. I nodded and didn't comment on the money we'd lose if she was out of commission for more than a few nights. He deserved a sweet homecoming. Money and business could wait until next week.

"You came back on a cold ass day. Been snowing for a week. Business is up, though. Guys want more than a pizza delivered to they door." I knew it sounded needy, like I was waiting for his approval, but it wasn't that. I needed him to know that I wasn't like Iceman, that I hadn't crossed or double-crossed him. That I'd been loyal as fuck while he was away.

"The house still here. No water dripping in from the roof, so I know you took care of things. Mama ain't doing the best, but that's on Alisha and not you."

He was right about that. His amputee mother's battle with diabetes hadn't been my job. My only job had been to turn over sixty percent of the nightly earnings. What his niece did with it after that wasn't my business. I hoped I wasn't there when he noticed that she'd upgraded his Lexus and had gotten herself a Mini Cooper to boot. That was family business.

"How you get here this early? I for sure thought you was in until July. This ain't California with people doing half time and all that because of overcrowding or liberal legislators letting out non-violent offenders."

Sledge winked at me. The purportedly convivial gesture made me shiver. I'd never been afraid of him exactly, but he'd always exhibited a coldness that was intimidating.

"I got friends in high places," he said. "I'm going to run Mama to the hospital in a minute. May be there tomorrow as well. I'll see Shonna tomorrow night. Then I'm going to need you to carry me over to wherever Iceman's staying."

I blurted out, "Why?" before I could think better of it.

"Prison ain't Mars. I heard that he out on bail. Gotta make sure that he doesn't plan to talk to no one about anything other than his name, rank, and serial number."

"Talked to him already. Bailed him out. Hired him a lawyer—"

"Casey?"

"Nah. She represent me...Intraport..."

"Why not Waters?"

"Cause even I know that's a conflict of interest. He talk or they discover something from that Arab girl's phone, and I'm going to need someone to have my back."

"Fuck me. You shoulda done it the other way 'round. Get her to represent Waters and find someone else. Some kind of Jew barracuda for yourself."

"Why? I'm confused. Casey Cort got you off that charge."

"That first one. Not that second one that put me in Conneaut."

"I thought that was because it was another county. I thought you took the plea because the feds was sniffin' around."

"Look, I don't need no help running my business. I'll tell you this. Casey got an in in Cuyahoga County. She used to date one of the judge's sons. Father still like her, and he run the courthouse downtown, like he in charge of other judges and stuff. That's how I got off. She ain't that good a lawyer."

I hadn't known even a tenth of that. He'd dragged me to her office and announced that she was our lawyer. I'd just made sure her bills were paid and kept her apprised of what was going on.

"I went to her when Ice got arrested. The police found—"

"The phone. I know."

I hadn't dared talk on the phone with him in prison, so a couple of visits where I talked mostly in code was all we'd had. Even I knew better than to share information over the phone, especially about an ongoing criminal enterprise. They recorded everything. Probably didn't have anyone to listen to it. But if they needed it, probably had every phone conversation ever on a computer or tape somewhere.

"She know the lawyer who took Ice's case."

"And?"

"And she said last she heard, he was going to plea. The guy...Mc...something Irish...McPhee wanted to go to trial, but she talked to him and he agreed to do what Ice asked, take a plea, and take the time."

"Any more runners?"

"Sorry?"

"Sorry? What—you some white guy now? Sorry." Sledge shook his head. I didn't like what that headshake implied, but I remained silent.

He continued, "I'm home now. Gotta get back to business. How many girls we got? Nobody left since Destiny, right?"

"Fifteen, including Shonna. She work out of the club a lot of days. Things been busy there now that we took over the upstairs."

"How that happened again?"

Coded prison talk had been brief by necessity.

"One of the vans kept breaking down." I pointed out the kitchen window. "It's in the garage. Anyway, guys in the club wasn't happy that you'd stopped offering extra services from the dancers, and business was down.

"The family that was living up there, they decided to move to North Carolina or some shit. I'll never understand black people moving back to the south. Anyway, it was vacant. I told you that I bought the building right. It was eighty grand. They just needed enough money to buy a place outright down south."

Sledge went to the fridge. Took out a beer, then put it back. Lifted the clean but empty coffee pot and shoved it back into its place—hard. My shoulders came down. I hadn't realized I'd braced myself for broken glass. Sledge didn't spare me a glance. He opened the fridge again, took out a soda instead. He didn't offer me anything, and I didn't ask.

"You got girls tricking out of The Place to Be."

"Consolidation. It's why car dealerships also do repairs, right. Unless you Coke or Microsoft, one line of business isn't enough."

"Do you remember when I shut down the extras the girls were selling?"

"Yeah, I mean, when you were facing trouble with the liquor control, food safety, and all that shit."

"This was the reason I went to trial. Because they knew I was promoting prostitution, they just couldn't prove it. And after I beat that charge, I shut that shit down. And now I'm hearing that you've reopened that door to liability."

Liability? I wanted to make fun of him for acting like more of a white guy than me, but that wouldn't have gone over well.

"It's not like that. They not giving blow jobs in the back room. A man's gotta know the password, pay up front. The dancers are not doing anything. They know if they asked, the answer is always no."

"I don't care. Shut it down. Shut that shit down."

"It's a hundred for a blow job, two hundred for half and half or straight. Easily clear three thousand a night if not more per girl. Our girls are not like the rough ones on Lorain Avenue, so the men willing to part with hard-earned money. Especially on Friday after they get paid."

"Did I ask you for an accounting? I said shut it down."

"Fine."

"Fix up the van and get back to how I left the business when I went to Conneaut."

"I've had no problems at the club. The cops haven't so much as driven by."

"I need a completely legit business. One that I can use to move money through. A place I can offer up any kind of investigator that starts sniffing my way. You know that. I told you that's how I run things. Now you've gone and messed all of that up."

"What should I do with the upstairs? No one is paying ninety thousand a month in rent."

"Use it for storage. Rent it to a family or some insurance agent, I don't know. That's up to you."

"Fine."

"With the numbers you put up, I assume the building and land is all paid for."

"Yes. With the usual deductions for taxes, improvements, depreciation. It's a separate LLC. Seventy-one twenty-five St. Clair, LLC."

"Where the paperwork?"

It was at my apartment, but I wasn't going to say that. "It's in the office. Intraport is here like we discussed."

"Let's go."

"Where?"

"Time to see the Iceman. Forget tomorrow. I don't want him getting wind of my return. I need to be the one to tell him I'm home. That it's his turn."

I lifted my phone from my belt. "Let me give him a heads-up that we heading over."

"Nope. Put that back. He don't need to know a damn thing. Nothing beat the element of surprise. Why you think the cops don't announce themselves until they at your house with a battering ram?"

Why indeed. I lifted the keys from the peg on the door and sent up a silent prayer for Derek Waters. I pushed at a button on the mudroom wall, and the garage opened.

"That a new Lexus? Well hot damn."

"Your niece—"

"Did a good job. Breakwater blue, she said. Nice ice-blue color. You drive. I like to ride."

I blooped the doors open and stepped up into the driver's seat. Backed it out and waited a minute. Sledge got in. Ran his fingers along the leather. Opened and closed the glove compartment. I was very happy right then that Sledge was a rule follower. As a felon, he wouldn't dare have a gun in the car. At least I knew that Iceman was only going to get a good talking to, not a bullet in the brain. Other "business" owners would have killed Waters for much less.

9

Ron: Hey there beautiful.

Me: Are we still on for tonight? I'm really looking forward to it.

Ron: Me too. Logistics later. Have to get back to work.

"The State of Ohio versus Derek Waters," the bailiff called. I shoved my phone away, so I didn't piss off the judge.

"That's a lot of people against me." Waters looked momentarily wild-eyed, like an animal that suddenly realized he'd been captured.

"Shhh," Justin hissed at Waters. He grabbed onto the too long sleeve of the ill-fitting sport coat nearly covering his client's fist.

Presiding Judge Patrick Brody looked out at the courtroom.

"This is more than the usual crowd," Judge Brody observed. Despite the fact that most court proceedings were public, courtroom galleries were usually empty. There were a few die hard court observers who believed in sunshine laws, or lawyers with a few minutes to kill, but few others ever came to watch outside of high-profile cases.

Judge Brody let his glasses fall to his chest. He lifted his hand in a salute against his forehead as if he were a seafarer looking toward the horizon.

"I see one familiar face back there. Ms. Cort, good morning. Good to see you. With so many judges I don't get to see you often enough." I tried not to let the warmth in his voice get to me.

He was warm like the snake in the garden of Eden was warm...a cold-blooded animal adapting to its environment.

"Can I hope that you being here means that you've taken pity on my family and decided to reconsider becoming a Brody?"

"I'm just here to observe, Your Honor." I shifted in my seat hoping that Judge Brody didn't comment on the fact that I was sitting on the side farthest from the empty jury box, the defense side behind Justin. That he wouldn't realize what I'd just done with one of them, that both attorneys at bar had been my lovers. I tucked my Catholic guilt far away so that it wouldn't show up on my face.

His eyes squinted for a moment taking in everyone while I tried not to feel...exposed. A quick nod to himself indicated that he was satisfied with what he'd seen. Then he lifted his reading glasses to his nose and looked down at the file before him, opening it and scanning its contents.

"Attorney McPhee, Tom, we're here today to take a plea from Derek Waters for the crimes charged in the indictment dated December twenty-eight. Have the parties reached an agreement?"

Both Justin and Tom nodded and said, "Yes, Your Honor," simultaneously.

"Before we move on to taking a knowing and voluntary plea, I need to make a statement for the record. Even though I'm presiding Judge Patrick Brody, I'm also a father. My son, Thomas Brody is an assistant prosecuting attorney for Cuyahoga County. This case, Ohio versus Waters, was assigned both to him and to me. Normally, I'd recuse myself in cases like this to prevent the appearance of bias or impropriety.

"However, in this case my only job today is to take a plea of guilty after a protracted negotiation by the defendant who is ably represented by Justin McPhee, a capable attorney who has appeared before this court numerous times.

"Both parties and, most importantly, Defendant Waters have agreed to waive any objection to my assignment on this matter for taking the plea and for sentencing as well. For the record, gentlemen, I'll need your waiver of objection.

"Counselor McPhee? On behalf of Derek Waters do you waive an objection to my recusal for my relationship to the prosecutor?"

"Yes, Your Honor."

"Tom? On behalf of the PA's office, do you waive any objection?"

"Yes...Da...Your Honor."

To no one in particular, Judge Brody said, "I rarely get to see my own son in action. Hazard of the job, I guess. Now that we have that on the record, I'd like to get to the plea. Will the defendant please rise."

Justin and Derek Waters stood in sharp contrast. Justin was clearly comfortable in his wool suit; the faint wrinkles saying that he'd worn it just enough to break it in. Waters looked awkward in his. I guessed that he'd probably only worn it for funerals or maybe a church wedding.

"Before me I have a plea agreement. Derek Waters, in exchange for consideration in limiting your sentence, do you agree that you'll plead guilty to possession of a controlled substance and to trafficking in drugs?"

Waters gave a stiff nod.

"I'll need you to speak out loud for the record, Mr. Waters," Judge Brody admonished.

"If I plead guilty, I'm going to jail, right?" Waters' voice was an octave higher than it had been moments before.

"Sentencing would not be today, Mr. Waters. You'd remain out on bond until the sentencing hearing. Before that, probation would need to do a report. Did your counsel not explain all of this to you?"

Judge Brody cast an eye toward Justin. The part of Justin's neck that I could see from my seat in the gallery colored slightly. It had been that same color when he'd been on top of me and...I shut that thought down before it could blossom.

"I reviewed all of this with my client, Your Honor," Justin said.

"Can I assume that we're ready to proceed, then?"

Justin nodded. His client glanced at his attorney, then Tom and the judge.

"Regarding the charge of possession of a controlled substance, to wit, methamphetamine, Mr. Waters, how do you plea?"

"Not guilty, Your Honor."

There was shuffling among the few in the pew-like seats around me. Another attorney closed the file he'd been perusing and leaned forward.

"Excuse me?"

"Not guilty. I want a trial."

"Mr. McPhee?" Judge Brody's tone had gone from warm serpent to cold and unforgiving god.

"I need to consult with my client, Your Honor."

"Indeed, you do. Five-minute recess." Judge Brody banged the gavel and abruptly rose from his chair.

Everyone stood hastily as the judge swept out of the door behind him, his robes swirling in his wake.

The possibility of me going to jail wasn't even on the table, but my heart rate was up, nonetheless. An angry judge was as scary as an angry parent. Maybe scarier because they didn't love you like your mom or dad did.

Tom stood and wandered toward the witness box. He lifted the phone there and pressed some buttons. I wondered if he were alerting his boss or doing something entirely different. I shifted my attention toward Justin and Derek Waters. Their voices were not as quiet as they thought.

"What do you want, Derek?"

"I don't think I want to go to jail. I mean, Sledge say it ain't no thang. But I could do like three years. That's a lot of time to be gone from here. I'd be like twenty-seven or even thirty. I'll be old, man. I don't want to miss out on shit. I mean, there's not even any girls there. I couldn't have sex, man. Could you go without sex for that long?"

I nearly died in my seat when Justin hazarded a quick glance in my direction.

"This isn't about me, Derek. This is about you. The first thing you have to consider is whether or not we think a jury of your peers would find you guilty. If so, what are the consequences of that? Because judges generally sentence defendants to longer stints in prison after they go to trial than after they plea."

"Is that fair?"

"It's neither fair nor is it legal, but it's the reality."

"Or I could be found not guilty."

"You were caught up in a sting, Derek. Narcotics officers pretended to be an up and coming dealer, ordered a large quantity of meth, and you delivered."

"Ain't that entrapment?"

"It would be if you weren't already a drug dealer."

"That's just it. That's not my main job."

"Are you willing to talk now about the thing I tried to talk to you about, but you shut down? If you're willing to give the police or prosecutors information about the people you work with, the people above you in the meth distribution chain, then you might not have to go to jail at all."

"Could they protect me?"

"What do you mean?"

"Like witness protection?"

I wasn't a mind reader, but I'm sure Justin was regretting the influence of television where everyone got an OJ defense and there was federal witness protection money raining from the sky.

"Maybe. It's a possibility. Are you afraid for your safety? If you…gave up your accomplices, most likely they'd go to jail and not be a threat."

"Meth ain't no thing. Cookers and dealers are a dime a dozen. I got something way bigger I know about."

"All rise!" the bailiff shouted. I turned my head from Justin and Waters toward Judge Brody who'd swept back into the room. He sat in his chair at the bench and re-buttoned the top of his robe around the ice-blue tie that matched his eyes. Tom hung up the phone abruptly and made swift work of getting across the well toward his own table.

"Mr. McPhee, does your client want to enter a plea to-day?"

"No, Your Honor."

Judge Brody blinked once slowly, then turned to the courtroom clerk. How much time does the defendant have left?"

"Two hundred forty-eight days, Your Honor."

"Mr. McPhee, how much time do you need to prep for trial? How many witnesses will you be calling?"

Justin glanced at me, then his client, then the clerk, bailiff, and judge. He wasn't truly seeing any of us. My best guess was that he was turning around multiple strategies in his head. He made a show of flipping through his leather-bound calendar.

"We could be ready in thirty days, Your Honor."

"Tom?"

"The same, Your Honor. This is a slam dunk case."

I didn't need to glance in Tom's direction to know that his face held a smug smile. I hated that about prosecutors. They acted like trials weren't a search for the truth or quest for justice, but about their own win–loss ratio.

"Trial motions will be due February twenty-third. Trial will be set for March sixth. Any questions?"

"No, Your Honor," Justin replied.

"No, Your Honor," Tom parroted.

"Well, then we're dismissed. I'm a little worried that to-day's Groundhog Day. I really hope this means I won't have to see a repeat of what just happened here. Have a good day, counselors."

With that, presiding judge Patrick Brody left the bench.

Tom approached Justin.

"Call me." Tom handed Justin one of the heavily embossed cards prosecutors brandished like the guns their police compatriots carried. "It looks like we need to have a long talk." Tom shouldered his bag and threw his coat over his arm. One jaunty salute, and he pushed his way out through the heavy wood double doors.

"What he mean by that?" Derek didn't look any calmer with his plea deal now history and the trial he very much wanted scheduled.

"Derek, I have another hearing. Call me and we'll make an appointment for Monday or Tuesday. You take the weekend to think."

"I'll call you first thing Monday morning. I can just go home now?"

"You're still out on bond, so just get home and think."

Derek threw on a puffy coat that completely mismatched his pressed suit, then he was the next through the courtroom doors.

"So?" I asked. I glanced at the clock above the bench. I was on the clock. In my representation of Dion Fortune, I had come to watch Derek take his plea and make sure that he didn't take Fortune or Carter down with him. Now it was all up in the air. I needed to plot out my next move. First I had to get a handle on whether Justin had client control. Although truth be told, that ship had clearly sailed.

"So?" Justin looked confused. Rightfully so. I hadn't really talked to him after that weird night in January. He'd texted a question about appearing before Judge Brody. I'd responded to him but hadn't answered the other implied question. Because I didn't have an answer to that. To anything about us. I needed an answer to Waters, though.

"No plea," I said. "Why did he change his mind? I thought you'd all agreed that he would plead guilty." I knew I'd said too much. That I'd need some kind of cover story as to why in the hell I was here asking about a referral. Attorneys never held that tight to cases they'd let go.

Justin looked around the nearly empty room. We'd become the stars of our own reality show. "Let's take this out to the hall."

"Fine." I agreed. I'd always wanted the courthouse regulars to know me, to greet me like Norm on Cheers, but for my legal prowess and my ability to win cases, not my effed up interpersonal relationships and possibly loose relationship with ethics.

Once we were outside the doors and down at the end of the hall, standing before a huge window that overlooked downtown Cleveland, Justin didn't speak until he'd caught my eye.

"Can I ask you a question?"

I shrugged. "Sure?"

"Are we going to see each other again?"

I did my best to not let the jolt his question caused show in my demeanor. I couldn't help the stutter in my answer, though.

"Uh…um. We're seeing each other now."

"Right. Okay. You seem upset about Derek not taking the plea. I was surprised to see you in court this morning. Did you come to support me? Or was it Tom? You guys getting back together? Judge Brody seemed to think it was a good idea." His pivot from one idea to the next threw me. Me and Justin. Sledge Hammer's operation. Derek's threat. A possible relationship with my ex fiancé. My brain was on overload.

"I'm not getting back together with Tom," I insisted. In case any of this got back to Ron, I wanted to set the record straight on that one. "I just came to…I had a hearing here and remembered that your plea was today."

"I don't remember telling you about that..." he trailed off. "I'm glad he's rethinking it."

I rushed in with excuses and explanations, because of course he hadn't told me a damn thing about a hearing. That had been Dion Fortune, and a search through the ancient court database had confirmed Fortune's information. I rushed in because I had to do something to patch this up, fix the one thing that could unravel everything—an examination of my motives.

"You're glad? What you said to him is one hundred percent true, though. If he takes this to trial and loses, then he'll be in jail for much longer than three years. He can kiss not only sex but freedom goodbye."

"You don't have faith in my skills?" Justin sounded almost injured.

"It's not that," I said. Honestly, I didn't have a true assessment of Justin's skills. I'd never seen him at trial. Our relationship was based on referrals and our shared belief in ethics in a world where honesty and truthful dealing weren't always valued. "But," I continued, "the system is stacked against defense attorneys."

"Oh ye of little faith."

"I've never been up against Tom, but he has a one hundred percent win record, so I'm not sure faith will be enough."

Tom's win rate was the stuff of legends. Now, obviously, that was probably ninety-nine percent plea deals like today, which prosecutors treated as wins. But he'd never lost an actual jury trial either. Part of that had to be kicking losing cases to other prosecutors to take that dive. But part of it was probably that he was that good. Or at least was better than everyone he'd come up against.

"There are many ways this could go. We will see." Justin was unusually confident for a defense attorney in a prosecutor-happy courthouse. He turned away from the window and turned the full force of his gaze on me. If there hadn't been a wall behind me, I'd have backed up.

"You free for dinner?" he asked.

For a full ten seconds my mind went blank and my mouth mute. What exactly did one say to their one night stand about dating? Dating for real? My best guess was the truth, so that's what I led with.

"Um, no. Sorry. I'm meeting Ron for drinks. It's gonna be a no work night."

Not that what we'd done had been work, but it had started out work related. We were colleagues. We were not dating. That's something I wanted with a guy like Ron. Not just a guy like Ron, but with Ron, I thought.

"Ron Pinheiro, right?" Justin asked, even though I knew that he hadn't forgotten. That long and drawn out warning he'd given me about his former classmate's questionable ethics still sat in the back of my mind. "You serious about him?"

My mind did that thing again, where I forgot my words. There was no book of etiquette about this kind of conversation.

"He's a great guy," I started, tentatively stepping into uncharted conversational waters. "You said so yourself. I'm actually ready for a serious relationship," I overshared. Then I did some more. "I'm certainly not getting any younger. He wants to get married, have kids. I want to get married and have kids. We want the same things, so I think it's a good idea that we get to know each other better and see if we're compatible for the long term."

The way he was looking at me shut me right up. I sounded like a desperate woman, a throwback to one hundred years earlier. A woman who would be nothing if she couldn't find the right husband. It wasn't a good look, but I couldn't take it back. And despite how sexist it probably sounded, it was the unvarnished truth. I wasn't meant to be single. I wanted what my parents had.

"Right. Marriage and kids. All that."

"Do you want that?" I asked. Maybe we were the same. Maybe we weren't so different, and I didn't come across as so crazy.

"I'm not sure, actually."

My phone buzzed. It was most likely Ron sending a text. We hadn't decided if I should meet him at the restaurant or if he was going to pick me up. Logistics demanded I cut this conversation short. I took a peek at the phone. Ron was cancelling again. Disappointment flowed through my body like blood.

Suddenly, everything—my coat, my briefcase, my heart—felt heavier somehow. I tried not to let the disappointment show on my face. I didn't want to go down that road with Justin. I needed to walk away before I began to overshare again. The fact that my best friend was wrapped up in her too old, married boyfriend was making it difficult to manage discretion. I needed to talk to someone, and Justin was too easy. I needed to bail.

"Well. It was great. I gotta go. Hearings. Work. Date. Have a great weekend."

I didn't wait for him to respond. Instead, I hefted my own briefcase, then walked as quickly as I could to the elevator. I did not want to take that slow ride down with Justin standing awkwardly next to me. I needed to spend those long minutes thinking about what I was going to say to Dion Fortune and his newly freed boss.

The biggest threat to their ongoing criminal operation was walking free throughout the city, and Derek Waters suddenly seemed like he might have an axe to grind.

10

It was too fucking cold outside. The arctic breeze that blew from Lake Erie cut through my parka like a knife. Couldn't be more than ten degrees outside at this time in the early evening. At least the few flurries blowing through the air weren't gathering into a storm like they had when I'd driven back from the prison in Conneaut.

I shook my head, marveling at either my utter bravery or utter stupidity for visiting Jarrod Carter. Back when I thought seeing him would be enough to eliminate my exposure to humiliation if not prosecution.

I wasn't at the end of this journey yet thanks to Waters chickening out. I thought criminals had balls of steel. This one had just regular, weak, fleshy testicles that obviously shrank at the thought of prison.

I lifted my hood on my short walk from the Justice Center to Public Square. I snapped the hood's closure more forcefully than was necessary. It was the only way I could think of to deal with my anger.

Derek Waters hadn't taken the fucking plea. I'd offered the shortest sentence I could get away with without raising Lori Pope's eyebrows. Generous didn't even begin to cover it. Ninety-nine-point-nine percent of the defendants sitting in the county jail would have jumped at the chance to take such a short sentence for so much meth.

Sledge wasn't joking. He was not the kind of guy who made jokes. If he said he had some kind of insurance, I was inclined to believe him. Videos of me and Destiny would not be a good career move. I guess he didn't have as good of insurance on Waters, otherwise this little problem wouldn't still be on my plate.

Now I was the one place I did not want to be, in between the proverbial rock and hard place. I wasn't planning on being there alone.

If, somehow, the worst happened and I ended up trying the case, I'd have to make sure to keep that phone out of evidence. There was no way anyone would accept that kind of fuckup from me, though. It's not that I thought I was brilliant or some kind of legal savant. I didn't lack that kind of self-awareness. That said, there was a certain expectation of how a Brody should conduct themselves.

I needed some help to throw the case. It's why I was stepping into the Tipsy Jurist instead of taking myself home and blasting the heat at eighty degrees. A chill had set in my bones that wouldn't go away.

"Sir, are you eating dinner?" the host asked when I pushed the heavy wooden door closed behind me.

Sir.

I was usually addressed by name, but this bar-cum-steak-house on the bottom floor of Casey's building was not a hangout for the law and order crowd. The establishment was much older than I was. My father's generation had hung out there when they'd first passed the bar. That was before it had turned into the de facto defense bar for the defense bar. The prosecutors like me mostly lived on the Westside, and we had our own hangouts.

"I'm not sure," I said, my gaze bouncing back and forth between the bar and the booths. "I'm looking for Nicole Long. Is she here?"

Nicole hadn't bothered to cover her tracks. The host hadn't even pretended not to know her. He tilted his head to the right.

"Check the back corner."

I did the barely-there nod as I wove my way through the booths filled with defense attorneys halfway to drunk. Someone should tell them they were on the wrong side of things. Winning one hundred percent of your cases did not drive you to drink. I knew that firsthand. I had a remarkably sober Irish family. Chalked it up to their ability to sleep at night.

Nicole hid out here with them these days because she'd alienated most of the prosecuting attorney's office which was no easy feat. Nearly a decade of showing up to court drunk, then recovering, then relapsing had not made the kind of collegial inroads one would expect of someone with her tenure.

"What are you having?" I asked. I'd pushed myself into the booth across from her without waiting for an invitation or acknowledgement.

"I'm not...this is just..." she stuttered. I assumed her wide-eyed expression was disbelief over seeing a fellow prosecutor.

Busted.

"I'm not here from the Supreme Court," I said.

Ohio's highest court was in charge of not only attorney registration, but discipline as well. I'm pretty sure that I'd heard that Nicole Long remaining sober was a condition of her probationary status with the bar, if not with the prosecutor's office too.

She was only a few drinks from losing her job and perhaps her license to practice. If she'd been a solo practitioner like Casey, she'd already have been disbarred. The prosecutor's office was a shield against discipline. Long's shield was battered and bruised, though. If life were a video game, she'd have been one step from her defenses being obliterated with her next sip.

"It's a good thing that Lori Pope doesn't fundraise from the defense bar," I said when Long didn't respond.

A waiter shuffled to our table, slipping a paper coaster onto the nearly black wood scarred from decades of abuse. He plopped down a glass of ice water that was sweating in the overly warm room.

"Sir?"

I thought about sticking to water, then realized I wasn't the one chasing sobriety. I glanced at her warm-hued drink. Looked like cognac. That was as good as any other at smoothing out the rough edges.

"Old Fashioned," I ordered.

"Right away, sir," was his obsequious reply. Head down, he shuffled away, his black sneakers squeaking against the highly polished floor.

"I've only had one," Nicole announced. She lifted her nearly empty glass, swirling the remaining contents. "It's all about moderation, like everything else. This is under control, here." She pointed the glass toward herself. If I were a betting man, I'd lay odds that it hadn't been her first. I stood and took my coat off. Hung it on the hook on the pole that separated our booth from the one behind us. Sat back down and folded my hands on the edge of the table avoiding all that was possibly wet or sticky.

"I need your help."

"What?" Long was too inebriated to be immediately suspicious. She continued, "I don't really have any cases. I'm on grand jury duty." She had that assignment because we all knew the rumors were true, you could get the grand jury to indict a ham sandwich. It was a suitable task for a fuckup.

"I need a second chair," I said. Someone who would sit next to me at trial and share any blowback that came the prosecutor's way. That last part, it remained unsaid.

"In major crimes?" Alcohol had made her brain slower, not stupider. The time it took for her to arrange her features into those of a suspicious person would have been comical if it hadn't been so sad. "Do you have the wrong Long?"

"Nicole, I don't have the wrong Long. The only way to get back on the horse is to do it."

She may have been tipsy, but she wasn't exactly buying what I had to sell.

"Why do you want me of all people? There are at least two hundred other attorneys who outrank me."

I took a deep breath. Paused. I was going to have to sell this one—hard. Fortunately, I had the background to do it. I'd seen my father and uncles, more than once, convince someone to do something that was in the interests of the

Brody family if not necessarily in the interests of that self-same person.

"After my uncle was convicted, I've had a lot of time to think about redemption and second chances," I started. "You and I, we came up together. You were one hell of a prosecutor once you got out of CSEA and came downtown to work in the felony unit. I was covering new filings over the Christmas break. Things were slower than usual, so I was cleaning out my file cabinet and came across some of the old cases we'd worked on."

None of this was true, but bringing up common memories was one of the better persuasion techniques. My uncle was always reminiscing about the "good old days" with the men who came to our house. When those men left, they were always happy to do whatever favor had been asked of them.

"Remember the Robert Thomas case? Thomas threw a brick at the guy hitting on his girlfriend, then tried to run him over with a car."

"After a case of beer," Long said without a hint of irony. "I still don't know where he put it." Nicole closed her eyes and smiled for a second. It had been a slam dunk of a case. Another where the defendant gave up the possibility of two years to roll the dice for acquittal. Thomas had come up "snake eyes."

"Got eight years," I prompted.

I could see it in Nicole's closed eyes when the memory came back to her.

"All because he wouldn't take a plea and apologize." She shook her head. "Classic example of 'Pride goeth before destruction, and a haughty spirit before a fall.'"

"I'm amazed you still remember all that." Before Nicole had fallen long and hard off the wagon, she'd given the most eloquent opening and closing arguments. She'd been a master at weaving religion into a morality tale that had defendants convicted before the jury had even begun deliberation.

"Religion major. I still think it's one of the most relevant ones for this job."

"Your opening and closing arguments have always been a thing of beauty," I said. That part at least was one hundred percent true. Nicole had been a master. "You made every defendant look guilty."

"For whosoever shall keep the whole law, and yet offend in one point, he is guilty of all."

"What's that from?" I hadn't learned much from twelve years of Catholic school.

"James two, verse ten."

"You always did have a good memory," I said. Though I had to wonder if the alcohol had turned it to Swiss cheese. For the briefest moment I had a twinge of guilt because I was hoping that she'd lost her edge.

"Holyoke was a good education," she said of the past.

"This is a good opportunity," I said of the future.

The rest of Long's cognac slipped down her throat as she titled the glass high. The empty glass was swept away by the waiter before it could even hit the table properly.

"What is it?" she asked. From the intensity of her gaze, I knew I'd hooked her. My biggest challenge right now would be not talking after the close.

"Defendant is charged with possession and trafficking of meth." I kept it dead simple.

"Did you move to narcotics?"

"Nope, this is still major crimes."

"What's the catch?"

"Neil Walsh says the kid is connected."

"To other meth dealers? Meth is a problem that mostly solves itself with the dealers using and overdosing or blowing themselves to smithereens. Since when is this an office priority?"

"The office's focus hasn't changed. Walsh says that the defendant is connected to organized crime."

"Mafia?" Long's shake of the head said she was unconvinced of the importance of the case. Of the likelihood that serving as my second chair was a true path to redemption. "This is Cleveland, not New York, not even Chicago. We don't even have Chinese gangs like the West Coast."

"Neither. Something bigger, maybe."

"You don't know?"

"Defendant came out of the gate with a lawyer. Didn't give the cops more than his name. I'd worked out a plea. He was to take himself to jail this morning."

"But…"

"He didn't. Whatever pressure his bosses brought on him, something else is going on. He's making noises about talking. Needing protection. This could be a news maker, this one." I took my hands from the table, shoved them in my lap, crossing my finger for luck like a superstitious grandma that this case didn't hit the papers.

"And you thought of me? Why was that again?"

I shifted in my seat. Took a deep sip of my own cognac-based drink. Let the smooth spirit momentarily numb my mouth before taking it down my throat where it warmed my insides. Even in the hot bar, my hands were still ice cold. I rubbed them together, then placed them back on the table, palms down.

"Everyone deserves a second chance. This probably won't be a hard case but may be one that gets publicity. Page three worthy, if not the front page of the Plain Dealer.

Having your name attached to us taking down a conspiracy can't be bad. There's no downside. Plus, I miss having you around." That last was the sugar, the sweetener as my uncle called it.

That last part was also the truth. She was smart and funny and didn't have a gloomy sourpuss face like the rest of the women working in the office who all acted like it was some kind of hostile work environment because of the men who coped with the horrors of what we saw with gallows humor. Unlike any of them, Nicole got it. She understood that rape and murder and brutal assaults needed to be lightened with a little levity now and then.

"It may not be much, but I am assigned to the grand jury. I can't just walk away."

"I'm sure Lori or one of her deputies would pull you off temporarily. There's got to be someone else in the doghouse she wants to task with that job."

Nicole reached across the table and punched me lightly in the arm. My heart lifted because with that punch I knew I had her.

"Thanks. Seriously. I've been worried I'd somehow end up back in the permanent hell of child support enforcement. It's literally a recurring nightmare."

With my name and connections, the "pay your dues" assignment in juvenile court had barely registered as a blip on my own resume.

"Worry no more. Major crimes wants you back."

"You have the file? I can get started this weekend."

"Why don't you rest up," I said. I hoped that my real meaning was clear. I needed her to sober up. "We can hit the ground running on Monday morning. Judge Brody set trial for March sixth."

"Judge Brody? Your dad, presiding judge Patrick Brody? Why didn't he recuse himself?"

"We all waived. It was a negotiated plea deal. No chance of bias."

"Is he going to stay on the case?"

"Unless defense counsel objects," I answered. I hadn't decided if having my father there was a blessing or a curse. It was something I'd have to work out in my own trial strategy. No need for Nicole to be in on any of that.

"Who's that?"

"Justin McPhee."

Nicole closed her eyes for a long moment. "Non-descript guy. Map of Poland on his face even though his name is McPhee."

"Mom was Polish."

"Why do you know that?"

"I had to ask with a name like McPhee."

"I don't remember anything about him. Is he any good?"

"He's not Jacob Schmidt. But I think he'll probably hold his own."

"Where am I going to sit? I have a cubby outside the grand jury room. Doesn't seem appropriate for someone in major crimes."

"I have an extra desk."

Nicole's mouth opened. Closed.

"You've never shared a space, ever. It's one of the perks of being a Brody."

"Make no mistake, this one isn't permanent. I don't like to share. Too much of that with my brothers and cousins when I was a kid," I said. "But this is a short prep time. I don't want to be running around looking for you whenever we need to talk. Plus this will be your only case."

Truth of the matter was that I wanted to…no needed to control the flow of information. I did not want Nicole going "off the reservation" so to speak, talking to Walsh, talking to investigators, or making her own decisions. Her sole purpose was to take the hit when we lost this case. Because that's what was going to have to happen.

I was going to have to sacrifice my perfect record to save my ass. I needed someone to point my finger at. Nicole Long, nobody's favorite drunk, was taking the fall. She just didn't know it yet.

I wanted to tell her to drink up, she'd need it. But I didn't. Instead, I patted her arm, then offered her a ride home. I'm pretty sure she no longer had a driver's license.

11

"Why didn't he plea?" Sledge wasn't happy. Wasn't one hint of a smile in his question. If I didn't come up with an answer quick, I was going to be on the hook for Waters. After I'd been summoned to his house, I bounced from one foot to another in his kitchen as I tried to guess at what my answer should be.

I'd barely scraped by last time Waters had fucked things up. Sledge had done jail and said the whole meth thing he'd done time for were bygones. Waters had been the culprit then, asking me to deliver some drugs and collect the money. We were driving that way anyway, and the favor had been easy enough to say yes to. But the police had been waiting for us.

I'd been getting burgers and when I'd come out bag in hand, Sledge had been on the ground with a boot kicking his head. I didn't stay to see what was going to happen. The business would have died with both of us in jail.

"I don't know," I finally answered, careful to keep my voice even. "Freaked out at the last minute? Didn't want to go to prison?"

"I didn't want to go to prison. Nobody want to go to prison. It's like school. You have to do what you don't want sometimes. What part of 'put him in the ground' didn't he understand?"

During our last little visit to Waters, I thought Sledge had scared the hell out of the Iceman. My boss had certainly scared the living hell out of me when he described just how he'd chop Waters up into little pieces and dispose of his body way out into the lake. After Dashanique, I no longer believed anything Sledge said was an idle threat.

He didn't threaten.

He just did.

"What we do now?" I asked. My boss needed to make the decisions. I wasn't at all ready to take the blame for Ice. Not last time. Not this time. "You think he'd talk?"

"Not if he knows what's good for him. We need another visit. Get the car," Sledge ordered.

I hesitated a moment too long. Sledge's right hand balled into a fist. Built like a heavyweight prize fighter, that fist was no joking matter. Fists like his had probably been the origin of the phrase "one punch homicide."

"He's gone," I said. He hadn't shown up for work on Saturday, our busiest night. It had been hell getting the girls to where they needed to go. Fortunately I had a couple of pinch drivers in reserve.

But I'd had to watch them like a hawk, to make sure they didn't help themselves to the girls or help themselves to some cash. Five hundred for a few hours of driving and waiting seemed like a lot. It was a lot until they counted the cash coming in. Then they suddenly felt shorted.

"What do you mean he's gone?" Sledge hammered.

"In the wind," I said quickly.

"If he talks, the feds will be up our ass." Sledge punched at the kitchen table. I looked at where his hand had landed. Hadn't made a dent. "The police will be up our ass. Everyone will be up there like it's a goddamn colonoscopy. I didn't get out of prison to go back in. You need to find Ice and bring him to me."

"On it," I said. I would need to figure out how hard I should look for Ice. If it came down to him or me, I chose me. But if Derek Waters was going to try to pull me down with him, I'd find his ass and leave it to Sledge.

"Now, get the car," he ordered.

"Where we going?" If it wasn't Ice, I wanted to know our destination. I didn't want to be the one in the lake.

"Two stops. First I got to show you something. Then we going to see the lawyer. Any more questions or are you going to get the car?"

I resumed the job I hadn't had in two years, chauffer for Sledge. This new Lexus wasn't much different than its predecessor. I followed his directions from his house to Warrensville Center Road, the street with the motels we used to use. It's where we'd lost half our girls when the Feds had discovered the container. Driving over here made me nervous. I didn't say a thing, though. Just swallowed air and willed my bladder to behave.

"Pull in at the Sleepy Time."

"I paid these guys off," I spoke quickly, trying not to sound guilty as I tried to figure out if I'd made some huge oversight or grievous error. "I haven't heard from the Hami Emad dude or that other guy at the Sunrise."

Sledge didn't respond. I needed to stop talking. Felt like everything I was saying was an explanation or an excuse for what had happened in the last couple of years. I didn't think I needed to keep doing that. I'd done a good job.

Our revenue was at more than ten million a year. Expenses weren't five percent of that. I'd paid his niece. I'd kept the lights and heat on in his mama's house. I'd run his dive bars. Except for Ice, there hadn't been a problem. And Ice was his problem. He'd switched up the operation so that we had to use the vans. It was a set-up practically begging for a side hustle. Ice hadn't been able to resist the temptation.

When we got to the front desk, Hami was there. It was like the Egyptian was an insect frozen in amber. He hadn't changed one iota.

"Mr. Hammer...you can't be here. I'm running a legitimate business nowadays. I don't want you to scare off our customers."

Emad's eyes slid toward a room off to the side that I hadn't remembered. It was filled with light-colored wood tables. A few people sat scattered in the room drinking coffee from to-go cups and eating store-bought donuts and muffins.

"Are you saying I'm scary? Why is that? You come from a country full of people who look like me. Anyone ask, I'm your cousin. Feel me."

Emad nodded quickly, then looked down at the computer in front of him at the reception desk.

Sledge barely nodded in acknowledgment that he was done before going behind the counter and into an office. I only hesitated a moment, then I followed.

My boss squatted on his haunches and turned the dial on a solid-looking black safe. It opened easily and he pulled out three video tapes that weren't much bigger than the palm of my hand. There appeared to be about five more in a shoe-box, but I didn't ask or touch.

"What's that?"

"Isn't it obvious?"

It was obvious in one way. Not so much in another.

"If it was obvious, I wouldn't have asked."

Sledge leaned down, shoved his hand into the very back of the metal box, then pulled out a camcorder. He poked his head in this time, then extracted some cords. He plugged them into an old TV—a little thirteen-inch cube—on the corner of Emad's desk, jammed the power cord into an empty wall outlet, then looked at the tapes.

They had names on them. Dashanique was number one. Destiny was number two. Shonna was number three. I knew what was on the Dashanique tape. I sure as hell didn't want to see that. Like he read my mind, he opened the tape labeled Destiny. I remembered her first night here. I did not want to see that, but I couldn't show him fear on my face.

After he punched a few buttons on the camcorder and TV, a grainy image floated on the screen. It was what used to be Destiny's room at the Sleepytime across the back parking lot from this place. Stephanie...Destiny. I'd had to think of her by that made-up name, otherwise guilt sat like a pit in my gut. Made it hard to do my job.

I focused back on the screen. Destiny came out of her bathroom. I remembered the set-up, before the vans. Each girl had a room with two full-size beds. There were three doors. The one to the parking lot, which only locked and unlocked from the outside, a small closet where they kept work clothes and pajamas, and a small bathroom.

She was rubbing her hands like she'd just put cream on them, then she swiped at her face and arms. All that skin was exposed because she was in a purple nighty. Victoria Secret-type stuff was far too tame for our customers, so I got Alisha's help picking out items from the Frederick's of Hollywood catalogue.

The kind of outfit Destiny had on was the most popular—see-through top and peekaboo underwear. Destiny moved toward the bed and made herself comfortable.

The sound wasn't that good, but I did hear the door open and close. A tall white guy walked in. Destiny said something, and he looked up and his full face was caught on camera. For some reason, it looked kind of familiar, but I couldn't place it. There weren't too many white guys in my life. Just the customers. I tried not to look at them too close.

Sledge punched at the volume button. I could hear them talking. Though they sounded like they were speaking through a long and noisy wind tunnel.

"Tom," the man in the video said. He stuck out his hand for a brief second, like he was looking for a handshake, then retracted it as he obviously thought better of it. "And you are?"

"Destiny."

"Interesting name."

"My mother was interesting." Her half-smile was both innocent and coy at the same time. "But I don't want to talk about mothers. Mothers and sex don't mix."

"Some might say that mothers can only become mothers because of sex."

"What you want, tonight?" she asked, cutting off all the talk. A lot of guys liked to leave as soon as the sex was over. Gave the girls some time to rest before the next customer. They got good at minimizing the talk and maximizing their free time.

"How old are you?" he asked, as if plausible deniability were didn't matter to him. He had to know the truth. If they wanted girls over eighteen, customers had all of Lorain Avenue. We charged more because we served a clientele with very specific tastes.

"Eighteen," she answered as required. "Some people say I look fifteen, though. You?"

"Only thirty-four."

Then Sledge turned the sound back off. Destiny came up onto her knees. She undressed Tom. Then he was all over her. MY mother would have said it was like "white on rice."

Sledge hit stop. Ejected the tape, then slipped it back into its plastic case.

"Insurance."

"Who is that?" I had to ask to pull it all together.

"Tom Brody."

I shrugged. That name didn't mean shit to me.

"He's a county prosecutor. He's the county prosecutor on Ice's case."

All that had been cloudy in my brain suddenly became clear. The tuxedoed guy who'd I'd asked for advice on New Year's.

"Did you fix it like that?" I said. After the story he told me about Casey Cort, I wasn't sure he didn't have his hands on a lot of puppet strings.

"No, he did. He's the one who got me out of Conneaut. He assigned himself the case. He worked on a good plea for Ice. Waters would be in jail for a real long time if Tom hadn't worked that out. Then Derek threw all the shit I'd worked at away for a slim chance at freedom."

"Isn't this a conflict of interest?" I asked. Not to mention probably ten kinds of illegal, I thought.

"I don't know or care about that. What I care about is Ice know too much and is running around with his big lips loose like a cannon."

"That's a mixed metaphor."

"What?" He shook his head, his smile real this time. "God save us from college boys."

Sledge closed the safe, spun the lock, gathered up the box of tapes and the camera.

"You got a bag?"

I shoved my hands in my coat pocket and pulled out the empty insides. "I'm not a bag boy."

"Fine. Then carry something so I can get back to the car."

I hefted the camera, while he shoved five tapes in one pocket, and a few in another. Tossed the box in the trash can under the desk.

Sledge hadn't said much of a hello, and he didn't say any kind of goodbye to Hami Emad. Didn't say anything myself because manners didn't seem all that important right now. I pushed a button on the key fob that gently lifted the trunk door. I laid the camera inside a mesh holder that kept stuff from rolling around in the back of the SUV. Then got in. Pressed the start button.

"Where to now?"

"Casey Cort's office."

I didn't ask why. I just put the car in drive and took us from the Eastside, through the empty spaces between eighty-eighth street and twenty-fifth until I reached the parking lot for the building. The garage was a dark and sketchy affair, and I normally didn't use it, but Sledge didn't look like he was in the mood to take a walk in the freezing cold weather.

This time, I did get a bag out of the back. Some old Hei-nen's canvas bag that had been rolling around in the trunk for who knows how long. I stashed the camera in, then the tapes.

"I assume we're taking these upstairs."

Sledge nodded.

"I need a new hiding place. Her office seems as good as any. Least she could do for the retainer we're paying."

When we got upstairs, the receptionist didn't look any less scared than she usually did at the appearance of two black men in her office in the middle of the day.

Without even asking who we were, she lifted the phone and informed Casey that there were two men here to see her.

Instead of her secretary, Casey herself emerged. The lawyer looked pissed in her brown plaid skirt and brown sweater.

"What did I say about appointments?" she asked, not budging from the reception area. "This is how it works. You pick up a phone—it can be a landline since calls to me can't be used against you—then you ask for an appointment. Lettie looks in the calendar, figures out when I'm not in court or seeing another client, then gives you a date and time. You mark that in your phone or palm pilot or scratch it on scrap paper, I don't care. You just remember when it is, then you come in at the appointed time. Why is that so hard to understand?"

"You done?" Sledge asked, a second smile of the day playing around his lips. He didn't take women too seriously. "Look like you're not busy right now."

Her nostrils flared. But she didn't say anything more. Instead she turned on her low-heeled granny shoes and stepped toward her office. We followed like it had been an open invitation.

"Mr. Carter. Mr. Fortune. How can I help you today? I'm on the clock."

"Money ain't no thang," I said. I may have laid on the Ebonics a bit thick. Something about white women made me want to jostle them a little bit. Probably in response to all the door locking, window rolling up, and purse grabbing I'd suffered in my lifetime. Was that pay it back or pay it forward? I'd have to think about that one.

While I'd been doing all the thinking, Sledge had been pulling the camcorder and a tape from the grocery store bag.

Sledge spared me a glance. "Where can I plug this in?" he asked, holding up the two-pronged end of the AC adaptor.

Casey jerkily gestured toward a socket next to the bookcase opposite her desk. Sledge pushed it in. He slipped the Destiny tape into the cartridge holder, pushed it closed. He flipped open the three-inch screen, tilted it up toward the ceiling. He fiddled with the tiny buttons until the tape started playing.

"What am I watching?" she said, though she was still staring out the window at the frozen surface of Lake Erie. Wasn't nobody going in there this week. Maybe the cold-ass weather was a reprieve for the Iceman.

"If you look, you'll see," Sledge said.

Casey shifted her eyes from outside to the tiny screen. She squinted. Pulled up one of her pink upholstered wood chairs so she was closer to the movie. I wanted to ask if she needed sound, but when I looked at her, I knew she didn't.

"Stop it. Stop the tape. I don't need to see anything more. How old is she? This...this girl?"

"She was—"

"No. Don't answer that. Excuse me." Casey stood stiffly, like she was ninety-something and not thirty-something. She took her coat off a hook on a rack, opened the office door, walked through it, and slammed it behind her.

I looked at Sledge, my eyebrows deliberately as high as I could make them. I didn't think she was coming back. Now I was going to have to make nice with her secretary to get the keys to the safe or wherever it was that the lawyer kept important client stuff.

12

It had to be some huge breach of ethics, what I'd done, leaving two clients in my office. They could open every drawer, look at every file, violate every confidentiality. I'd wanted to vomit, though, and didn't want to do that in front of them, so I'd walked…well, maybe I'd run out.

I had sudden compassion for the parish priests and their stiff robes and their swinging balls of incense, for all the things that they heard at confession and had to swallow down. I had no idea how they slept at night.

Tom, my Tom. The man I'd thought I'd marry not once, but a second time. We'd been engaged. That man hadn't thought twice about having sex with an underage girl. Not only was she probably well under the age of consent, but she actually looked like a child. That's what had propelled me out of my own office. Not her age, exactly, but that she looked like a twelve-year-old.

There were kids in my very religious Catholic high school who were having sex with each other at fifteen, maybe even younger if rumors were true. It had all been consensual as far as I'd known. But even when I'd been that age, sex had kind of squicked me out.

I couldn't imagine, back then, knowing someone well enough, loving someone enough, being vulnerable enough to do it. The situation had been different a couple of years later with my first boyfriend, but I had matured by then. Even looking back on it now, though, I'm not even sure how mature I really was. But I knew one thing: I sure hadn't been at fifteen.

On top of all that, I was representing men who'd willingly taken advantage of that girl. Who'd somehow signed her up to have sex with strangers—many of them in one night. God knows I didn't have or need the exact numbers, but this well-paying defendant, who was probably single-handedly keeping me afloat, had zero morals. Not that there was a big intersection between criminality and morality.

I was supposed to be having dinner with Ron. That's what had kept me going all day. That's where I was walking toward now, my legs freezing even under my full-length wool coat. My favorite one with its faux fur trim. Fortunately for my legs, the Blue Point Grille was only a five-minute walk from my office.

When I got inside, I waved away the hostess who was looking at me expectantly.

"Gotta make a call to my office. I'm meeting someone who should have a reservation. I'll be a sec." She shoved the menus back in the wooden stand and went back to scrutinizing the reservation list and table set-up.

I tucked myself in the vestibule, which while cold, wasn't in the hypothermia range. I flexed my fingers to bring feeling back into them before I slid my phone open and called my office.

"Lettie, it's me, Casey. Sorry to walk out like that. Did my clients leave?"

"They left, but left some stuff behind for safekeeping."

"Where did you put it?"

"For now? In the locked bottom drawer of my desk, where I normally keep my purse."

"Thanks. That should work overnight while I figure out somewhere to put it."

"I'll research safes or safety deposit boxes in the morning. I'm sure we could get something delivered. Is there a budget?"

"That would be a godsend, thanks. No, no budget. Whatever works." I'd charge the safe to Carter. "There's always something new," I said, looking for commiseration.

Lettie's "Copy that" was all I was going to get. It was not her problem to solve, she was just an employee. One who didn't need to stick around running up the hourly tab I'd have to pay in two weeks' time.

"Go home. I'll see you on Monday."

"You need me tomorrow?"

"No. Enjoy the long weekend." I didn't tell the truth, that I couldn't afford her tomorrow. Every year I thought I could make her full time, and every year I was unexpectedly no further along than I'd been the year before. Something was going to have to change. I wasn't sure that more criminal clients was going to be my way out of the seemingly permanent financial rut I was in.

I snapped my phone shut and shoved it into my pocket, since I didn't have my purse or briefcase. I'd have to go back for those, or maybe not. I may just save all that until the morning.

"Hi, reservation for two. Ron Pinheiro," I said to the hostess when I came back into the main restaurant area.

"Yes, of course. Follow me." She took two heavy leather-bound menus in hand and wove through tables to a single booth near the carpeted stairs leading to the upper level. I gave her my coat, because I'd been so rattled that I'd blown right by coat check, then slid myself into the booth.

"Can I get you something?"

"Water, and an Old Fashioned if you don't mind."

Normally I'd wait for my date before starting in on the alcohol, but after today's little private screening, I needed something to help me blur the edges.

"Coming right up."

When she returned, I accepted the drinks and looked out into the huge room. There were some things about Cleveland that were absolutely beautiful. The county courthouse on Lakeside. The Federal courthouse not far from it on Superior. The rotunda of the City Hall. This building was like those, massive Greek columns, intricate plaster work, gleaming antique chandeliers.

It made me feel like I could be any place in time. Like I could look up and it could be 1940 where Europe had taken a deep breath between wars. Before the world had taken the next step toward crazy again. A place where time stood still. A place where I felt stuck.

I glanced down at my drink—empty. I checked my watch. Ron should have been here by now. As if he'd heard my thoughts, my phone buzzed.

Ron.

"Hey there. I'm one drink in. What do you want me to order for you? It'll be ready when you walk over."

"I have bad news."

"What?" I asked, though I was sure I had an idea what his news was. I'd been coasting on one good date through these last few weeks. Now I wasn't too sure that I hadn't been imagining our connection.

"I can't make it tonight." Though my prediction was sound, it still hit me like a kick in the gut.

"Are you working late? I can pick up something to go and bring it to you."

"I'm not downtown, actually. I'm caught up in something in the Heights. Rain check?"

"Sure. I guess." My "Call me" was a Hail Mary.

I took another look around. This time it wasn't about the architecture or the décor. It was to look and see who else was there. Even in a downtown restaurant, on a weeknight, it was full of couples. Lots of men and woman—together. The men leaning forward in earnest. The women curling hair behind their ears as if to hear better.

And me.

Alone.

With an empty glass.

When the waitress offered me a second drink, I took it.

"Are you going to want some food with that, hon? Or do you want to wait for your date."

"He's not coming."

"Oh. Sorry."

"I've been stood up. I had this really great first date, then he's been too busy to see me. Sorry. I shouldn't be telling you all this." I opened the menu abruptly. "Can I have the calamari, a crab cake, and the seared scallops?" I scanned down to the bottom. "And a side of the roasted sweet potatoes."

"I'll put it in. To go?"

"Box it up. I'll take it with me," I said.

When the server disappeared, I did a quick calculation in my head. I could cover it, tonight's dinner. I'd put it on the emergency credit card I carried in the plastic holder for my RTA pass. Now I'd have to remember to pay that when the bill came. Hopefully it would come due weeks from now when this humiliation would be a distant memory.

I took my phone from the table and punched in another number.

"Want to have dinner?

"I was about to head home."

"I'll bring it to you." When he didn't protest, I pushed forward. "I'll meet you there in thirty. Hopefully it won't be too cold."

I hung up before a second man could turn me down.

Forty-five minutes later, I arrived at Justin's place.

"Took me a little longer than I expected." I'd had to find a cabbie who'd take my emergency credit card. There were very few of those, I'd found. "Where can I put this?"

"In the oven. I have it on the warm setting."

"Perfect."

"So…this is a surprise."

"I found myself in the Blue Point Grille. Got hungry. Wanted to share. I know you like seafood."

Justin walked forward. I walked backward until my back hit the stone counter of his small kitchen island. He leaned in close. Part of me knew what was coming. Another part was taken by surprise.

"I can't be in the same room without wanting to kiss you."

Then he did just that. Kissed me. It took me a long time to pull away.

"What does that mean?"

"Pantsfeelings."

"What?"

"I have pantsfeelings…raging pantsfeelings for you. That's all."

"Is that even a word? What does that mean?"

"You know what it means, Casey. With seven years of advanced education, I think you can figure it out."

"Do you want dinner?" I'd lost my appetite, but I needed something between us that would give me enough breathing room to get myself under control, figure out what in the hell I was really doing here. Fixing my client's problems, or getting my baser needs met? Maybe it was both.

He blinked long and slow like he'd needed a moment to get his raging pantsfeelings under control. "Sure, what did you bring?"

I slipped around him, held up the large black bag dinner had been packed in. The restaurant's name was in gold across a five-pointed blue star.

"Blue Point Grille?" he read.

"I got stood up."

"Stood up?"

"For a date. Your former classmate didn't show up for our date tonight. He wasn't even downtown. Said he had some big emergency on the Eastside."

"Sorry."

"Don't be. It's the second time. There won't be a third. I know I should probably learn something from this. Not sure what."

"That maybe he's not for you?"

"We had the best date, though. He sends the best emails and texts." My body warmed and I hoped my face hadn't as I remembered his complimentary messages. Ron thought I was pretty, and smart, and funny, and a great date. I wanted more of that. Being with Ron was like having the warm sun bear down on me. In the bleak Cleveland midwinter, any hint of sun was more than welcome. "It's a woman thing, you wouldn't understand. I'll reschedule. How's Derek Waters? Is he seriously ready to go to trial?"

"Don't know if that will be necessary. He is in protective custody, though."

Whatever blood had been in my face had probably drained. Protective custody meant the county thought Waters had information worth the cost.

"Did the county win the lottery?" I asked. Protective custody wasn't cheap. The cheap motel, now that was cheap. Round the clock cop, that was expensive.

"The feds are putting up the money."

"Feds?" I was drowning. Ten minutes ago, the downside for Waters and maybe Fortune was eighteen months if all counts were consecutive. Maybe five or fifteen years depending on what the county could prove. The federal government? Twenty years. For each count if they threw the organized crime book at them. Unless there was some kind of end of life compassionate release, they'd die in jail.

"If what he says is true, we're talking RICO," Justin confirmed. "If he can take down organized crime, nobody's going to care one iota about some meth. Every prosecutor knows that if they put one meth dealer away, they're like roaches, there are dozens more that will just move in to take his place. The war on drugs has been a failure. No one from the law and order side of the aisle would say that out loud, but they all know it's true. Ten or twenty years from now, they'll probably say the same about the war on terrorism. If they used any of that money to fund education, then they wouldn't need any of this on the back end."

"That's one hell of a soapbox you have," I said. Five years ago, ten years ago for sure, I'd have made the same speech. Especially when I'd been standing in juvenile court and the judges condemned the kids for growing up in foster care right before they sentenced them to another juvenile institution.

"Do you disagree?" Justin asked. His back was to me because he was pulling the food from the oven. The smell of fried seafood brought back my appetite. I opened all the containers while he turned off the oven and brought out utensils.

"Some people need to rot in hell." I pulled the calamari toward me. Dipped it in the sauce from the tiny plastic cup. "In lieu of the afterlife being an option, there's jail."

"Crime is a poverty problem." Justin speared a scallop. Chewed it. Swallowed. "This is good."

It was expensive. It had better be good.

"Organized crime is a depravity problem," I said.

"You're not usually so cynical. What's up? This is about more than Ron."

That name was like a punch in the gut. I didn't want to think about Ron. It made me sad or angry or both. Maybe sad. Angry had to be saved for men like Jarrod Carter and Tom—definitely Tom.

"Everyone should be cynical about organized crime. It's not stealing food to feed your family or dealing drugs because there aren't any jobs in your neighborhood. It's crime for the sake of making money. Kind of like Wall Street, but without the Series 7 securities license."

"Ouch. You still on the defense bar side?"

"I'm sorry." I pushed the food away. My appetite was all over the place. The dog sniffed my legs. I'd forgotten about Morro. Maybe he could eat the rest. I wondered if seafood was bad for dogs, or fried food. Maybe I should get a dog, he was a great distraction. I sighed long and hard. "I had a hard day. A harder week. And I've got a hard month ahead. I read somewhere that we should be careful of what we see, because our brains can't unsee. That happened today. A client was like, look, I need to show you some evidence. I didn't think to ask what that evidence was before I looked at it. Now, I want to wash my eyes out with bleach. Disinfect my brain. I can't do that, obviously."

"Do you want to talk about it?"

Would it violate client confidentiality if I told him about Tom, about the sex trafficking ring? Could I talk about it, but make it hypothetical? I wanted to talk about it...so badly. No one told you that holding secrets made you lonely.

Law school didn't prepare you for the horrors clients shared that you had to keep to yourself. On top of that, there was the tiny matter of Derek Waters. This potential federal witness, he was a threat to my client's freedom.

I finally spoke.

"It was a sex crime."

"Why does your client have his own crime on tape? Should he be on one of those world's worst criminals shows?"

Morro licked his chops. I think that Justin must have given the dog something. Or maybe Morro had stolen something. I looked into the dog's brown eyes. It was all innocence.

"He's far brighter than that. He has someone else on tape. The two are playing a game of chicken. I don't know who will cluck first."

"Wow."

"Yep. My client's freedom hinges on someone else staying silent. The other guy talks, and I think everyone is going to prison for a good long time."

"What kind of crime?"

"Sex with an underage girl."

"And you saw that?"

"One minute of it, tops. Enough to cure me of empathy for the downtrodden defendant."

"This is what happens. You've moved up the chain. Fifth degree felonies are in your rearview mirror. No wonder you handed off Waters. You're rolling with the big guns. It's like you're one of those Mafia lawyers you see in movies."

"The ones who get corrupted by their clients?"

"Maybe not that. You're the farthest thing from corrupt I've ever seen."

I hope the untruth of that didn't show on my face.

"Do you have a prosecutor?"

"In the basement?"

"Assigned to the Waters case."

"Funny you should ask."

"I'm not in a laughing mood. What's so funny?"

"Miles Siegel is the assistant US attorney on the case. Word on the street is that he's been gunning for a big case."

"My ex fiancé, the ASUA."

"You've got a lot of those."

"Two. I only have two of those."

"And they're both on this case. Is this why you have an unhealthy interest in what's going on? Are you trying to get back together with one of them? Tom seemed like he'd be game."

Justin was getting too close to the truth for comfort. I needed a distraction.

"I'm not getting back together with either of them. Ron looks like he's history. That leaves me with only one guy in my sights. Want to tell me more about your pantsfeelings?"

Justin wiped his mouth and hands on a cloth napkin. It was like a light switch. I could see the exact moment his mind switched over.

He stood. Pulled my hand with his.

"I think this is the kind of thing that's much better with show and tell. I have just the place to show you."

For an entirely different reason, I needed the distraction as much as he did. I squeezed his hand, then followed him from the kitchen to his bedroom where I learned all about raging pantsfeelings. It was the best lesson of the day.

13

I'd lost the first battle of the turf war. I really needed to keep control of the Waters case, and this visit to FBI headquarters was ceding a lot of control. With Derek Waters in protective custody, courtesy of the Federal Bureau of Investigation or the U.S. Attorney's office—whichever had the budget—I didn't have a leg to stand on when I'd demanded they bring the defendant over to the Justice Center.

"Can I help you?" the receptionist at the FBI office asked. He was all suited up in full uniform, brass shining, well-oiled gun at his hip. All behind bulletproof glass.

"Tom Brody and Nicole Long from the county prosecutor's office. We're here to see..." The name stuck in my throat longer than it should have.

"Miles Siegel," Long interjected. "He's an AUSA. Supposed to meet us at one thirty for a suspect interrogation," she finished.

"Right. Have a seat over there. I'll put in a call upstairs."

Long retreated to one of the gray lobby chairs and I followed her there, reluctantly. She sat and fiddled with the black nylon strap of her bag.

"Tom, you want to sit?" she asked.

"We shouldn't be here too long. It's twenty after."

The truth was that I felt at a disadvantage if anyone caught me sitting. I especially didn't want to be sitting when Miles came in. I wouldn't admit it to anyone out loud under pain of death, but I would not sit down around Casey's ex-fiancé. The one who'd come on my heels. I was pretty sure I was taller. He was a black guy, though maybe only half. I think Lulu had mentioned his background once, but it was a hazy detail I hadn't paid any attention to at the time.

I didn't want to buy into stereotypes, but I knew my bedroom performance with Casey had probably been underwhelming. She wasn't really my type. The "all cats are gray in the dark" adage hadn't really worked all the time either. Pretending that she was darker with African features used up a lot of energy I probably should have dedicated to pleasing her.

If I ever got another chance with my ex, I'd surely make her a priority. I'd been immature back then, assuming my family name was enough. I knew now that women needed more, that she would need more to marry someone like me, give me the legitimacy I sorely needed.

"Tom Brody?"

A short and stocky man had come from behind some kind of hidden door. I looked more closely and saw a key card entry box, though no handle. This new federal building had been started before 9/11 but finished after. It had state of the art security. Nothing like the Oklahoma City bombing could ever happen here.

I nodded in greeting. The man ran his hand across his salt-and-pepper brush cut before he extended his hand to me.

"Lou Valdespino. FBI. AUSA Siegel and Waters and his lawyer are upstairs. We've reserved an interview room."

"This is Nicole Long. She's an assistant county prosecutor who's been assigned to work this case with me."

Nicole stood. Valdespino shook her hand.

"Ms. Long." The receptionist came around the desk through another hidden door, this on the other side of the lobby. He handed us visitor badges. While I clipped mine to my lapel, Nicole mimicked my actions, though she failed to get hers affixed.

Lou screwed up his eyes at her.

"You need help with that?" he asked.

"No. No. My lapels are just smaller. That's all." Finally she got the clip on the fabric. I wondered if she'd had a little morning pick-me-up. Half of me felt sorry for her if she did. The other half of me was glad that she was being herself, that if this case tanked, she could take a good share of the blame.

Badges taken care of, Lou turned.

"Follow me," Lou said. We kept close behind as he swiped his ID card against the reader. A nearly silent click followed, and he pushed through a door. I held it for Nicole then brought up the rear.

In front of us was a small elevator lobby. Valdespino swiped again then pushed the call button. Once the elevator doors opened, we all stepped inside. He swiped again before pushing the button for the third floor.

"You guys need coffee or water or something?" Valdespino asked when the elevator opened on the top floor.

"Coffee, for both of us," I said. Nicole didn't exactly smell like a distillery, but she didn't smell like a teetotaling church lady either. My guess was that she could use a legal pick-me-up. My plan, though, did not involve outing Long at any time during this Waters thing. I'd let Lorraine Pope or the media pick her apart later—after we lost the case, after I lost my perfect win record, and everyone was picking us apart during the autopsy.

"Here's the room. Make yourselves comfortable. I'll be back with your coffees."

He swiped again and the door to an interview room opened. There were four brand-new chairs around a table that had yet to be scarred by an angry man in handcuffs.

Nicole turned to me the moment the door closed behind us.

"We locked in here?"

"Probably. I'm not too worried that he won't let us out." I took a pause. Took the time to push air in and out. I met her eyes with mine. "Can I tell you something?"

A line pinched around each corner of her mouth. I only knew she nodded because her ponytail swung.

"When I first met you, I thought we'd make a great team." I made the statement an admission.

"We're on a case now," she said in misunderstanding.

"Outside of the courtroom, Nicole. Outside." I dipped my head in false modesty. "Despite the speech we'd gotten about not fraternizing at work, I was planning to ask you out."

Her eyes widened a bit. She leaned closer an inch or two.

"Then what happened?"

That first part, the asking her out part, it had been the truth. She was meek enough not to intimidate or alienate my parents. She was attractive enough, especially when she didn't have her hair in what I thought of as her "serious lawyer" bun. The thing that had killed the idea dead in my mind had been the drinking. The last night of our training, we'd gone out to a bar, on the Westside, to celebrate our freedom forever from classrooms and our introduction to courtrooms.

Nicole had one or maybe three drinks too many. Next thing I knew she was practically dancing on the bar. Any interest I'd had in her died right there between the shiny brass railing on the bar and the scarred wood floors. The last thing a prominent Irish family needed was a drunk. She'd been crossed off my potential dating list immediately.

"You started dating Michael Betancourt," I lied. He was a half Irish, half Puerto Rican prosecutor who'd been murder in the courtroom from the outset. Betancourt's reputation from the Manhattan district attorney's office had proceeded him. He hadn't stayed in Cleveland long. He'd defected to a big firm, and he was working in white collar crime in D.C. faster than any of us could blink.

"Michael. Yeah. He was a great guy. More career than family oriented, though."

"Aren't we all," I said.

From under her lashes, Nicole really looked at me. The smile that took over her face was the first genuine one I'd seen in a long time. The little white lie had been worth it. Nicole was going to be just that more loyal during this meeting, that tiny bit more deferential. Whoever had said flattery gets you nowhere was dead wrong. The door swung open, blowing in cool air from the hall. I hadn't realized until that moment how stuffy the room had gotten. Maybe the FBI was from the "make the defendant sweat" school of interrogation.

"Coffees are ready." Valdespino entered the room, handing each of us a Styrofoam cup with a thin plastic lid. He dropped a couple of creamers, some packets of sugar, and tiny wooden stirrers on the table.

I pointedly looked at my watch. "When—"

Before I could finish my question, Miles Siegel stepped into the room.

I stood, pulling myself to my full height. I couldn't quite see the top of his head, but I did have a couple of inches on him. I took his extended hand and squeezed it—hard.

"Tom." He gripped me hard right back. "Glad you could make it over to the federal side of things."

"Happy to help where I can."

"Derek Waters should be escorted up here in a minute," Miles said. "We had to arrange special transport since he's not in lockup."

Nicole hadn't exactly cleared her throat, but she'd shifted in her chair. Brought my attention right back to my case strategy. "This is Nicole Long. She's going to be second chair on the case."

"Ms. Long," Miles shook Nicole's hand. "Nice to meet you." Dismissing her, he turned back to me. "Tom, my man, you're never going to get to trial on this one."

I ignored his too-familiar tone. We weren't friends or buddies. He'd relentlessly gone after my elderly uncle a few years back when that amount of zealousness hadn't been necessary. "Why not? Why do you think we're not going to trial on this one?"

"The AUSA's office is not the housing authority providing him a bed for free. We think he's got a story to tell. A RICO-type story."

"You are familiar with Revised Code section 2923.22 right? Ohio has its own organized crime statutes." I'd never tried anyone under the law I'd quoted, but we did have one.

"I know you didn't go to a top-tier school," Siegel started. Then he spoke slowly. "But surely they taught you about federal supremacy. Article four, Clause two? That's the U.S. constitution in case you were wondering."

"Thanks for that primer. Why don't you get Waters in here. Make sure he actually has something to say. Then we'll figure out the prosecution angle. But since you can't seem to win a case, I'm not seeing you on this one."

A perfect win record was a good sword.

"Your uncle was as guilty as the day he was born. It's why he's in jail."

"A jury you guys selected wouldn't convict him. He's only in jail on a technicality," I said. That was true. He'd run from the cops and had gone through a fierce battle on Contained, and was away on what I considered the shakiest conviction ever. He'd have won his appeal, but once he'd run out on his appeal bond, his tenure in jail was all but assured. He was in federal custody now, living out the remainder of his days.

"If that's what helps you sleep at night."

"When Casey's next to me, I sleep just fine." I knew using my ex—our ex—was like throwing lighter fluid on a fire, but I couldn't help myself.

Miles' eyebrows shot up to his curly hairline.

"Casey's back with you? She wouldn't date you if you were the last man on earth. Do we really want to get into that? In front of Long here or Valdespino? If we do, you'll be sharing a cell with your uncle."

My heart sped up. I kept my cool. Then I got out ahead of things.

"Are you one of those people who think that all Brodys should go to jail just because we're a successful law and order family?" My uncle may have been in jail, but my uncle Liam was still attorney general, and my father presiding judge of the common pleas court.

"Maybe you should all be in jail because you're all crooked."

Valdespino clapped his hand on the table.

"Gentlemen. Waters and his attorney are ready. Can you keep it together for this interview? If not, one of you will have to leave."

"It's actually my case as I actually have an indictment. I'm sure you wouldn't interfere with an active prosecution. We have a trial date in a little less than three weeks. So I'm thinking it's up to me who's in the room."

Miles held up his hands in defeat.

"I'll be as quiet as a church mouse," he said. "Let's just see if this canary sings." He left the room abruptly.

I was about to lift the lid from my coffee and make it to my liking when Nicole put her hand over mine.

"Already did it. Two creamers, one sugar. Right?"

Miles had just come back into the room. I didn't dare glance in his direction as he shoehorned a chair at the head of the table.

"Right. Thanks for that."

"I remember from training," she said.

Target hit, I guess. My goal had been to insure her loyalty, not turn her into the next Mrs. Brody. That ship had sailed a long time ago. I turned and gave her my best smile anyway, because she wasn't privy to the predetermined outcome of us or the case like I was.

The door swung open again. This time Valdespino wasn't alone, he had Derek Waters in tow along with Justin McPhee.

Valdespino escorted the defendant to the chair opposite me. Waters looked from me to Miles to Nicole, then back to me. I was starting to think it was all much bigger than Waters had thought when he'd said that he had something to share.

"Good morning, Mr. Waters. I'm prosecuting attorney Tom Brody. You may remember me from the courtroom."

"Yeah, I do."

"We're here to discuss what you may know about an ongoing criminal enterprise."

"Uh huh."

"Before we go on the record here, I want you to be clear, Mr. Waters, why cooperating with the feds may not be a good idea."

"Excuse me," Miles interjected. I waited for him to say something else. When Miles closed his mouth, I continued.

I laid a hand on Waters' forearm.

"Without an ironclad deal on the table, you could go away for a lot of years for each and every RICO count you're found guilty of. That's safely the rest of your life. When we were in court a few weeks ago, you were quite clear that going to jail for three years wasn't something you wanted to do. I want to make sure you know that was one sweet deal."

"Do we have a deal, man?" Waters asked McPhee.

"We have a cooperation deal. If the information you disclose leads to successful prosecution, then the charges against you get dropped," McPhee answered.

"My ass is relying on whether or not Sledge can beat a charge. That nigger can beat almost any charge. His lawyer's that good and he's that lucky."

"Who is Sledge?" Valdespino asked.

"You know what? He right. I don't know what I was thinking. I want to talk to the county prosecutor here."

"Siegel, Valdespino. If you could give us the room."

"Mr. McPhee?" Miles said the name like a question.

"Let us talk. Then we'll get back with you."

"If I leave this room," Miles postured, "this cooperation deal is off the table."

"My client hasn't been charged with a federal crime. Unless you're going to charge him, he's free to go."

"Without that cooperation deal, there's no protective custody either."

"Give us thirty minutes, and let's see what happens. You can wait that long before tearing up the deal, right?"

"Fine. Thirty minutes, no more."

Valdespino stood and swung open the door with more force than was necessary. Miles snapped his leather folder shut and followed the FBI agent out of the door. I lifted an eyebrow at Nicole. She took the hint and moved across the table so that both of us were bracketing Waters, one of us at each of his elbows. McPhee, who'd been standing awkwardly, took the chair opposite Waters.

"Let's talk," I said.

"You going to prosecute me?"

"We can't drop the charges at this point. Again, though, we're only talking three years versus lifetime."

"And if I talk?"

"We can make the charges go away. The prosecuting attorney, Lorraine Pope, she makes that decision. But...in this case, I don't see any problem. I'm a senior trial attorney. My decisions are rubber stamped."

"I work for the guy behind the container case," Waters said without preamble. Justin's eyes widened. I'm guessing his client had refused to preview this information.

I tried to arrange my face into suitable shock by mirroring Nicole's.

"He trafficks girls, not meth," Waters added. "Meth isn't his business. He doesn't allow drugs. The ice—that's my own side business."

"Tell me the story," Nicole said. It was the perfect move. Waters wasn't a question-and-answer guy. He was the kind of person who wanted to tell a tale. Nicole was pretty and could be soft spoken or at least softer spoken than me. I gave her a glance that said, take the lead.

Waters paused a long time. Then he spoke, "A couple of years ago the word went out on the street that Sledge Hammer was looking for some employees."

"Who's Sledge Hammer?" Nicole asked. Most younger prosecutors would have pulled out a yellow pad, clicked a pen, broken the rhythm. Nicole was better than that.

"The top guy. I thought I already said that."

"Go on." She sounded very encouraging, even though he hadn't really answered her question.

Waters looked between all of us, took a deep breath, then spoke. "So I went over to his club, The Place to Be. He and Grand were there. They told me they needed drivers who could keep they mouth shut. I was like, I can't do anything that would put me in jail, like moving drugs from place to place. He was like, I don't do anything above a misdemeanor. That sounded good, so I waited until he called me back one night. He say all I needed to do was drive a girl from one address to another. He'd give me a list, I was to memorize it, drive the girls. Collect cash, then return the girls home at the end of the night."

"Did he tell you what the girls were doing?" Nicole asked.

"It didn't take a genius. That first night I drove a girl named Candi. At the first address, she rung the bell and went in. Came out about forty-five minutes later. Asked me for a mint and some water. I had a cooler in the passenger seat. Gave her a bottle of water. At the next stop, the girl rang the bell and the guy came out. They got in back and shut the doors. When the van started rocking, I got out. Did that for eight more stops. Brought Candi back home. Went home, went to sleep, did it the next night. Kept it up for years.

"How much were you paid?"

"Started at five hundred, then six-fifty. I was up to a grand a week before I got arrested. He take out taxes, though. It was like a straight legit job. I filed a 1040 and everything. Caught up on my back child support and shit. Got my bench warrant dismissed. It was legal and illegal at the same time."

"What did you do with the money you picked up for the customers?"

"I put it in one of those bank things. You zip it, then lock it. Money go in but can't come out unless you have a key. No one has a key other than Sledge or Grand.

"You've mentioned Grand twice. Who is he?"

"Grand is Dion Fortune. He's the right-hand man. When Sledge was in jail, he took over."

"Sledge was in jail?" Nicole asked.

"Meth. It was kind of my fault. Not prostitution. He was charged."

"What is Sledge Hammer's real name?"

"Jarrod Carter. I thought I said that."

"Jarrod Carter?" Nicole lost her cool, glared at me—hard. "Fuck me. Jarrod Carter? I tried a prostitution promotion case. He slipped out of that charge like an eel from...from wherever eel come from. He's the fucking sex trafficker of the century. Him?"

"I remember him saying something about beating some case." Waters shrugged. I looked at McPhee. He was nonplussed.

"Your fiancé was his lawyer." Nicole said as her memory came back in full force.

"Casey Cort? She's my ex fiancé, by the way. We're not friends," I said looking at all of them. "Okay. We're all over the place here. I need to think about what we can prove in court. Do you happen to have any of those lists? The ones that had you drive from one address to another?"

"I probably have one or two. Ninety-nine percent of the time, Grand took them and shredded them at the house. On busy days, though, or if there was a bunch of new spots, I may have folded it and kept it. Got them at the house...somewhere."

"You have a phone for work?" Nicole asked.

"Burner. Changed out every month."

"How many girls?" I wanted to know. The more girls, the more charges, Nicole would think. The more girls, the more people who could maybe identify me, was what I was thinking.

"Eight in Cleveland Heights. Another seven more work at the clubs. At least that's how it was a couple months back."

"Where do they live? Where'd he move them after the containers were opened?"

Waters didn't pretend not to know about the containers.

"Cleveland Heights."

"Cleveland fucking Heights!" Nicole exclaimed. She was loving the swear words.

"At his mother's house."

"Are you serious? Of course you're serious." Nicole's eye roll was dramatic. "He wouldn't be the first criminal to use his mother's house."

"Where does he keep his files or records?"

"Not at the club, that I know of. Maybe at the house. Not sure."

"Has he talked to you about insurance?" I asked. I needed to assess my exposure here. Fifteen different girls who may recognize me plus videotape was a big problem I needed to solve.

Waters' eyes widened. "How do you know—"

"Did he?" I pressed. I didn't need anyone asking how I knew things I couldn't know.

"Yes. He says he has videotapes of people committing crimes."

"Prostitution?" I asked. A lot of lawyers could survive misdemeanors. I probably couldn't, not unless I was willing to go the Nicole Long route and live in obscurity.

"Not exactly," Waters hedged. "Some of the girls start when they are like fourteen or fifteen. I think he takes videos of the johns. Also I think that some girl may have died early on. I think he has a video of that."

"Of a murder?"

"Like they meant to kill her? No. Not like that. I heard one of the girls talk about it. That first night a bunch of guys were with her and something happened. When Sledge and Grand went to check on her, she wasn't breathing."

"That's all you know?"

Waters nodded.

"Also the phone. The phone that the police found, that was used in some other thing they did. I wasn't supposed to keep it. But when the police left the scene—this was in Toledo—it was there. Rather than them coming back and finding it, I took it home. It was a mistake to use it, but I was out of phones."

"Okay. Let me step outside a minute."

I stood and turned the handle. The door was locked. I resisted the urge to jiggle the handle or kick the door. Instead, I looked for a button. When I finally found it, I pressed, hard. It was only a few seconds before I heard the click. I signaled Nicole.

"What's the story?" Valdespino asked when we emerged into the hall.

"I need to talk with my colleague. Can you give me a second, please?"

Valdespino stepped away.

"What the fuck?" Nicole said.

"What the fuck is right," I mimicked.

"What do we do? You were right. This is the case of the decade. This could save my career. We have to ride hard on this. Get his statement down, get a search warrant, get arrest warrants, get the media. We'll be the heroes who've saved girls and women from a life of hell."

"And what about our fed friends down the hall?"

"Fuck them. We'll drop the charges in exchange for his testimony."

"You want to break that to them using some of those fucks, or do you want me to give them a more nuanced response?"

"Certainly you shouldn't deliver that nuanced response." She bent her fingers in scare quotes around nuanced. "I thought you and that AUSA were going to come to blows.

It's so weird how small this city is. I think I met him. I think he was there for Casey Cort's closing argument in the Jarrod Carter case. I can't believe I had him, the container guy, but let him go. Didn't know who he was. Who investigated his case anyway? How is it no one noticed?"

"When the FBI made that big bust, they didn't look further. You know we don't have those kinds of resources. Vice isn't doing big cases like that now. No budget. It's all going to terrorism." I tried to sound critical, but the focus on terrorism was going to save my ass in this case.

Nicole shook her head like the past didn't matter.

"We got this. We're going to take down a criminal enterprise. We can save some girls. Reveal some bad guys who take advantage of girls. And if I can move back to the Justice Center, then that would just be a bonus."

I shook her hand, then brought her into a half-hug. Started to walk towards Miles and Lou. I was more than ready to break the bad news.

"Let's go dole out some justice."

14

"Did you talk? That why they let you walk?" Sledge asked Derek Waters. "How you home all of a sudden?" Waters was the last driver in the house. We'd sent the rest home. Cancelled the night's work. There was only a handful of nights we'd done that. Sledge always said that consistency was important to meet customer expectations.

The snow was coming down again, three more inches combined with yesterday's two and last week's fifteen; it was a mess outside. We did not need any kind of accidents happening.

A delivery van wasn't suspicious when there was a road full of traffic. But as the lone vehicle on a snowy road...that opened things up to too many questions. Even the big boys in brown were suspending all but critical deliveries during this week of bad weather.

"No. Not one word," Waters insisted. "They thought they had something. Ran me through the feds and then back through county. But I'm straight."

"Why you here?" Sledge pressed. "Must have been a hell of a night to drive over. Nothing but snow and ice out there."

Derek held his left fist with his right hand. Shook them toward us, sitting at the kitchen table. He was standing as Sledge hadn't invited him to take a seat.

"Can I be back on the payroll?" He shifted back and forth in his boots. His nerves were getting to me. For a guy who didn't get agitated by meth dealers, he was losing his cool. "I still got bills to pay and I don't want child support on my back."

"First, no one driving tonight. You heard why. As for the rest, now's not a good time. You need to spend your days and nights working on beating that meth rap. You still got that problem as far as I can see."

"That ain't no thang. Deal's back on with the prosecutor. Feds closed their investigation." Derek was talking so fast, I wondered if he was on meth.

"That was awful quick," I said. Something wasn't right. I couldn't put my finger on it, but Derek being here was strange. He could have called and asked for his job back, not driven a few miles in a snowstorm over icy roads to ask in person.

"They got bigger fish to fry. Someone else talked maybe. They can take down the meth ring. Either way, I'm out of jail for now. Gonna beat this case too, maybe. That lawyer you hired, he's really good. Took the feds straight down. FBI only questioned me for about five minutes before they gave up."

"Glad it's working out," I said, not because I cared but for something to say. Derek was feeling like a loose cannon that needed to be contained somehow. He'd fucked up. I'd done my best to handle it. From here on in, it was a waiting game.

"So are all the girls here now? No one's out tonight?" Derek was pacing in tight circles now.

"Nothing has changed, man," I said. Sledge looked about ready to pop a vein.

"You know, the cops and everyone asked me a lot about bookkeeping. Like if I kept papers and books on my business. I know you guys are big on running things clean. So maybe you'd want to make sure that you have a good place where you keep things. Do you keep them here or at The Place to Be?"

"We'll take it under advisement," Sledge said. My boss pulled himself to his full height then leaned forward and pressed his hands on the table. He was in full intimidation mode.

"You seemed to be all about the business these days. Wish you'd been all about the business before we did you that favor in Toledo. You know I took your three years for you. You better make sure you take these years for me. I'm not going back to jail under any circumstances." Sledge banged the table so hard, glasses in the sink across the room rattled. "You owe me."

"Yeah, man. I know. It's why I asked for my job back. I need to earn as much as I can before I go. Help my baby mama and all that. You're a family man. Your mama still here with you? Is she in the downstairs room you set up?"

"I think it's time you go home. Don't know about you, but I got a business to run. You got to handle your own affairs. Hand off whatever you need to hand off. You feel me?"

Sledge's face was so far from friendly that it even made me a bit nervous. Derek needed to read the room and get his ass out of here. I was trying to work out why in the hell he was here in the first place. In my gut, I knew it wasn't about asking for his job back.

"I feel you. Did I leave anything down at the club? Any papers or anything?"

Sledge reared up, his boots hit the chair. It scraped back noisily. He got right up close to Derek. I don't know what prison is like, but from all the TV shows I understood that vibe, the one that said violence was just around the corner unless something stopped it. The kitchen was electric with it.

Sledge threw an arm around Derek's neck. It was a move that could be friendly or choke a man out.

"Man, you know I don't keep no papers that ain't required by law. Grand, come over here. I think Ice here ain't on the up-and-up. I think he's working for the cops. You pat him down and make sure he ain't wearing a wire."

Not two seconds after the word "wire" came out Sledge's mouth, a loud boom filled the house. The back door splintered into pieces and what looked like a thousand men came through the door, in black pants, black shirts, black boots, bulletproof vests, and black helmets over they faces.

I knew how this was going to go. I might die tonight. I took a deep breath and got ready to meet my maker. Didn't want to go down having shit myself like a punk. Thought about my mama, my sister.

"Police! Get down! Everyone get down on the ground and put their hands on the back of their heads."

I got out of the kitchen chair and fell to the floor, prone. The boot in my back was expected. I waited for the bullet to come next. After the shooting of Troy Duncan had gone unpunished, it was open season on us. My arms felt like they were being wrenched straight out of my sockets. Then cold cuffs snapped, metal tightened around my wrists. I heard a second clink. That had to be Sledge.

"How many people are in the house?" a voice demanded.

I didn't say a word. Wasn't my house. Think the cop figured that out right quick.

"Look, I'm going to lift you up, put you both in a chair. Then I'm going to ask you some questions."

I was lifted from the ground. Put back in the chair I'd just been sitting in when Derek had been betraying us. Sledge was pushed into another. A tall white cop took off his helmet. Flipped a third chair backwards and sat across from us.

"Neil Walsh. I need to know if there's anyone else in the house. If there are any weapons. You need to tell me the truth if you want to keep everyone safe."

"First, I want you to know we have a lawyer," Sledge said. "I'm not answering any questions."

"Waters said your mom is here. If you want to keep her safe, you'll answer this one."

Sledge was quiet for at least a minute.

"My mom. She in that three-season porch. She's either in her wheelchair or the hospital bed set up in there on account of the fact that she's missing one of her legs. She can't run away or walk. My niece Alisha should be in the room with her or upstairs in her own room."

"What about the girls? Where are they?"

Sledge looked from Walsh to me.

"What are we under arrest for?" I asked.

"Promoting prostitution for one," Walsh said.

"Feels like déjà vu," Sledge responded.

"Charges are going to stick this time. Got you dead to rights. Now tell us where the girls are so we don't have to tear apart your mom's nice house."

Sledge looked toward me. His nod was slight.

"Attic," I said. "Key's in my right front pocket."

Another officer hauled me up and Neil Walsh felt around until he located the brass in my change pocket.

The key was passed, followed by the sound of at least a dozen boots clomping up the stairs. Two women with bulletproof vests, but not the helmets and automatic weapons, came in. A third man in a sport coat came up behind with a pile of silver blankets in his hands.

Though some of the cops had gone up the back steps, I could hear muffled steps through the walls and figured they were congregating in the living room.

"Weapons?" Walsh looked between us.

"Nah man," I said.

Walsh gave Sledge the stink eye.

"Nothing. I don't roll like that," he said. That was mostly true. Guns did not go with his whole misdemeanor theory of crime. I did know he had one somewhere, though. I was guessing it was in the wall at The Place to Be or under some floorboards at The Dive Bar or somewhere else the cops couldn't find it without a treasure map.

"Media's here," a woman cop said after she came into the room.

Walsh practically ran from the room like the TV news reporters was handing out winning lottery tickets. My guess was that all the cops would pull off their helmets so they could cheese for the cameras. Promotions were made from busts like this. Even I knew that.

"What happens now?" I asked Sledge.

"What do you mean? They'll march us out of here right downtown to county lockup. I'll call Casey. She'll get us bailed out. Should be back home by tomorrow afternoon at the latest." He recited that like it was the Lord's Prayer or the Pledge of Allegiance, not the plan to thwart those who wanted to separate us from our liberty.

"You worried?" I was worried.

"Nah. A lot of bluster. Lot of flash. Can't turn into anything."

"How are you so calm?"

"Insurance ain't gone away. If we go down, I'm not going down alone, you can be sure of that."

The cop named Walsh stomped back into the room. It was cold in the kitchen with a hole where the door used to be.

"Get up." He pointed to Sledge. "It's your turn."

"Where's my mom?"

"Someone from county elder care is here. They'll bring in an aide for the night. That's my guess. She doesn't deserve this, you know. If anything happens to her, this'll be on you."

"Right." Sledge stood. "If it's time to go, let's go so I can get back here."

"Can I have a coat?" I asked.

"Why?"

"Cold outside. It's the blue one on that chair."

Walsh threw it over my shoulders. We walked through the living room, which was empty now, then out the front door. I was first, and I was prepared. I leaned down until the coat covered most of my head. I could see the bright lights from the cameras but kept my eyes on the snow crunching under my Timberlands. The questions started almost immediately.

"Are you behind the container case?"

"How many girls have you exploited?"

"Is it true that you were charged before but got acquitted?"

Sledge exercised his right to remain silent. Someone pushed the top of my head, and I was in the back of a cop car—alone. Sledge probably went in another. My heart sped up when the car engine revved. Not because of trial or jail or prison. But because I was going to have to call my mother and tell her the truth about my job.

15

"Glad you could make it," Tom said. I'd barely made it off the Justice Center's slow elevator before he'd put his hand on my arm and escorted me to a small room in a corner of the ninth floor. "I think working this case means that our no contact pact is broken."

"I guess I didn't think we'd ever come up against each other," I said. For someone I never wanted to speak with or see again, we were going to have to do a lot of speaking and seeing.

"And yet, here we are. So good to see you." His hand trailed down my arm. Grabbed one of my hands. Then he grabbed my other with his other hand. Looked me up and down. "Looks like life is treating you well."

Glad that I was still wearing my gloves and could barely feel the warmth from his hands, I pulled mine back anyway, tucked them into my coat's pockets. Hugged myself so I was completely covered, not that there was a thing that was provocative about the plum tweed suit I was wearing under my full-length coat.

"Thanks for the compliment," I said. I tried to smile, but I wasn't sure it was even bordering on genuine. He was making me nervous for no good reason. "That thing I said all those years ago about us not speaking? That still holds outside of work."

I wasn't at all interested in doing this "pretend friends" thing Tom was trotting out. We could speak when necessary. Like when I needed my birth certificate, or when we were on opposite sides of a case. There wasn't a need for anything else.

"But you're talking to me now."

Tom's smile belied something. Rueful maybe. I couldn't read him like I'd been able to all those years ago. Although maybe I hadn't really been able to read him. If I had, I'd have known all along that he really didn't have feelings for me. That I was only his cover story.

"There's no reason for this kind of freeze out. We could be friends. Maybe we should be friends. We have a lot in common."

In many ways he was right. There was that shared experience I'd hung my hopes on in law school, and that second time we'd tried to be together and I'd accepted his proposal. But it's not enough, now. Any feelings I'd had for him were squelched when Miles and I saw him go into the hotel with that girl. I shuddered at the memory of what we'd seen on the videotape because it mirrored that long ago night exactly.

"It's not prostitutes that we have in common," I deadpanned.

Tom's eyebrows shot up. "Touché."

The room was hot and close. I pulled my hands from my pockets, took my gloves off, and looked at my watch.

"So we're supposed to have a meeting at ten, Tom. Are we going to have it here in this closet? Do I need to squeeze my clients in here?"

"No, we'll go back to the conference room down the hall. Nicole Long is there."

"Nicole Long." I nodded my head. Of course all of this would come together. Sledge Hammer's real name was no longer a secret. His business was done. And Long was back.

"The original prosecutor on the first Carter case," he acknowledged.

"She remembers back two and a half, three years ago?" I asked. It was an oblique reference to her well-known problem with alcohol. "She's back in major crimes? Hope she doesn't hold a grudge." I was only partly kidding. I'd won my fair share of cases, and prosecutors had longer memories than elephants.

"Look Casey, I know that I'm not in any position to ask you a favor, okay. My behavior hasn't been the best."

Here it comes, I thought. The reason he'd pulled me into the closet with him.

"Nicole doesn't know about you, does she?" For the shortest moment ever, I pitied a prosecutor. "She's flying blind."

"No one knows about me. And I'm done with all that, anyway. There's nothing to tell. I'm ready for a change. I mean, looking at that news footage of those girls coming down the stairs from that attic, they'd been locked in for months or years, it really woke me up, Casey. I know I did something wrong. Very wrong for a long time. But you know what my family's like. Knowing right from wrong is sometimes a little fuzzier than for most people."

He had to be kidding. I wondered if I were in a fun house and not just a tiny interview room in the Justice Center. His family's corruption was his excuse?

"Fuzzy? I think if you just avoid violating statutes, you should be good to go. Seems like an easy bright-line to me." I set my bag on the small table. Took my coat off. Sweat was pooling between my breasts. I didn't know if it was heat or nerves or what, but I was getting uncomfortable. I was keeping entirely too many secrets, some protected by law. Others because of displaced loyalty for my ex.

I made my glance at my watch obvious and deliberate. "It's ten after. Nicole's going to be wondering where we are."

"Casey, I get it. I did wrong. Now I'm trying to make it right."

"How? How are you trying to make it right? Those girls can't get their lives back."

"Look, I don't have any interest in locking your clients up forever."

"You have no interest in prosecuting the case of the century? Or the decade or whatever? It's been wall-to-wall news for the last week about how Neil Walsh and you and apparently Long are heroes for doing what the feds couldn't, solving the container case. That reporter, Victoria Greenlee, has practically moved into my little corner of Shaker Square.

"It's like her and her camera guy are following me everywhere. And if I have to see my clients' perp walk one more time, I'm going to have to ask for a change of venue because I'm not sure there's a single person left in Cuyahoga County who hasn't seen that damned news report."

Tom shrugged. His nonchalance was maddening. He wasn't doing my clients a favor out of the goodness of his heart. He was all about himself. Keeping his secrets. Saving his own skin. In ten long years, not a single thing had changed.

"Walsh wants to retire with the biggest pension possible."

"Big get for a narcotics detective."

"So, Casey?" Tom was too close for comfort.

"What do you want?"

"Your clients are coming, right?"

"Of course. It's their lives, not mine. They'll make the decision about accepting any offer on the table. I assume there's an offer coming. We didn't come down for a dog and pony show where you asked them to walk themselves into prison for the rest of their lives."

"Then let me lead the meeting, okay? If you do right by me, I'll do right by you."

"Funny." My dry laugh held no humor. "That's how we got into this mess."

Having bought more silence from me, Tom leaned away. His loose-limbed frat boy persona was firmly back in place.

"Let's get out of this steam bath."

I hefted all of my stuff and followed him to the real conference room. A deputy with one hand on a gun and the other on his belt stood outside the door. He looked down at me.

"You the defense attorney?"

I nodded.

"Your clients are in there. Mr. Brody, I'll be out here if you need anything."

"I'm sure we'll be fine, deputy." Tom gave a jaunty salute, then twisted the knob and pulled open the door.

I was done being walked over for the morning. I bustled into the room ahead of Tom and took charge.

"Mr. Carter, Mr. Fortune, good to see you. Tom, Nicole, can you please give us the room. Let's convene in ten minutes."

I eyed Tom. He poked Nicole on the shoulder and the two of them took their files and left the room silently.

"What's the plan?" Fortune asked the minute the door closed.

"To see what they're offering."

"Dropping all charges would be good," Carter said.

"I'm not seeing that happening. That twenty-four seven, wall-to-wall news coverage of that perp walk in the snow. The girls coming out of the attic in practically see-through pajamas. The girls in the container from three years ago. You're not Jeffrey Dahmer or Charles Manson, but to the fine folks of Northeastern Ohio, you might as well be. There's no way that you're not seeing the inside of a prison unless we beat them at trial. But they're not coming back in here offering you a misdemeanor and probation. Any questions on that?"

Jarrod Carter didn't look happy, but shook his head, resigned.

"Let's see what they've got."

I opened my briefcase, took out my file, plopped it on the table along with a fresh yellow legal pad and the Cross pen my parents gave me. The pen seemed fitting as it had already been at the scene of at least one Brody crime. While I decided whether it made me lucky or not, I went to the door, opened it, and peered down the hall. Nicole was there waiting like an impatient dog told to stay.

"We're ready. Let's talk," I said.

She nodded and disappeared around a corner, presumably to get her superior, Tom.

I ducked back in the room when they started down the hall.

"You all don't talk. Understand? While we're in this room you are exercising your right to remain silent and your right to counsel."

"You will have no problems from us," Carter said.

I knew he was telling the truth. Except for their horrible, nauseating crimes, he and Fortune were model clients.

"What are we here to discuss?" I asked when everyone was sitting down and the door was closed on the nosy deputy.

Tom tilted in the chair, the back hitting the wall. I had to admit I was surprised when Nicole Long took the lead.

"After watching the news, I think we can all agree that a trial is not in anyone's best interests."

She looked at me as if waiting for an answer. But two could play this game. I wouldn't blink first.

"So, I want you to know that we've had a long meeting about this," Long continued. "Tom really went to bat for you. He knows that you're not like the rest of the defense bar and won't be unreasonable. So here's our offer."

I tried not to roll my eyes at the drama and backhanded compliment...or insult, I wasn't sure which. The characterization was up in the air.

"The indictment has one hundred counts of compelling and promoting prostitution with a human trafficking specification. Throw in section 29 23.32, engaging in pattern of corrupt activity, and we're looking at some serious mandatory jail time. With this kind of publicity, there's no way a judge is going to sentence you to concurrent terms, so we're clearly looking at life in prison...if...if you take it to trial."

I was already over her drama and we'd only been in the room together for five minutes. I didn't want to think about how unbearable she'd make trial this time around.

"What the deal you're putting on the table?"

"Fifteen counts of each charge. One for each girl we rescued. Concurrent sentences. Jail time is still mandatory otherwise the public will have pitchforks out."

The nudge from Carter was subtle, but I felt it.

"That's ten years for each of you," I said. I looked each of my clients in the eye. Then at Tom, then Nicole. "That's the bottom line, unless I miscalculated."

"She's right," Long said. "Ten years. You'd still be young when you get out. No life sentences. No dealing with parole boards or hearings. You'd go in, do your time, pay your debt to society, and be done with it. It's the best offer you're going to get."

I stood. Proffered my right hand. "Thanks so much, Nicole, Tom. My clients will take it under consideration. If you'll excuse us."

I didn't need to signal. My clients were savvy enough to follow my lead. Dion and Jarrod gathered their coats and bags. I marched down the hall, then bundled them into the tiny room Tom and I had shared earlier. It was still overly warm.

"Why we in here?" Carter asked. He was clearly the one making the decisions. I tried not to think too much about whether there was a conflict here. Whether I should be advising Fortune to get his own lawyer. Carter's second-in-command could probably turn state's evidence and minimize his own punishment. He was the more well-spoken and less intimidating of the two.

"No need to go across the street to hash this out." I turned to Carter. "I want to know what you think of the offer. I can get back to them now."

"What you think?"

"I think it's a good offer considering the publicity on this one. Considering the scope of the crimes involved. Most prosecutors would try to bury you to make themselves look good."

Jarrod Carter shook his head. "You know he's not making this offer out of the goodness of his heart."

"I know that." I didn't mention that I'd had a front row seat to Tom's perfidy. "What's the verdict?"

"I'm not planning on going to jail," Sledge concluded. I didn't bother to ask Dion Fortune his opinion. It would be the same as Carter's. At least while the three of us were in this room.

"That will mean a trial. I have to warn you as I would any other clients. You get convicted at trial, you'll be in prison for the rest of your natural lives. You should be grateful there's no death or murder, otherwise they'd be throwing the death penalty at you."

Jarrod Carter shrugged like we were debating paper versus plastic at a grocery store.

"So we take it to trial. That's easy enough."

"What about the tape?" I asked. If it were up to me, that thing would never see the light of day, but I didn't exactly trust Carter not to do what he needed to do to save his own ass. And it wasn't as if Tom didn't deserve some kind of consequences.

"What about it?"

"What's going to happen to it? I don't like to be surprised."

"It's my get out of jail free card."

I tried not to shiver as steam hissed from the radiators. Jarrod Carter and Tom Brody were playing three-dimensional chess. I hadn't graduated from checkers.

16

I brushed leaves from the sparse grass and knelt at the gravesite. The tombstone was shiny, its crisp and neat engraving out of place among older, aged stones. It read, Maria Zamjoski, 1917-2006.

"Where is our father? Shouldn't their names be on a stone together?"

"His body is lost," Erika answered for Anna. "Let me think how to say this in English." She paused for a long, excruciating moment. "He is buried in a mass grave that was made along the roadside between Poland and Germany. He had to, probably, dig it himself. They did it like that during the war. After the hole was dug, they'd shoot half the people into it and make the remaining prisoners shovel the dirt back along top."

I didn't have any questions after that. After Anna had shown me the pictures from last night, I'd had so many vivid dreams of what I thought Poland was from when I was three or four. I hadn't mentioned them to anyone at breakfast in the hotel basement because I still wasn't sure if the dreams were real or just from my overactive imagination filling in gaps that I hadn't known were missing.

Anna knelt down next to me, fresh tears coursing down her cheeks. She touched my arm gently.

"You remember nothing of me?" she asked in halting English. She must have practiced the phrase just to speak it to me today.

I'd stood in the hot shower, staring at the intricate patterns of the Polish tiles thinking about this question I knew would come. I suspected the answer would be hard for her to hear, but I decided to speak it anyway. Even though my answer was in English, and it would be for Anna's daughter to translate, I looked directly in my sister's eyes that were so much like my own.

"When I was adopted to the von Kraus family, an older girl was taken in at the same time as me. She was Polish. My aunt said we spoke the language to each other for a time until we didn't anymore. Her name was also Anna. She neatly fitted into the sister space in my brain, I think. Maybe that. In America, they would say it was the trauma of the situation that altered my memory. I like to think, though, it was enough to have an older sister around. To have someone to make me feel safe. Keep me protected."

Anna said something in Polish. Her daughter said, "She is happy that you were not alone. Her greatest fear had always been that you were some scared little boy somewhere, the camps maybe, waiting for your death. She wants to know if you talk to the other Anna?"

I had to blink away my own tears then. In many ways, I was grateful that I'd been taken away...kidnapped, really, at such a young age.

The brain, I'd learned, is an amazing organ. It does an amazing job of protecting our psyches from traumatic memories in many cases.

The other Anna's brain wasn't so good at that, though. Maybe because she was older. Maybe because her own brain worked differently. She had been, in many ways, more damaged than me. She'd been kind of somber. Rarely talked unless someone had asked her a question. Stayed in her room most of the time. I'd tried a bunch of times to get her to go out with me on what Greta called her big adventures, but as often as she said yes, she also said no.

I mostly hadn't been surprised when Anna had taken Viktor's suggestion to work for a hat maker some distance away. She would get a trade and build the kind of solitary life she'd seemed to have wanted. After she hadn't responded to my first few letters, I'd given up. I regretted this now, so very much. Maybe I could have been a friend to her. Maybe I could have brought her to America. But as it stood, now, I knew as little about this second Anna as I did the first.

"I lost track of her when I went to America," I said.

"Mama would have been so happy that we have found each other," Anna's daughter translated. "You were her lost boy. She lit a candle for you every year on your birthday."

"Remember that year we were in Chicago and they were doing a whole Bastille Day celebration and I thought it was just for your birthday." It was the first thing Casey had said since we'd arrived at the cemetery.

"Bastille Day?"

"It's a French holiday. Celebrating revolutionaries storming the Bastille? I'm not sure, but it's cool to have a national holiday on Daddy's birthday."

"Is Bastille Day not in July?" Erika said, her eyes suddenly full of confusion.

"Of course. It's July fourteenth," Casey answered, sure of her facts as lawyers were.

A long look passed between Anna and Erika. Then rapid Polish passed back and forth between them.

"Your birthday was on the fourteenth, but in January," Erika finally said.

My Casey, who took nearly everything with grace, visibly paled.

"January? During the middle of the winter? Your birthday was always in the summer. Mama always complained about baking in the heat. Remember the hot summer in nineteen eighty-eight? The candles melted before Mama could light them." Casey turned to Erika. "Is your mom sure? January?"

There was a lot more Polish before Erika spoke.

"It was cold and dark. It snowed the day you were born. We had one of those huge heaters in the apartment. The ones that are nearly two meters tall and covered in green and white tiles. Papa made sure it was hot. So it was cold outside, but we were sweating in the apartment so that you wouldn't get cold. I'll never forget that, Marek...Pietrek...Peter." Erika stumbled over the last bit, naming me.

"Someone at the meeting did say something about shaving off months to make a younger child more attractive to adopting families," Casey supplied.

"I am sorry," Erika said. Whether it was her genuine expression of regret or Anna's, I didn't know. I was going to ask for clarification, but then realized it didn't make a difference either way. It was a sorry situation. One where the people at fault were all long dead.

"What's done is done," I said. Then I stood as quickly as my creaky knees would allow, which was not quick at all. I brushed off the twigs, a few stray leaves of grass. It was like Marek Zamojski was dead and buried in the ground with my mother. I don't know when it happened, but on that day in 1942, I think he ceased to exist. I was ready to go back to Peter Cort's life in Cleveland. I missed my wife. I wanted to be back in my kitchen with its old, too loud phone and the smell of baking. I wanted to wake up on West Boulevard where I knew there would be no surprises.

As we prepared for goodbye, Casey hugged her cousin and aunt. I hugged my sister and niece. They wished us a safe trip back to America. We promised to keep in touch. I could only breathe and relax once we were back in the car.

"You okay, Dad?" Casey asked while maneuvering through the winding streets.

"You need a new car."

"Probably should have bought a good used one and not spent my money on Arhaus furniture."

"You deserve both."

"I can't afford both."

"But I can. Let's go shopping on Tuesday. There are more sales at the end of the month. It'll be from us to you for your birthday."

"Dad, you don't have to do that."

"Tomorrow, all three of us are getting on an airplane and going back to the United States. Look at what happened to me during the war, what happened to so many people. We...all of us spend too much time thinking and stressing and worrying. I don't want you to worry. I don't want to worry about you in that ancient car. Seize the day and all that. No one knows about tomorrow."

"Will Mama be okay?"

"I'm sure she will be fine. I love you, my dear heart. I don't say this enough, but I love you. I'm grateful that I got to spend every night of your childhood under the same roof. I'm grateful for all the times we can spend together now. The last thing I want to worry about is you stranded on the side of some road in an old car because of your pride."

"Thank you."

"You are very welcome." Casey's safety was only a third of it. Another third was that I did want to give her something while I was still alive and could help her. But the last bit, the part that had motivated me was a bit of what Americans called "retail therapy."

Shopping for the car, I hoped, would help soothe her after she broke her second engagement. Obviously I was biased, but I thought my daughter was beautiful and smart and any man should be grateful to have her in his life.

The men of Cleveland didn't seem to agree. I didn't want her to have to wait any longer to have the things in life that she wanted and deserved. I was one man who would love her unconditionally, always. I vowed to show that bit to her more often. Maybe then she'd know what real love was like when it finally came her way.

17

That prosecutor hadn't been able to fix her mistake in the hour she'd promised the judge, so by noon, Judge Brody had sent us all home for the day. Home for me right now was my sister's place. Reporters had camped out at my apartment building, so I stayed away from there. I didn't want them at my parents' house either, and Retta's house wasn't too far, but far enough, from my parents these days.

I'd made it my singled-minded mission to avoid my parents. Whenever they were on their way to my sister's house, I managed to be gone. It wasn't mature by any standard, but I still didn't know what I'd say to them if I had to look either one of them in the eye. Some nights when I woke up in a cold sweat, scared to death about my future, the promise of jail didn't feel as awful as the inevitable confrontation with my parents.

I'd just dropped Sledge off, switched cars, and was pulling up to the garage behind the house when I realized I'd made a mistake. The front bumper of my father's car was kissing the third door of the three-car garage. If my mind hadn't been back in the courtroom, or thinking of how to best dodge reporters, I'd have noticed it long before I was parked next to it. I'd have turned around and bided my time somewhere until my sister let me know that the coast was clear. That Camry said that a complicated conversation I'd hoped to avoid was ahead. For a long moment, running on foot was a viable option until I saw the kitchen curtain flick.

Not that I had anywhere to run to. After two months, I was out of options.

"How long did you think you could avoid us?" my father said the moment I stepped through the back door. The disappointment in his voice had my stomach plummeting to my toes. Anger I could have tolerated, but this tone pierced my heart like the sharpest knife.

I'd been hoping to avoid this conversation forever, but I didn't say that out loud.

My mother stepped around him. There were tears brimming over her lower lids.

"Sex trafficking in underage girls. What did we ever do that would make you think this would be an acceptable line of work? How many times has your father offered to set you up with a job? He's been in the perfect position to help you."

"Mom, I couldn't be perfect like Dad."

"I didn't ask you to be perfect. I asked you to do one thing, not to get involved in a life of crime." That last had been a constant refrain in my childhood. After we'd gone to see Boyz n the Hood, I'd gotten that first lecture on the importance of securing a future free of crime. John Singleton's lesson for my father had been that black boys couldn't be trusted to steer their own future. From that day, he'd watched me like a hawk second-guessing and double-checking every decision I'd made.

"I know," I lied. I hung my head because the shame was still real.

"Why did you do it?" My father whispered the question, his voice hoarse like he'd been crying. "Can you answer us that? I'm seeing it on TV every day—girls coming down from an attic. They were locked in there night and day. Before that it was a container. Before that it was hotel rooms. While you escorted men into those rooms or those vans, what were you thinking? Were you thinking about your mother or your sister?"

"It was a job." It wasn't an excuse. It was the truth. It's the way Sledge treated it. It's the way I had to treat it in my mind to keep me from thinking about the other stuff, the bad stuff that sometimes happened, that no one other than Sledge or me could clean up.

"A job?" My father fell into a kitchen chair. His head fell heavily into his hands. "A job is driving a bus. Your mother and sister have jobs at Cleveland Clinic. I have a job. What you did was an abomination."

"This is why I haven't come to your house." I could hear my own voice unnaturally high-pitched with indignation. "I knew you'd react this way. What could I say to appease you? The answer is nothing."

"You could say that what they're saying on the news isn't true. That somehow you got caught up in this and weren't a willing participant," my mother offered.

I closed my eyes against their shame. Shook my head. "I can't say that."

"Do you have any explanation?"

"Mom, give him a break," Retta said coming into the room. She'd no doubt stashed the kids somewhere far, far away from our little family drama.

"Give him a break? A break? How can you say that? He's staying in your...house. How do you know that he won't have your daughter working?" I couldn't believe my mother said that, had such a low opinion of me.

"Mama, that's crazy." Retta dismissed our mother's concerns with a wave of her hand.

"What's crazy is you let him in here."

"It's my house."

"Is it money? Has to be money. I'll pay you whatever he's paying you. I'll pay you double to get your brother out of here."

"You don't get to decide what goes on in my house."

"That's obvious. I wouldn't have all this junk food. Cookies. Chips. Chocolate covered pretzels. What is all that? You've gotta make sure your kids don't turn out like you or like him. Obviously we've done something very, very wrong here."

I shook my head. I felt bad, but my mother comparing what I'd done with eating too many calories was one step too far. I raised my hand to stop the madness, but my sister was one step ahead.

"Mama. Enough," Retta shouted, cutting off the rant. "Let's all sit down in the living room, okay? I think it's time we talk."

Mama shoulders were shaken with silent tears by the time she got to the couch. Finally, she looked up, using the sleeve of her white cardigan to dry her face. "I can't believe that you're on trial."

AIME AUSTIN

"It wasn't my plan, Mama, trust me." I'd never planned to be anywhere near a courtroom. And for all these years, I hadn't even been close.

"What was your plan?"

"I am on trial, and my lawyer tells me conversations with anyone other than her or someone who works for her aren't confidential."

"I'm your mother."

But she wasn't a doctor or lawyer or priest or therapist. She wasn't bound by law to keep my secrets. I didn't share those with anyone who wasn't.

"The prosecutor could call you to testify," I said.

"When they came around, I told them that neither me nor your father would have anything to say to them."

I was both surprised and not. Casey Cort and Sledge kind of shared information with me on a need-to-know basis. I guess neither of them thought I needed to know every last detail.

"So if I talk to you about anything, it has to be hypothetical, okay? I shouldn't be doing this, but I know that I owe you an explanation."

The tightness that had seized my chest for months eased a bit. I hadn't realized how much stress it had been holding onto all of this—alone—for years.

"Retta, put in a video for the kids. Something long."

"I'll put in that latest Harry Potter. It's over two hours."

My sister disappeared to the family room then came back and gave my parents a nod.

"Dion. You were always a good kid," my mother started. "You were my easy one. Always went to school without a hassle. Got good grades. Didn't let your pants sag around your behind. Didn't get involved with those bad kids from Cleveland or East Cleveland. Didn't do no drugs. Your biggest problem was being vain, and if that's the worst, I knew I had a good one."

"I wish I had a better answer for you, Ma. I graduated from Cleveland Heights. I went to Clark Atlanta. I even got a job. Remember when I graduated, I worked for the Sun Newspapers. I was driving all around the county doing stringer work for a bunch of their different local papers. I was hoping that would morph into something more substantial. But the journalism industry had started imploding by then—"

"I know editors at Crain's Cleveland Business, the Jewish Journal, Daily Legal News," my dad jumped in, his brain like a personal Rolodex.

"Dad, I know you know people. That doesn't change things. Clinging to a sinking ship don't make it float."

"Go on."

"So remember when I told you I was thinking of starting my own business?"

"You went to the chamber of commerce entrepreneur program. I was so proud of you for going out on your own. Our community always needs more of us."

"I met Sledge...Jarrod Carter there."

"Why was he there?" My dad asked that like what Sledge had done wasn't a business. I wanted to tell him that Jarrod Carter had been one of the smartest businessmen I'd known. If he'd been one hundred percent legit, and not an intimidating dark-skinned black man, he'd probably be running one of those companies that had their own entire building downtown.

"He came there to get some help on his bars. I think he was having some licensing issues. We were the only two brothers there and got to talking. At first he asked me for some help at The Place to Be. I filled out papers. Got his liquor license squared away. Managed some stuff with the city taxes, county, state, worker's comp. I mean, he went to Heights High school too, but he wasn't—isn't so good with the paperwork part of business. But he took those two bars from dive bars with only a few hardcore drinkers during the day to really profitable in only a minute. Most new businesses fail, but it was like he had a golden touch."

"The Midas touch?" My dad had the annoying habit of always trying to show how smart he was. I nodded at his reference to Greek mythology, then soldiered on.

"Yeah, sure. But he made two businesses successful—in the 'hood." I hated how my voice sounded like I was seeking their approval for associating with someone who had been successful albeit not in a traditional manner.

"And the girls?" My mother's voice was a whisper. In those three words, she pierced at the heart of the matter. That I'd treated the women who'd worked for us no differently than our ancestors had been handled—as human chattel. I blinked away the comparison.

"Yeah, look, Mama, Retta, I'm really sorry about what I did. I want you to know that I love you both very much."

My mother's "That's nice" was heavy on the sarcasm. "Go on."

"Adding the big screens for sports was a really good idea. Patronage was up and profits tripled. Jarrod hired me on full time when the liquor license on the second place came through. He said I was worth my weight. Paid me more than I was earning from the newspapers. It started small.

"First it was just girls dancing. Brought in money on the nights there wasn't a ball game. There was no sex in the beginning. Then the guys wanted extras. Didn't see any harm. It was a victimless crime. The girls were happy to get bigger tips and extra money, and we got lots more customers at the bar. No one was doing anything against their will.

"Then some neighborhood girls came and asked for work. They were too young to work in a bar, but were over the age of consent, so Sledge—"

"Do you have to use that name?"

"Jarrod…Jarrod figured we could stake them, you know. He'd partner with a couple of local motels that were failing. Paid double the room rate, the girls could work there, then we'd screen the customers.

"Then, I think, some customers wanted younger, and Sledge knew some people. We added a couple of girls. The demand we had outstripped the supply. So we got more girls."

"Got girls. This isn't slavery times."

"I'm not proud, but I helped recruit people who may have been less than willing." Following Stephanie Wells into the park that first day flashed through my mind. I pushed that thought as far away as I could. Focused on the real reasons I'd stayed on when things changed. "The money was amazing. Business was growing."

"Didn't I raise you with a conscience?"

"It's not my best moment. But you have to understand. It was a business. We were successful. It was challenging, but I was growing and expanding, fixing problems."

"Containers? That solved your problems?"

"Things got complicated."

"They were dehumanized. You stopped treating them like people."

"I let two of the girls leave. When it looked like they weren't going to be okay, I drove them home."

"What your boss Jarrod say to that?"

"He didn't know. I came up with some excuse."

"Why didn't you quit?"

"I'd already committed the crimes. There wasn't a lot of reasons to go straight. I mean, most of the crimes were victimless, they were misdemeanors. And a business is not just something you can leave. At some point you're bound by those first false turns, by those first…mistakes."

"Don't you see the irony?" My mother's head was in a permanent shake, like a palsy. "Now you're not going to be able to leave jail. You know they don't let you out of there. You could have left Jarrod Carter. No one's going to get you out of prison."

"My hope, Mama, is that I don't have to go."

"How is that going to work? I saw the news like everyone else. I saw the video of you. I saw the video of the girls coming down the steps in the snow, half dressed. I don't know of a jury that would acquit you. I'm not even sure I would and I'm the one who raised you, who knows underneath you probably still a good person."

"I have a good attorney, Ma. We have a good case. Got more than half the charges dismissed on day one."

"I'm your mother and I will always love you. I'm not thrilled with any of this. But if you get out from under this, I'll support you in building a new life even if you have to leave Cleveland."

My father took my mother's hand in solidarity, like they'd always done when lecturing or chastising me and Retta.

"Me too. Son, me too," Dad added. "I think we gotta go now. This was a lot to process. Kids' eyes may bleed from that TV if they're watching too long."

"Thanks, Mama. Thanks, Dad, for listening." Even with their condemnation, I was happy that they hadn't abandoned me altogether.

"Thanks for finally telling us the truth," Dad said. They stood at the same time. Then they ran out like the house was on fire. I know they wanted to get away from me, from what I'd come to represent.

"I didn't know all that." Retta sounded sad. I wondered if there were anyone left on earth I hadn't disappointed. "Why didn't you tell me?"

I looked into the eyes of the sister I'd known my whole life. We were close and distant at the same time. But our parents had forced a wedge between us years ago when they'd pitted us against each other. We're closer now, but I don't think we'll ever heal that wound. If I'd told her, there was a fifty percent chance she'd have told my parents as deflection during one of the moments they were harping on some perceived deficiency of hers. I closed my eyes for a long minute.

"Sledge is pretty smart," I answered. "He was right about one thing, and that's a secret's not a secret if you share it."

"Dion. I'm a vault. I have my share of secrets. Especially from Mom and Dad. You know that. If they knew that my kids didn't have the same father, they'd blame me worse than they already do."

I didn't contradict her with the truth. I was the vault. I'd kept every single one of her secrets, even the one about her baby daddies. She'd never done the same for me. I'd always taken the hits, because I was the boy. I was the one who'd gone to college. I was the one who could face our parents' obvious displeasure without wilting. She had never been that strong.

"Can you turn the heat down?" I was sweaty and light-headed. Maybe I wasn't as strong as I thought.

"You know Cleveland will get cold. I don't want my babies to freeze overnight."

"It wasn't the kind of job I wanted to tell people about," I said in answer to her first question, the why.

"I know. You sleep at night?"

"Most nights," I admitted for the first time. My mother thought that my Achilles heel was my vanity, but it was really my conscience. "Some were harder than others. Any girl's first night was hard as hell."

"This is why you don't have a girlfriend, huh?"

"I didn't think I deserved it," I answered truthfully. "Still don't. Either I couldn't tell her about my life, or I'd have to come home and look her in the eye. I couldn't do it."

My sister took one deep breath. Let it out. Sat up straight, squared her strong shoulders.

"What now?"

"Keep my fingers crossed that Sledge can pull a rabbit out of a hat. He's done it before. He may do it again."

My sister grabbed my hand and held it. Squeezed it. The fact that she hadn't abandoned me meant everything.

18

"Good morning, counselors. The jurors are all in the assembly room."

"Are you ready for opening statements?"

"I'll reserve, Your Honor," I said. Given the press and the crimes, I'd spent all weekend thinking about case strategy. I'd decided to let the prosecution do their thing. Get the lay of the land before I stood up ready to defend the indefensible.

"Mr. Brody, Ms. Long, is the prosecution ready for opening statements? Ready to call the first witness?"

"Yes, Your Honor," they chorused. I glanced at the prosecution table. Maybe they were finally on the same page. They hadn't been so far.

"Ms. Cort, is there anything?"

I shook my head slightly. I needed to worry about my side of the street, not what was going on between Tom and Nicole.

I stood to do my job—defend Carter and Fortune.

"Your Honor, in light of the first superseding indictment I received only this morning, I object to some of the people on the witness list."

"Do you mean the victims?" Long argued.

"Your Honor, I don't want to get into the characterization of those on the list. What I want to discuss is the duplicative nature of the testimony of the fifteen witnesses on this list who were allegedly employed by the defendants."

I took a breath because I needed to win this one. Woman after woman pointing to my clients would put the defense in a hole too deep for me to dig out from.

"Evidence rule 403 applies here," I continued. "Having so much testimony will be more prejudicial than probative. Additionally, I want to be clear that not one of these…victims…can testify regarding events that occurred before the dates on the new indictment…August eleventh, 2004, the day after Mr. Carter's first acquittal."

I hadn't yet exhausted Judge Brody's goodwill, but I could sense his impatience.

"Mr. Brody. Ms. Long?" the judge probed.

"Your Honor, we concede to the dates specified," Tom said. "We will choose a single representative to testify. The stories are harrowing enough that we're sure one girl's testimony will be sufficient to start the jury down the path toward conviction."

I tried not to let my knees go weak with relief. Maybe there was some way I could win this. Some way that wouldn't scorch the earth behind me after the jury verdict.

"You won that first point, Ms. Cort. Anything else while you're on a roll?"

"Your Honor, I did not receive notice of prosecution's intent to introduce any prior bad acts allegedly committed by the defendant. I ask for a ruling that—pursuant to rule 404—those will be excluded as well."

Judge Brody looked between the prosecutors. They didn't object.

"So ordered. Let's get the jury in here, my coffee and doughnut budget will be exhausted otherwise."

"Ready to proceed, Your Honor," Long said.

"Ready to proceed," I mimicked.

It took a couple of minutes, I imagined, to separate the jurors from their breakfast of caffeine and sugar. Tom let Nicole do the opening statement.

It was typical. She painted my clients as the worst of the worst and promised the jury that the only true justice was conviction. I watched the jurors intently, looking to see who I could win over. I only needed one.

A young man with Buddy Holly glasses sat in the back corner. He was a little less wide eyed than the other eleven and watched all of us with a touch more scrutiny. When he winced, I turned to Nicole. She'd stumbled on her way back to the lectern. Surely she was sober. That had to have been one of the conditions of her return to the courtroom. No one else appeared to have noticed. I looked up when Judge Brody spoke to Nicole.

"Call your first witness."

"We call Shonna Townsend to the stand," Long said.

A deputy yelled that name into the hall. The woman who came through the doors was thin and lanky and ethnically ambiguous. Her black jumpsuit had white ruffles at the collar.

The moment she stepped through the little door between the gallery and the well, she bent down.

"Someone drop this?" she asked. She lifted her hand. In her palm was a single cufflink.

"It must have fallen out of my case," Tom said, grabbing the small gold stud.

An explosion of memory filled my head. That was Tom's cufflink. His father had given it to him when he'd turned twenty and had bought his first tuxedo. Up until that first Advocates Ball, I'd never met a man who'd owned his own tuxedo. When you rented, the shirts had buttons. When you owned, it came with French cuffs.

I stole a quick glance between Shonna and Tom. Had he really dropped it, or had Shonna done the thing I'd seen a magician do once? Pretend to find something in their hand that they'd had all along. Had he been with her? Was this Jarrod Carter's way of intimidating the prosecutor? Did I need to worry about witness tampering?

I glanced at Tom, but his eyes wouldn't meet mine. Either way, there was more going on right here in front of me than I could see. I tried to push all that from my head and get back to my job. When I looked up front again, Shonna had already placed her hand upon the bible and had been sworn in.

She stated her name and an address that I thought was a halfway house on the Eastside.

"Ms. Townsend, how old are you?" Nicole's voice was soft. The sounds of shifting in the gallery came to a near silence as everyone leaned forward to hear what this witness was saying.

"I'm not quite sure. I lost track of time. What year is it again?"

"It's 2007," Nicole was happy to answer.

"I'm twenty-one. Hey, I can drink legally." A few laughs from the gallery lessened the tension in the room.

"Had you had alcohol before you turned twenty-one?"

"All the time."

"How often is all the time?"

"Every day, maybe? Every time we asked for it. Sledge didn't hold back the wine."

"How did you meet the man you call Sledge? Can you point him out to the jury?"

"That's him right there." Shonna pointed dramatically in a manner I'm sure she'd practiced more than once. "Dark-skinned guy at that table."

I wanted to object. Practically had to hold myself in my chair. Anything I said would only emphasize what I wanted the jury to ignore.

"Let the record show that the witness has identified Jar-rod Carter."

"So noted," Judge Brody said.

"Let me repeat the question, Shonna. When did you meet Sledge?"

"When I was fourteen my stepdad said I had to get a job, start paying for myself. I was working at a burger place on Euclid. Sledge came in most nights. Started out ordering one or two things, then he would put in a bigger order. It's, like, fast food, so you can't put in an order in advance or any-thing, but he would pass me a twenty if I could get his food ready before he came in. So he didn't have to wait."

"Did your relationship change?"

"One night I was putting out the garbage in the dumpsters in the front, and he happened to be driving by. When I realized I knew him, I waved him down. I was kind of hoping he would give me a ride home. It was cold outside, and I didn't want to walk."

"Did he give you a ride home?"

"He rolled down the window and asked me if I wanted to be passing out burgers and taking out trash for the rest of my life. I told him no. Who'd want that? He say, let me talk to you. I punched out and got into his car."

"Then what happened?"

"East Cleveland ain't but a minute long, so he pulled down to the park. He asked me what I was making at the food place. I told him, $4.25 an hour, minus all that taxes they take out. It wasn't a lot, but it helped with clothes and...you know...personal stuff. Plus, because I was under sixteen, I couldn't work but a few hours a week. I told him I wouldn't be able to work full time for two years. Then he passed me three hundreds and said that I could make that in a night if I worked for him. That was like half the rent for our house. I was like, I could make that in a week, and he was like, no a night. I was like, what I have to do. Then he said I just have to—"

"Objection, hearsay." Hearsay was my true objection. But I had another motive as well. I needed to stop the story. Break the jurors out of the grip of Shonna's tale. Who wouldn't be on the edge of their seat waiting to find out how a girl went from hawking fast food to giving up her body to the highest bidder?

"What happened next, Ms. Townsend?" Nicole continued. Her question this time was completely opened-ended and proper for direct witness examination.

"Sledge kissed me. We made out for a minute. Said it wasn't no harder than that. I wouldn't be dealing drugs or nothing. I just had to kiss men, maybe give them a hand job or something. Nothing different from what boys wanted at parties."

"Okay, then what?"

"He'd given me his pager number. Told me it was up to me. A couple of nights later, when I was off from the burger place, I told my mama that I was working, and I paged him. He picked me up and took me to a place called The Dive Bar."

"Where is The Dive Bar?"

"Superior and seventy-eighth."

"So Sledge took you to The Dive Bar."

"It's like a two-story building. The bar was on the bottom. There was an apartment upstairs, that's where he took me. Got me food from downstairs and a couple of drinks. Piña coladas. They was good. He told me to wait, and when I heard a knock, that would be my first customer."

Shonna paused and swallowed. I could tell that she was probably remembering something difficult or unpleasant. If I could read that from her face, there was no doubt the jury did too. I was impotent to do anything about it. To get her to speed up, be more clinical. This was the Tom and Nicole show—for now.

"What happened next?"

"Do I have to? Do I have to talk about this...here...in front of all these people?"

"Shonna, if you want that man to get what he deserves—"

"Objection to Ms. Long's characterization," I said without standing.

"Your Honor, I'm sorry, but this is very hard for the witness," Nicole said. "Can you give me a little leeway to lead, Your Honor?"

"Given the sensitive nature of this testimony, I'm inclined to give the prosecution some wiggle room on this. Ms. Long, you can proceed with caution."

"Thank you, Judge Brody. Shonna, please tune out all the people in the courtroom except me. Okay. I know this is hard, but you'll only have to do this one time. It's important, though, that you say what happened. It's the only way we have in this country to enact justice. You with me?"

Shonna nodded.

"Good. Look at me. Tell me what happened after that knock on the door."

"I was happy when the door opened, because it was Sledge. It wasn't some stranger. He looked at me and asked if I was ready. I nodded. I was ready. I thought I could turn off my brain and at the end of the night I'd have money. It wasn't one guy, though, it was three. I didn't say anything. Sledge was like, it's easier this way. Pop my cherry and all that. So he gave them a forty and left."

It took all I had not to look down or look away or look at my clients in disgust. I had some idea what happened in this business. After nearly a decade of practice, I wasn't naïve or stupid. But what I tried not to do was live in the details. Like everyone else in the courtroom, though, I was holding my breath. I let it out slowly, stole a look at my juror. I glanced down at the wide dot matrix printout in front of him. The juror was Castillo. He worked in the administrative offices of the Cleveland Orchestra. His eyes were closed. I looked back toward the witness stand.

Nicole nodded, locked eyes with Shonna.

"So then they took turns. If there had only been one guy, maybe I could have controlled it. It started out okay. They wanted me to kiss them. They handed around the bottle. Then they took off my clothes, and even that wasn't too bad. Then they drank some more, and they got fresh." Shonna closed her eyes. Shook her head. When she opened them again, I could see the spine of steel that had kept her alive all these years.

"That's not the right word, I think. Because of course they was there to get fresh, but they were less…nice. When they came in, they said I was pretty and that we were all going to have fun. That didn't sound so bad. But after I was naked, they lost they patience. One of them held me, took my arms behind my back and gripped me hard. One guy, he put his…he put his thing in my mouth. Pushed it all the way to the back. I couldn't breathe. When I gagged, they laughed and said something about me being a sloppy girl.

"I was trying to get my breath back when another guy— not the one holding me—he put it inside me. They took turns for a long time. Then Sledge knocked on the door and they left. He took me down the hall to the bathroom. He said I had to clean up before I went home. I brushed my teeth. I put some toilet paper in my panties. I put on my clothes. When I came back out, Sledge handed me five hundred. It was two hundred more than he'd said I'd get. It was a bonus, he said, because the customers had left happy. I went home, gave my mother fifty dollars, and kept the rest for myself."

"How old were you on that night?"

"I was fourteen."

"Did Jarrod Carter know that—your age?"

"Objection, Your Honor. Knowledge of age is not required," I said. "I'll stipulate." I did not want the jury to think too long and hard about three men gang raping a fourteen-year-old child. I was very much willing to concede the fact that she was underage at the time they'd employed her.

"Next question, Ms. Long," Judge Brody instructed.

"Ms. Townsend, did you go back to work for Mr. Carter again?"

"Yes. I went back a couple of days later. After I'd bought myself a phone with the money. I didn't have anything left."

"How many nights each week would you work for Mr. Carter?"

"Every night that I could. Not when I had my period, though, but the other nights. It was mostly not more than one date at a time."

"How many dates did you have most nights?"

"Five, maybe, sometimes ten."

"How did you end up in Mr. Carter's house in Cleveland Heights?"

"Sledge said a hotel would be easier. So we moved to the Sleepy Time. It was better because there was a bathroom in the room and everything. But it was worse, too."

"Worse, how?"

"He wouldn't let me leave. He decided that it would be easier if I didn't go home in between. So I was living there."

"Did your mother and stepfather notice?"

"It wasn't good at home. I threatened to run away a lot, after my stepfather put his hands on me and my sister. He would twist my arm so hard it would leave a bruise. He did that to my sister and broke it. So it wasn't like he was missing more than someone he could hit or someone who brought home money. It wasn't like the police was coming looking for me, if that's what you mean. It wasn't like TV where they put out an ABP and that Amber thing…"

"The AMBER Alert?"

"Yeah, that. No one was looking for me. I didn't have anywhere else to go."

I looked down at my notepad. Pretended to scratch out notes. I'd seen all sides of the justice system and it wasn't pretty. It was as if all the people who'd been thrown away by society got together and did their best to hurt each other. In my head, I sounded like senator Moynihan or something. I didn't agree with a lot the former New Yorker said about poverty and welfare and crime, but he'd probably been right about the nature of the cycle of dysfunction. Without something to break it, all of these broken people seemed doomed to repeat it.

"Did you continue to get paid?" Long asked.

"No, I don't know. I think Sledge said something about holding money for me. I kind of stopped thinking about that. It was just about getting through the days and nights. I took the pills he gave me to even it out."

"Did you move again?"

"There was a big police bust, Sledge said, so we were going to have to stay in these big things, kind of like the back of a tractor-trailer truck."

"I believe they're called shipping containers."

"Okay. We were there for a while. I don't know how long. Then Sledge said the police were getting too close to his business again so then we went to a house. We were on the third floor. There were eight of us there. It was okay. We had to share a bathroom, so that wasn't perfect. I'd had my own for so long at the motel. But it was better than the…container…because it had real water and stuff. The food was good too. Like chicken and dumplings and eggs. Real food. Not burgers. I'd loved burgers as a kid, but I hated them after a while."

"How did you work if you were in this house?"

"Sledge and Grand changed it up."

"Who's Grand?"

"That guy there. The smaller, medium-skinned one sitting next to Sledge."

"Please let the record reflect that the witness has identified the defendant Dion Fortune."

"So noted."

"How did Grand and Sledge change it up?"

"We went to our dates. They stopped coming to us. So at seven at night, we had to clean up, get dressed up. Each of us went in our own white van. We got in back of the truck, and then we went from house to house. Sometimes the guys would come out to the van. Sometimes we'd go into the house, like we was a delivery."

"How many times a night were you…delivered?"

"Eight maybe. Not sure. It was less than the hotel and stuff because there was a lot of driving in between."

"Then you were rescued."

I made a choice not to object to that characterization. I needed the jurors to not hate me as much as they may have hated my clients by now.

"I guess. One day a lot of police showed up. We've been in this house since then. Some of us girls. Until we figure out what to do next."

"Thank you Shonna, Ms. Townsend. Thanks for telling your story. Your witness."

I stood. I'd spent a good long time this weekend thinking about how to cross examine sex trafficking victims. There was no easy way to do it, so I'd opted for a minimal approach that I hoped would be the least alienating for the jury.

"Ms. Townsend," I introduced myself. "I'm Casey Cort. I'm the attorney for Jarrod Carter and Dion Fortune."

"Okay."

"I have only one question for you. No, two. Sorry two. Did you come into some money lately?"

"Yes. About two hundred thousand dollars. Grand had held it back for me, like he'd promised. It was all put in a bank account in my name. I'm not sure what I'm going to do with it."

"What's next for you? What do you want to do when you leave the house you're living in?"

"I'm going to Nevada, I think. Brothels are legal there and it's a job I think I'm good at."

The answer was perfect for my defense even though it felt tragic for Shonna.

"No further questions."

19

Tom

April 26, 2007

I always came to Lakewood when summoned. The moment court had ended, I'd gone up to my desk. In the middle had been a pink message slip with two words: Tonight. 7:00. It was unsigned, but I knew full well who it was from. With a wave, I'd left Nicole alone to prep for Friday and made the short drive to my parents' estate, the longer walk to my father's study.

I kissed my mother on the cheek. She'd been standing in the kitchen when I came in, a glass of white wine her only companion.

"Your dad's in his study." Glass in hand, she gestured toward the back of the house.

"Good to see you too, Mom." My heart squeezed. Up until this moment, keeping my secret had been about me, my father, my brothers, my career. I tried not to think what my mother would make of Destiny if that tape came out. She knew the ways of men. She had to, but I wasn't sure she wanted to know any of that about me. I'd worked hard for years for her to see the clean and sanitized version of me. The me who dated the right women and had the right job.

"I miss you at Sunday dinner," she said, her voice wistful. There had been a time I'd never missed a family dinner. The last year or so, I'd enjoyed my autonomy for a day or two where I didn't have to play the role of the perfect Brody.

A ready excuse came easily to my lips.

"This case…"

"I know, honey. I have a television. There's always a case. I've been married to your father a long time. It never ends. You'll learn that. Always put family first. The job won't last forever. Family will."

"Maybe not this week, but next week if this case has gone to the jury. I promise." I crossed my heart. My mom batted my hands away, smoothed my hair, and kissed my forehead.

"Go on. He's waiting."

I went through the front of the house this time, walking the path between the twin spiral staircases, through to what I'd always thought of as my father's domain. Once I stepped into the study, it took a moment for my eyes to adjust.

Darkly stained wainscoting covered three quarters of the wall. The rest was the stone of the fireplace, with more dark wood in the large mantle and built-in shelves. What was left was painted a dark navy. I blinked twice, looking through the eye-level haze of cigar smoke. My father sat in his leather chair behind his desk. He'd done his Mr. Rogers switch, exchanging his suit jacket for a cardigan. His tie was probably still back in chambers.

"Dad…" I stopped when I realized he wasn't alone. My brothers Andrew and Simon were there as well. The full brigade. I was in bigger trouble than I thought.

I pulled one of the wood chairs from behind the desk so that I was between the couch where my brothers sat and my father's desk. My father lifted a pen, scratched it on a pad, drawing big circles, then pointed the fountain pen at me. His eyes bored into mine.

"You are throwing the case."

My heart sped up in panic. I had honestly thought I was being far more subtle. I should have insisted on a different judge. Any other judge would have assumed that I'd gotten the job through nepotism not competence and couldn't prosecute my way out of a paper bag. My father, Judge Patrick Brody, knew better.

"Nicole Long is worse than I thought," I started by way of explanation. It was never too early to start my plausible deniability defense. "I know she has a history of alcoholism, but she promised that she was clean. I'm not sure if that's true. But as they say, hindsight is perfect sight. It was a mistake to let Nicole take the lead on this. I hoped it would build her confidence. That ultimately I could count on her to be a loyal and trusted deputy because I don't have any of those in major crimes."

"That was quite a speech. Might want to polish it for whoever is buying what you're selling, son. You can't bullshit a bullshitter. Took me a few weeks to put it together. You wanting to try the case in front of me, even though you know I wouldn't favor you. You having a known drunk as second chair. You putting up the weakest fight I've ever seen."

"Dad, I…"

"What does he have on you?" That was Simon, the middle child. Both he and Andrew were older than me. It was hard to lie to people who'd seen me grow up, who'd seen me lie a hundred times, who could read me like a book. It was probably why my father had invited them.

"Who?" I was still playing dumb. I figured there was still a ten percent chance I could sell Nicole's incompetence.

"Jarrod Carter a.k.a. the Sledge Hammer. Clearly he's in charge. He escaped the authorities for years. Made a pretty penny. Hired Casey Cort. He's playing the system like it's a violin made especially for his own orchestra."

Andrew, the quieter one, turned to me.

"What does he have on you, Tommy?"

It was quiet for a long time while I considered my answer. I didn't know what I should say. I wanted to continue the lie. Continue under the guise that all blame lay at Nicole Long's feet. If Jarrod Carter turned on me... If I got in trouble, the only people I'd be able to count on were in this room. I took a deep breath. Got ready to tell the truth.

"I...I sometimes...I've patronized...pros...sex workers," I stuttered out. I'm sure it was something we'd all done. It was not the kind of thing a sober man discussed.

"Oh good God, that's hardly a crime," Simon said. If I had to guess, he did working girls on the regular. Not one of the three of us had settled down even though we were all more or less creeping up on forty. I didn't want to think too hard as to why. Instead I stepped up to the proverbial confessional.

"It's why Lizzy Cofrancesco broke up with me," I admitted. "It's why Casey broke up with me the second time." Every day it became more and more clear that not having a wife was a fuckup I needed to rectify.

"What? You couldn't do both? Satisfy your woman and your libido?" Andrew asked. He shook his head. Where were they when I needed to know that I was playing it wrong? Securing their own futures. My eyes shifted toward the windows that looked out on the backyard. I couldn't meet any of their eyes.

"I fucked it up. I assumed they wanted money or kids more than sex with their fiancé or husband."

All three of them laughed. They'd gotten the memo that I hadn't. Being the youngest had a downside. They'd always kept all the secrets between themselves. I'd been my mother's favorite, but how to find a relationship and get married weren't among the things we'd discussed. I could make a hell of a soda bread, though.

"Maybe that was true in the fifties or something, but not since the sexual revolution and certainly not since the nineties after AIDS, but newsflash: women enjoy sex as much as men," my dad said.

"Noted, Dad. This is not a conversation I want to have with you."

"Then we won't have it," he said. Dad tapped the pen on the pad. "Back to the trial. You're coming up on closing arguments soon if Casey doesn't put up witnesses, and given her clients, I'm pretty sure the answer to that one is no. I need to know there aren't going to be any surprises come tomorrow."

"Not in trial."

"But…" Andrew and Simon said nearly simultaneously. I hated when they ganged up on me.

I was glad I hadn't eaten dinner, because it might have come up all over my father's vintage oriental rug.

"It's bad. Like I could lose my job, bad. Like maybe I could be disbarred." I hated how my voice quavered. It was like I was ten and waiting for my father to punish me after either Andrew or Simon had ratted me out.

"What's your plan?" Andrew asked. "You have a plan, right?"

"Throw the case. Dad was right. That's what I was doing. Losing. If Sledge gets off then he won't use his 'insurance.'"

"God, Tom," Simon said like I was the stupidest person on earth. Like I was the first person ever to be blackmailed. "What is this insurance? How bad could it be? It's not like you killed anyone."

"Videotape of me and this girl, Destiny."

"So?" Simon said. "You have a sex tape? Did you use a stunt wang like Screech?"

"This is stupid," Andrew interrupted. "Soliciting a prostitute is the very definition of low-level crime. Steve LaTourette and Bill Clinton both survived sex scandals. You're a tiny fish compared to them."

"There's no stunt organ. Everything in the tape will be all mine," I said.

My father wasn't smiling. He'd heard the testimony against Carter. When his lids came down, I knew that he knew it was worse than any of the politicians of the past. It wasn't the hint of a sex scandal. It was full color, three hundred and sixty degree sex scandal.

Andrew, Simon, and I had seen that look on my father's face before. It meant serious trouble. They looked at each other, then me. Dad stood up and came from behind his desk. He got up right in front of me.

"Thomas Patrick Brody, how old do you think Destiny was when the tape was made?"

I thought back to that first night Sledge had introduced me to her. My mind screeched to a halt like the arm had come across a vinyl record. This case had gotten to me.

"I'm going to guess under the age of consent," I finally answered.

"Statutory rape, Tom?" Andrew asked.

"She's black," I retorted.

Rich. Poor.

Black. White.

Man. Girl.

Perpetrator. Victim.

Those were the first four strikes against me. I could practically hear the nasal voice of that reporter Victoria Greenlee taking me down one peg at a time.

My father steepled his fingers. Covered his nose and mouth with his hands.

"Are you asking me to grant Casey's motion for judgment of acquittal the next time she makes it?"

I tried to keep a smile from stealing across my face. My father had just offered the perfect, unassailable solution. No one would accuse him of bias if he ruled against me. But I couldn't accept that kind of favor.

"I'm not asking anything," I insisted. "I think there's probably a fifty percent chance we get a hung jury."

"I think you've pushed me into a corner. I think I'm going to have to do it. Take the political hit."

"I don't think you can do that," Andrew said. "You could lose the next time you're up for reelection. The press is watching this one…closely."

My father paced across the room. Paced back. Paced across. Came back again. This time he was a foot away from me when he locked gazes with me.

"So you're relying on a jury to see past a black pimp selling out girls like chattel to acquit him because he, what? Paid them a lot of money right before he got arrested? Didn't kill them?"

He had a point. It was *the* point. Systemic bias could win the case for us without either Nicole or me having to so much as lift a finger. Cleveland wasn't Jim Crow Mississippi, but sometimes it came damned close.

"I haven't thought all the way through yet," I admitted. "I've been playing it step by step. First, I kept it out of the feds' hands. Then, I got Long on the case messing up as I knew she would. Every morning she tried to use Chanel to cover cognac. She lost the first Carter case which has her pretty unsettled, so she's gunning too hard and making mistakes. So yes, maybe I thought the jury would acquit."

"I've been on the bench for a long time and I'm going to tell you. They're never going to let these defendants go. Jail time is mandatory. Whether it's two years or ten, whether it's consecutive or concurrent, there's going to be time."

"What are my options?"

"Make the tapes disappear," Andrew said as if we were all going to suit up and break into the Watergate hotel.

"How do I do that? I'm in enough trouble as it is without adding breaking and entering to my list of reasons to be disbarred."

"You won't be disbarred," Andrew said. "No Brody has gotten disbarred and we're not going to start today."

"Just humiliated, then," I said

"No one ever died of humiliation."

"You think we could get the tapes?" I asked. I'd never really considered it, but Andrew made retrieving them a possibility to consider. His job on the liquor commission probably meant he knew a lot of people who'd be happy to do him a favor.

"I could have Lizzy's dad give it a go," Andrew offered. "Where are they?"

"The Dive Bar? The Place to Be? They can't be in the Cleveland Heights house because they weren't booked into evidence. That place was searched top to bottom. Maybe the bars not so much."

"Tom. I can do a lot. Random searches of random locations. That would cost more favors than this is worth. If you can't pin down the exact location, this won't work."

"I'll try," I said. I wished I'd thought more about ways to avoid this rather than doggedly focusing on the only thing I could control, the prosecution's case. "Is there anything else you can think of?"

My brother Simon threw up his hands. "I'm in house at Strohmeyer. Unless the problem can be solved with free beer, I can't help you."

"I don't think the defendants can disappear at this stage of the game," Andrew mused. "The reporters might notice."

"You could do that?" I asked. I was both surprised and not at the same time.

"Maybe." Andrew's shrug was no different than if I'd asked him if he could make shortbread cookies from scratch without a recipe.

"Jesus," I muttered.

"Tom how do you think this works? We join hands with your defendant and sing Kumbaya?"

"I just want to keep my job. Keep my name out of the papers except as the prosecutor who lost the case of the century, if it comes to that. That's humiliation enough."

My father clapped his hands then walked back to his desk. He opened a drawer that I knew contained a custom humidor and pulled out a fat Cuban cigar. Clipped off the tip with a double guillotine cutter then opened a different drawer. Pulled out a torch lighter I'd given him last Christmas. He rolled the cigar in the flame. Blew on the tip, then turned it toward his lips. He took a long draw, blew out smoke. Ashed it on a crystal ashtray. I think Simon had given him that on a different holiday. He looked at each of us, his sons. "If it comes to that..."

20

"What's the plan?" I asked. We were in the parking lot under the justice center because we were early. We'd been more than a half hour early every day because being late would have been inexcusable.

"We're going to go to jail." I sighed hard and laid my head back against the car's headrest.

"I don't exactly know," was Sledge's response. I bit my lip against saying something I'd regret. Sledge hadn't used his fists that I'd seen since he'd come back from jail, but if he wasn't worried about going back he might no longer be on his best behavior. I'd seen his worst behavior and I didn't want to be at the business end of that.

"What about your insurance?" I couldn't figure how he'd reveal the tape of that prosecutor with Destiny when she was underage without taking us down, but he was super smart, so I was waiting for him to reveal his plan.

"I had a good run." He ran his hand across his close-cropped hair. Smoothed down the lapels of his dark gray suit. Straightened his glacier blue tie. "A really good run. Grew this business for nearly ten damned years with no problems. Beat the last charge fair and square." He sounded resigned.

For the first time ever, I regretted hitching my wagon to Jarrod Carter. He'd always had a plan. Always had a way out of trouble. This was the first time I think he hadn't figured out something. I certainly hadn't. I was counting on him. My heart nearly leapt out of my chest at the idea of spending the rest of my life in a cage.

"Does this mean you don't care? That you're ready to go to jail? They're talking at least ten years, man. I don't want to be in jail for the next fucking decade. Where's your fight? Where's your plan?"

Sledge turned to me, his face coming apart in laughter. "You look like a scared rabbit. Calm down. You used to have balls of steel, man. Don't you see what's happening?"

"No." No I didn't see anything happening. That was the problem. "No. What?"

"We're going to win this case." His voice was so sincere, I almost believed him.

Almost.

But it was like saying he was going to win the Browns game. Nothing left to chance was a foregone conclusion.

"Your plan is to leave my future to a jury?" I heard my voice go up a full octave. Wasn't my finest moment, but it was looking like my finest moments were long behind me.

"Worked for me last time." Sledge nodded looking smug.

"That was for pimping out exotic dancers at a club. This…these charges are next level serious."

"Look, Casey's been eyeing a juror. I know that means she at least thinks it could hang. The prosecutor's done a shit job on the case. I'm sure the judge won't let it get to a jury if his son is in trouble. That's at least three ways this could go our way. You have to have faith."

Faith? I didn't believe in God or no other higher power.

When the car clock rolled to nine thirty, we got out and went upstairs to get in the long line for the elevator. We were up and at the defense table with ten minutes to spare.

Casey was there, ready and waiting.

"Good morning. There's a late juror so we have a few minutes. I want to talk to you about what's going to happen today."

I leaned forward. I was looking for anyone who could give me a line on the future. Hope and knocking on this wood weren't working.

"You remember yesterday Nicole Long gave the closing argument for the prosecution. This means today is our turn. First, I'll do opening arguments. As we discussed in the office over the weekend, I don't plan to call either of you as witnesses. I am calling the two women who worked for you, who were of age, and who retired happy.

"I'm calling that expert on sex workers. Then I'm going to ask the jury to acquit you. Oh, but first things first, I'm going to ask for a judgment of acquittal. It's never granted, but it's necessary to preserve your rights on appeal."

"Appeal?"

"If we lose, Mr. Carter, Mr. Fortune, then you're going to want to have as many avenues to appeal as necessary to either overturn a possible conviction or somehow minimize the time in jail."

Appeal wasn't a word I wanted to hear. That meant I'd be in prison as days of my life slipped away while I was hoping for some kind of Hail Mary.

"All rise!"

We turned away from Casey and toward the jurors who were sliding into the box. One made eye contact with me. I tried not to flinch under the heavy weight of her judgment.

"Mr. Brody, Ms. Long, Ms. Cort, yesterday the prosecution made their closing argument. Are you prepared to present your case today, Ms. Cort?"

"Yes, Your Honor."

"Would you like to make a motion?" Judge Brody asked without even looking up from the stack of papers he was shuffling and signing. Looked like he was working on other cases while hearing ours. I tried not to take that as a sign he'd already pictured us in jail and wasn't wasting time to make sure our trial was fair.

"Yes, Your Honor."

Casey stood and adjusted her blue blouse so it was evenly tucked into her black skirt.

"Pursuant to Rule twenty-nine, I make a motion for judgment of acquittal."

"Your grounds, Ms. Cort?" Judge Brody asked while his pen scribbled across another document. I looked at the pen tip. It was one of those that needed its own ink cartridge. Probably cost him a pretty penny.

The judge's other work didn't seem to bother Casey. She droned on like she was the star of the Dion and Jarrod show.

"There was insufficient evidence presented by the prosecution to sustain a conviction on the offenses charged in the first superseding indictment."

There were so many words flying around, and it was taking all my energy to keep my hand on my knee and my leg from bouncing, much less make sense of what she was saying.

"Thank you, Ms. Cort." Judge Brody paused then moved a stack of papers to the courtroom deputy sitting to one side of him. Removed his reading glasses. Finally looked at all of us in the courtroom. "Before coming in this morning, I've had the opportunity to review the case that Ms. Long presented. I'm inclined to agree with you, Ms. Cort. Pursuant to Rule twenty-nine, I'm granting the defendant's motion for judgment of acquittal. The charges against the defendants, Jarrod Carter, and Dion Fortune are hereby dismissed."

I couldn't hear anything. I'm not sure if it was because of the uproar from the people sitting behind me or because of the blood pounding in my ears, but I was almost one hundred percent sure that the case was over—and we'd won. Sledge was hugging me with a hard pat on the back. Casey was shaking my hand. I was doing all I could to not fall out of the chair I'd sat back down in after being grabbed up in the bear hug.

"Simmer down." Judge Brody banged his gavel for the first time during this trial. "This is a courtroom, not a bar. If you can't be quiet, then you must exit the courtroom."

It got quieter—a lot quieter real quick. Didn't no one want to miss a word the judge was going to say. The judge said a lot about the jury doing their duty and justice being served or some shit.

Bottom line was, I could go home. I did not have to come back here ever again. I didn't ever have to see Sledge again. It came to me then, I needed to get out of Cleveland. It was the only way I could start over without the past hanging over my head. As I was swept out of the courtroom on a wave of euphoria, I realized that I'd finally found a favor to ask my father.

21

Casey
May 2, 2007

"Are you happy?" Justin asked. He'd been waiting in the reception area of my office after I'd pushed through a lot of reporters on my way here. I'd been hoping for an hour to work through the adrenaline shaking my limbs and addling my brain before I called a cab home.

There was no way I was going to walk through Public Square on the day my clients were acquitted of sex trafficking. I wasn't generally paranoid by nature but couldn't see how I'd be safe from an ambush of one kind or another if I didn't protect myself with the canopy of a yellow cab.

Normally I'd have driven myself if I'd been expecting a verdict. To say that Judge Brody's ruling had been a surprise would have been a massive understatement.

I'd wanted to send Justin away and get home. But the people pleaser in me had invited him in.

"I'm not sure." That much was true. I'd won, but I'm not sure justice was served. "I think anyone who has seen the news or who has read the coverage of the trial thinks my clients are guilty. Thinks they got off on a technicality. Thinks they somehow rigged the system in their favor."

"Did they?" Justin tilted his head like he was a little bit unsure of me. Like I might have magic powers I'd kept hidden from him.

"Obviously I couldn't know that," I said, my voice rising. "Do you think I'm corrupt? That I'd suborn perjury or be involved in some kind of bribe? If that's what you think of me, then you might as well tell me now."

Justin laid the coat that had been hanging over his arm onto the back of one of my chairs. He walked over to the window. Gazed out on Lake Erie.

"My client is going down, you know." He spoke to the window. Right. Derek Waters. He was the catalyst that had probably started all this, and I'd forgotten all about him. Waters was a sacrificial lamb with no one else to offer up in sacrifice. Waters had played his hand and lost.

"I'm sorry?" I shrugged, but Justin had his back to me. "He was dealing meth on the side. That's still a crime. These are the consequences."

Justin turned towards me, his hands and butt leaning on my sill. I tried to read his face, but it was inscrutable.

"You can imagine that he doesn't feel that way," he said.

"He gave up a sweet deal, then turned on my clients. Now that they're out from under, he's bitter. Nothing to do about that. At least he has you."

"So—"

"Gimme a sec," I said. My phone had pinged loudly in the room. I got it from my coat pocket, opened it, and looked at the text. It was from Ron Pinheiro.

Ron: Want to meet up for a late lunch or dinner? I'm free from now until…

I texted back yes. He texted an address in Shaker Square and a time, five. I closed the phone and turned my attention back to the man in my office. The one I wasn't dating.

"I was going to ask if you wanted to get dinner later," Justin said. "To celebrate."

I looked at him and tried not to think too hard about what was or wasn't going on between us. I tried to let the win from today and the time I was going to spend with Ron later buoy me past this uncomfortable moment.

"I have a date. Ron's free. Maybe some other time. Are you going to try to switch judges?" I rushed out, using words to push through the feelings of guilt and change the subject all in one fell swoop.

Justin didn't try to pretend not to notice what I'd done. Fortunately, though, he didn't comment. Took my question at face value. Answered it.

"No reason," he said. "Judge Brody suddenly seems very defense-friendly all of a sudden."

I small talked him into his jacket and as politely as possible, pushed him from my office.

After he left, I pulled on my own coat and made my way as fast as I could through Public Square, through the falling snow, down through Tower City, and onto the Green Line tram. Calling and waiting for a cab would have necessitated doing the one thing I couldn't stomach right now—spending more time with Justin. I'd played the reporter lottery and won.

I got out at Shaker Square and checked my watch. I had time to spare. I walked to my apartment, dumped my briefcase, changed into corduroys, a fluffy mohair-like tur-tleneck sweater, and low-heeled boots. Simba's meows sparked a second pang of guilt. I stopped to pet my ne-glected cat until he ran away in full sensory overload. He'd be licking himself for a good hour to get the smell of me off his fur. Satisfied that I was at least a halfway decent pet owner, I pulled my coat back on. Made the short walk back to the square and around to the Mexican restaurant on the southwest side.

Once inside, I looked around hoping to see Ron waving at me, fresh margarita in hand, but the restaurant was only half full at the early hour and there was no Ron.

"Can I help you?"

"Table for two." I scouted the room looking for the best seat where I could have a bird's eye view of Ron's entrance. "Can I sit at one of the high tables?"

The hostess nodded and smiled. After escorting me, she laid down a couple of menus and asked if I wanted anything. I ordered a scratch margarita. When in Mexico, my standard drink didn't seem appropriate.

It was six thirty-three by the time that margarita came. I tried not to gulp it to chase feelings about Justin away, to make me just a little less tense around a guy I really liked and had unrequited hopes for about a shared future.

Ron's "You started without me," startled me. I'd been so focused on how much to drink or not that I hadn't caught him coming through the door.

"Hi...um...hi." I was unaccountably nervous. Like eighth grade dance nervous.

Instead of sitting across from me, he pulled the chair around so that we were sitting side by side. His shoulder bumped mine.

"Heard about your big win today. That never happens." He lifted his water glass in a mock toast. "Heard that drunk prosecutor bungled the case."

"Or they just didn't have the evidence," I countered, already spinning the story I'd tell to everyone who asked. Already burying the truth of my former fiancé's crimes...again. Tom didn't deserve my loyalty, but he still had it anyway. "Looks like a grudge case on her part. She lost against me the first time, and the second time."

When his own margarita came, he toasted me for real.

"You're a rock star. Don't let anyone tell you different. I'm so proud of you. So proud that I'm here with you over all your other boyfriends."

I tried to parse his words with my newly tequila-soaked brain. Was he saying that he liked me, that he wanted to be my boyfriend? I wanted to shout yes in answer to his unasked question.

I settled for, "I'm glad you're here too." We were so close, our faces only an inch apart. His cologne swirled around me. Either that or the tequila was making me light-headed.

"You haven't kissed me yet," he whispered. "Every guy likes to be kissed by a winner."

I didn't hesitate to bridge the tiny gap between us and put my lips on his. My world started to spin, just a little, when my lips touched Ron's.

He was worth the wait.

22

Tom

May 5, 2007

My home phone rang. I looked up at the clock on the mantle. It was eight forty-five in the morning on a Saturday. The only person calling could be my mother. She'd have to wait until tomorrow when I could stomach family dinner.

I got up, went into the bathroom, cleared out my bladder, and got back on the couch. I wasn't sure I'd ever made it to bed. I'd watched all of season one of *The Office*. I think I'd fallen asleep to *Nacho Libre*. I fished out the hard plastic DVD cover that was poking into my back. No, maybe it had been *Talladega Nights*. Either way I'd had the first full night's sleep since this case had started. Since Neil Walsh had walked into my office with that phone in a sealed evidence bag.

My father had taken this bullet for the family. I'd be in his debt for the rest of my life. I was ready to start paying on that debt...tomorrow. I needed just one day where I didn't have to walk on eggshells or wait for the other shoe to drop or worry about clichés that portended doom.

The phone rang again. I wondered if cell phones would ever replace landlines. I pulled myself off the couch. If she'd called twice in ten minutes, I couldn't ignore her. Otherwise my mom would be at my doorstep in less than half an hour.

"Hello."

"I got a courtesy call from Lori Pope and Tobias Whelchel." It wasn't my mother, but my father. He'd spoken without preamble.

"Whelchel? Aw Jesus, Mary, and Joseph," I said, taking a phrase from my mother's playbook. Tobias Whelchel was the special investigator who had it out for me and anyone else he thought violated some moral code only he followed. Now I'd owe a debt to Nicole Long as well. I'd only meant to throw the case, not get her disbarred.

"What's going to happen to Nicole, Dad?" I asked. "The two of them can't pull her ticket. That would be up to the supreme court. Are they saying prosecutorial misconduct? I don't think she was the best. Maybe she was drinking, I don't know. But she didn't hide evidence or offer up any-thing prejudicial. I worked with the witnesses with her, so that was on the up-and-up. Did she threaten the defendants or Casey when I wasn't there? I know that as a woman, this had her back up, maybe made her a bit overzealous? I'm happy to meet with them. Maybe get everyone to make some compromise."

Guilt had made me verbose.

"From what I can see, Nicole Long is in the clear," my father said. His voice was as flat as Lake Erie on a windless day. "The courtesy call was for you."

I picked up the phone to take it back to the couch, but the cord wasn't long enough. I stood awkwardly while I waited for his next words. When they weren't forthcoming, I asked the question I didn't want an answer to.

"For me?" I searched my brain for what could have them coming after me. Whelchel hadn't been in the courtroom when Shonna had dropped the offending cufflink. Casey wouldn't spill the beans after so many years of loyalty. So what? "Do they suspect?"

"They don't *suspect* anything." His pause was so long I'd have thought he disconnected if it weren't for the faint static on the line. "They know."

"What are you talking about? Pope and Whelchel know what, Dad? Don't beat around the bush. You're freaking me out."

"It appears that Mr. Whelchel had the most interesting special delivery today. Apparently it took him half the day to locate a VHS player, this being Saturday and all, and the county forensics lab at the medical examiner's office being closed. But he finally found one because it's not quite obsolete yet, tape that is. Do you know what was on the tape?"

I dropped the phone and ran toward the bathroom. I'd forgotten to flush, and that smell pushed me over the edge. I lost the two Lender's bagels I'd eaten. And the orange juice. That burned coming up. I flushed this time. Rinsed my mouth and splashed water on my face. When I went back to the phone, there was only a dial tone. I dialed the number I'd known nearly all of my life. My father picked up before it even rang.

"When do you want to do it?" he asked without making sure it was me calling.

"Do what?"

"Turn yourself in, Tom. Nothing will come of it, I've been assured, but they're going to do the show."

I knew "the show." They'd done the show on Carter and Fortune. It was always some combination of evidence display, perp walk, and news conference. Not always all three. Not always in that order, but it was a display, nonetheless. Kept the good citizens of the county voting for law and order candidates and their funding. Made the good citizens feel safe. Ruined any chances of the defendant getting a fair trial. And now I was the show.

"They're going to arrest me?" I asked in resignation.

"Arrest you. Perp walk you. Fingerprint you."

"For a misdemeanor?" The show was for felonies, the more serious the better.

"It's a felony."

"Since when? Whenever there's a vice raid, the johns are always charged with misdemeanors. The girls' age never matters."

"It matters now. You know what happened when you threw that case? There was no one to rip apart. No one who took the blame. Everyone was left without a sense of justice, so they went looking for a new scapegoat. I think this goat had a tag around its neck that read, 'Tom Brody.'"

"I didn't think…"

"You didn't. There's ample evidence to this effect. I saved your ass because you didn't think, and now it may not be enough. Water under the bridge. If we do it today, we can get a jump on the press. If we wait until Monday, you'll be on the front page of the paper."

"Won't I be on the front page either way?"

"You want it without a picture. You want to keep some anonymity. So you can have a life after this."

"Am I going to lose my job?"

"No one could save that. Lori Pope is a climber. She can't have a pedophile on the payroll."

"I'm not a pedo. That's...she was..." I didn't have any shred of a defense. "When do I need to be ready?"

"Simon will be in a black car. The driver's off today. He'll be there in forty-five minutes. Wear a suit. A red tie. Some kind of lapel pin, flag, prosecutor badge, something that says you're a boy scout gone bad."

"You won't be there?" I didn't want to sound like a baby, but I wanted my father to come save me, fix it, make it all better like he'd done so many other times for me and my brothers over the years.

"I played that father/judge thing in the courtroom. Can't do it in a police station. Simon is more than capable."

***

"Drive me somewhere," I said to my brother twelve hours later. Twelve hours after I'd been treated like a common criminal. Searched, fingerprinted, photographed, humiliated. Now I was back in the car with Simon.

"Where?"

"I need to get something from my office," I said. On the way from collecting my belongings from the less than friendly Cleveland police officer and heading back to Simon, I'd made a call. Asked for my last favor.

"How?"

But I left his question unanswered. When we got to the Justice Center, I took the elevator to the ninth floor, swiped my keycard against the door lock, and pushed into the prosecutor's office. He'd followed without any more questions.

"Do you need a box?"

"I don't have anything worth keeping from here," I said as we approached the office I'd been sharing with Nicole for the last few months.

"Then what?"

"This," I said. I was holding up a small clear evidence bag. I looked at the log that had been left with the bag and signed someone else's name, Neil Walsh.

"I'm confused." Even as the peacemaking middle brother, Simon had his limits. I hadn't pushed past them yet. I was using his high need for people pleasing in my favor. I wasn't sorry. Not now. Maybe later.

"You don't need to understand." I took a pen, scratched it against a Post-it. I wrote: *You had insurance. I had reinsurance, also known as a back-up plan.*

Eventually that note would get to its destination. I used some Scotch tape to make sure it was affixed to the zip-top bag, then tucked it in my pocket.

"Now drive me to the federal building."

It took ten minutes to drive the circuitous route required by the city's archaic one-way streets and post-9/11 security barriers.

"Just wait in the car," I ordered my brother. "I'll be back."

I buttoned my coat, pulled on my gloves, and walked the cold steps until I reached the door. A guard let me in, though he didn't hide the surprise in seeing my face. Despite Simon doing a really good job of avoiding reporters when I'd turned myself in, it didn't stop the three major news outlets from flashing my "eligible bachelor" photo every half hour. I was wearing the same suit now as in that picture. It was my lucky suit.

"He'll be down in a sec," the guard finally stuttered out after he'd completed his scrutiny.

"Miles, long time no see," I said when the attorney finally made it to the lobby. Neither of us made to shake hands. "I come bearing gifts."

"I have to admit, you're the last person I thought I'd see." He blew into his hands in the cool lobby.

"We have a lot in common, you and I," I started.

"I wouldn't think so." He shook his head like I was some kind of roach not even good enough to grace the bottom of his shoe.

"Don't be weird. Of course we do. We both loved Casey."

He winced. "She saw you, you know," Miles said. "I did too."

"Saw me?"

"I'd come over to her apartment after you left one night. She pulled me down four flights of stairs, got into my Jeep and did the 'follow that car' thing. So I stayed one car behind a blue sedan Acura. It drove from Shaker Square over to a motel on Warrensville Center Road where a guy got out, could have been your twin, and met a young black girl at a hotel room door."

Casey had been keeping more secrets than I thought. I didn't need any more evidence that I'd made a huge mistake. Loyalty like that couldn't be bought. I'd have to think on a strategy to get her back. I needed her legitimacy now more than ever.

"All of Cuyahoga County now knows about that." I shrugged.

"Carter got off twice." Casey's ex pointed an accusatory finger at me. "How is that justice?"

"It's not. It's why I'm here." I handed him the evidence bag I'd retrieved from my office. "I'll need you to sign this receipt."

"Unorthodox."

"Yet keeps the chain of custody." I shook the paper under his nose. "Are you going to sign?"

"What am I taking?" He looked at the bag without touching it. "It's just a burner."

"And a cigar is just a cigar, right?" When Miles didn't even crack a smile, I continued. "You know this is what cracked the case open. Kid named Derek Waters worked for Carter and Fortune. Either Carter or Fortune used this phone when Rida Emad disappeared. Your guy Valdespino with his fancy equipment is going to want to trace those calls."

"Why are you doing this?" Miles' face was screwed up in genuine wonder.

"Call it my good deed for the year."

"You could have done a good deed years ago." Miles shook his head in disgust. "But protecting yourself was more important. This is no different. You're throwing up the world's biggest smokescreen so everyone forgets about the story that's been playing out on the front page of the *Plain Dealer*."

"Maybe I'm killing two birds with one stone."

"You're full of clichés. Maybe you're just one big cliché. Rich guy with all the advantages in the world throws it all away over a sex scandal. Maybe your next move should be to D.C. with like-minded folks."

"My next move is to untangle myself from these charges."

"Because you're not planning on going to prison."

"Nah, man. Prison is for Carter and Fortune."

"You're so sure I'm running with this." Miles wanted to be disgusted with me. Wanted to walk away from me. But he was just like me. A prosecutor who wanted to win cases above all else.

"You can't help yourself. At least something will come of this. Your career will be the Phoenix rising from the ashes of mine. Everyone wins."

AIME AUSTIN

Miles hesitated a long moment. But I knew he was like me, self-preservation would always win.

"I guess I have to call Casey," Miles said. He turned to go back into the building. Start the wheels of justice turning one more time.

"Go easy on her. She's a nice girl."

23

Dion
May 12, 2007

"Thanks for coming," I said when I let my father into my apartment.

"I don't think I've been here since you moved in." He looked around like he'd traveled to a foreign country, not two miles down the road.

"I'm glad to be back," I said. I loved my sister, but there was a reason we hadn't lived together in ten-plus years. "The reporters have left."

"Got bigger fish to fry." My father shook his head ruefully. "Want to say I'm surprised about that prosecutor. Did you know all along that he was one of...that he...?"

"No," I lied. I needed to keep him on my good side, not tarnish what was left of my reputation. "Sl...Jarrod kept that to himself for a long time. Told me right before trial."

AIME AUSTIN

"Sometimes I think this country is moving forward, is changing. Then something like this happens. Could have been a trial in Mississippi or Alabama during Klan times where the prosecutor is just as guilty or maybe even more so than the black man on trial." My dad went to my window. Looked down onto Overlook Boulevard. His hand lay on the windowsill, the entire weight of the history of unfairness to blacks bearing down on the wood.

"I don't know about the country, Dad. What's going to shake out in America. But I do know one thing."

"What's that?"

"That I was wrong." I hung my head in contrition. "What I did was wrong."

"Why did you do it, son? I know you talked to me and your mom. I still can't figure out why."

"I wanted to be successful," I said as plainly as I could. "I just couldn't figure out how to do that. Jarrod was starting something, and I was really good at it. Really good. I could solve almost any problem. It started out innocent enough, I think. Then it got worse. Then it was something I had to hide—cover up."

My father hefted himself from the windowsill. Walked from one side of the living room to the other.

"What now?"

"That's why I called you." I took a deep breath, ready to lay out the plan I'd been thinking about for a couple of days. I wasn't ready before, but I was now. That trial had scared me straight in a way that nothing else had.

"What do you need?"

"I can't stay in Cleveland. I don't have a record, so I should be able to get a job. But not in a place where everyone knows my name. I might even change it, but I'll leave that decision for later."

"Makes sense. Fortune isn't so fortunate anymore." I knew it took a lot for him to tell that joke. I gave him the best smile I could muster which was admittedly pretty weak. "Where do you want to go?"

"Atlanta? Grandma and Grandpa are there. I was hoping you could call them. Ask them to let me stay while I look for a job. Get on my feet."

I had no idea if they knew about the arrest, the charges, the trial. I didn't want to make that call myself. I wanted my father to smooth it over.

"You need money?"

"No, that I've got covered. The county doesn't forfeit. So after paying off the girls, I've got some savings put aside. I don't need a place to stay, actually. It's just that I don't want to live alone when I get there. I need someone to keep me accountable. So I don't get sidetracked by someone like Jarrod again."

There was some truth to that. What I needed even more, though, was to live with some people who had a regular life. Went to the grocery store. Went to church. Went to places like Applebee's and ate too much. My parents loved me, but with a whole lot of conditions. My grandparents' love was unconditional.

"I didn't tell them, you know."

"Thanks. I...didn't know."

"I didn't want my mother thinking the worst of you. They kind of loved having you down there when you were in school, since you visited them every other week. Drove your grandfather around when he broke his leg."

"Grandma made me some great food. Better than the stuff they served in the cafeteria."

"I still think that's too bad that all the schools turned to corporate food. It was good when there were people really cooking in the kitchen. Now it comes off a truck. Truly a shame."

I needed to wrangle what I wanted before Dad went down a road that would only lead to some long lecture about the state of…corporate America to start, rounding on the state of food production, then ending with these all being reasons I needed to earn a graduate degree.

"So what do you think of the idea? Atlanta?"

"It might be good for you. What exactly are you going to put on your resume?"

"That I worked for Intraport. That was the last LLC name I filed for. I'll tell them the truth. That I handled bureaucratic government filings. That I handled logistics. That I took care of human resources. That it went out of business. I can do what I did anywhere." When my father's eyebrows rose, I rushed to clarify. "For a paycheck. Not cash under the table. Just honest work. Maybe I'll even meet a girl…a woman down there. Someone I can build a life with. A family with. For so long I thought I wanted something different, but now, Dad, I think I want something like what you and Mom have."

There was a long moment of silence where I thought I'd maybe oversold it. Not that what I'd said wasn't true exactly, but not all at once. Maybe over the next ten years, at least some of that could happen.

"I'm proud of you, son. Proud that you are ready to own up, make a change. Jesus forgives you. I forgive you. You have to forgive yourself."

"Working on it."

The chain on the front door to my living room rattled when someone pounded on the door. My mind immediately went to Sledge. I had been careful, though, very careful not to cross him. But after he released that tape of the prosecutor even though we weren't under threat anymore meant that he was mad and out for blood. It was another reason I had to leave. I didn't want to be having to look over my shoulder all the time worried about him.

"Who—"

"FBI. Open up."

I locked eyes with my dad. His shrug was slight. I walked to the door and flipped the deadbolt, turned the knob. The door flew open, banging against my arm.

"Dion Fortune?"

I nodded automatically even though I didn't want to admit it was me. My father had been calling that name my whole life, though, and I couldn't help but respond. I almost laughed because this was looking like one time I wasn't going to be fortunate.

"What you got?" my dad asked once the agents poured into the room.

Stocky white guy with a salt-and-pepper brush cut came forward. Handed me what looked like court papers. I skimmed it quickly. United States District Court for the Northern District of Ohio was the header. On the left was the United States against me and Jarrod Carter. On the right in bolded letters were the words "Arrest Warrant." I didn't read any further before handing it to my dad.

Before anyone asked, I put my hands behind my back. I was cuffed.

"When can I call my lawyer?"

"After you're processed," the agent said.

"Who are you?"

"Lou Valdespino. And this here is Miles Siegel. I think your lawyer already knows who we are."

I nodded my head and let them push me down the stairs and out the door. I hope my dad locked the door on the way out. I wasn't worried about being gone too long, but still didn't like to leave my door unlocked. If I'd listened to anything Casey said, it was about Contained.

Once that prosecutor's father had dismissed the charges against us, there weren't any more anyone could do to us. Unless the United States government had come up with a list of bogus crimes, I couldn't be charged again. Once in the back of the FBI's SUV, I laid my head back against the seat and closed my eyes to relax before the relentlessness of mug shots and cavity searches and fingerprinting.

I'd miss my sister and her kids and my mom and my dad, but maybe I needed to get down to Atlanta sooner rather than later.

24

Casey
May 16, 2007

"Ms. Cort," the county deputy said. "Long time no see." I glanced down at his name badge. Didn't remember him.

"Hi?"

"It's okay. White guys in law enforcement uniforms are a dime a dozen around here. It's *your* name that I remember. I think it's cute." He said it in a way that suggested he thought I might be cute. Took me a long few seconds to realize that he was probably flirting. It was such a foreign concept that it rattled me.

I looked at him a little more closely now. The deputy was cute if not a few years younger than me. In another lifetime maybe, I'd have flirted back. But I was over law and order guys. Dating a prosecutor hadn't worked out—twice. There was something about Ron that made me think maybe I'd figured this dating thing out. It was slow going, but that was a good thing. I'd jumped in too quick before when the promise of marriage and family had been dangled in front of me like a carrot before a donkey.

"I'm here to see two people," I said handing over my bar card. "Jarrod Carter and—"

"Dion Fortune. They're famous. You're practically famous too."

I thought infamous would have been a better word for my clients but didn't correct him.

"I didn't know you had federal people here." My only experience in federal court had been with clients who were not in jail. I'd always thought there was some fancy federal facility that housed those charged in the district court. I'd been surprised when Dion had called from the county jail.

"Contract. They don't have their own facility."

"Right. Well, can you get them down to an attorney room?" I wasn't interested in prolonging my chat with this guy, cute or not.

"That's their right," he said. "Can I ask you, though, why you do this? You seem like a smart girl. Do you want to represent criminals the rest of your life?"

Right then he stopped being cute. I sighed. I didn't have time to do this dance. I waved my hand.

"Yada, yada constitutional rights and all that. Which room?"

"Sorry. I didn't mean to offend," he said, as if backing away from his bold statement was going to increase his chances for a date.

I didn't tell him he'd gone from maybe five percent to well into the negative digits. That I had a suitor and a lover, and that was enough to juggle. Instead I smiled. It's what women learned to do to placate men. I was no exception. "No apologies needed."

"Room six." He pointed down the hall toward the last room on the right.

"Thanks." I smiled again. "I'll see you later."

I hefted my bag onto my shoulder more securely and started down the hall when I heard my name again.

"Casey! Hold up."

If I'd moved to New York or D.C. or somewhere with millions more people, maybe I'd be more anonymous. I turned around at the familiar voice. "Miles. Lou. What are you doing here? Surely you weren't going to question my clients after they invoked their right to counsel."

"When you called to make sure they were here, we figured it would be a good time," Miles said.

I lifted my bag and put it on the floor. My shoulder was starting to ache.

"Good time for what?" I looked at my watch. To maximize the time I could spend with clients, visits were best arranged between counts. When the deputies did one of their five or six time a day counts, the inmates had to be in their cells. Between the flirty sheriff in the front and Miles, I was burning daylight.

"To talk deal. A lot of money and resources have gone to these guys. Two trials. Federal investigation. Where there's smoke in this case, there's a huge amount of fire. We don't want a month-long dog and pony show. It's time to put this to bed."

Miles didn't sound any different than most prosecutors. They made it sound like your clients agreeing to go to jail was doing everyone a favor somehow. If I were in charge, I'd require every defendant go to trial. Prosecutors weren't half as good as they thought they were. If the two trials against Carter hadn't proved that, I don't know what did.

"So you can get back to counterterrorism and jailing non-violent drug offenders?" I asked. The last was a poke straight at my ex. I knew it was the one part of his job that he had moral qualms about, as he should. The unbroken line from slavery to Jim Crow to the prison industrial complex was a hard one for any prosecutor to defend.

"It's the job." Miles shrugged. Though the flick of his eyes away from mine told a different tale.

"I'm going to talk to them, alone, in confidence as is their right," I said. I had no need to accommodate Miles and Lou. The fact that they'd come looking for me told me all I needed to know. My clients were starting out with an upper hand. "If you want to cool your jets out here, that's up to you."

"We'll be across the street getting some coffee." Miles bounced in his leather ankle boots. "Text me, if they're open to a deal. Do you need my number?"

I cut my eyes at him. "I'm sure I can locate it."

***

"How long before we're out?" Carter asked the minute I stepped into the room. I took off my coat, set my bag on an empty chair, and sat before I answered. I looked from Jarrod Carter to Dion Fortune then back to Carter.

"I don't know." I shrugged.

"What do you mean you don't know? My niece has the funds to post bail or bond or whatever you call it here. We go home, you file whatever papers you need to show Contained, then this case is done once and for all."

Carter had it all figured out in his mind. For once I had the upper hand. He wasn't at all going to like what I was about to say.

"I'm going to disappoint you, then."

"What you mean?" Carter leaned forward. Got into my space. Tried to intimidate me. I didn't lean back. There wasn't a thing for me to worry about. Not in here. Not from him.

"Your little stunt may have cost you your freedom."

"Stunt?"

"Why did you release the tape of Tom Brody? Why did you send it to the prosecutor's office and Victoria Greenlee? You were already free. What in the hell did you hope to accomplish?"

The *why* didn't matter, but I was curious. It was the one piece of the puzzle I couldn't figure out. He'd been acquitted—twice. Tom was guilty and had gotten away, but so had Carter and Fortune for that matter.

They'd all done bad. No one had paid the price, really. I'd figured everyone would take their toys, go home, and live to be free another day.

I'd thought the prisoner's dilemma had played out exactly as it should. No one talked. Everyone was free. Then I'd turned on my TV to see a picture of my other ex-fiancé on the news on a split screen with some heavily edited and blurred video of him having sex with a prostitute—presumably one of Sledge's girls.

"He was so smug," Carter said. "I thought everybody should know he was as dirty as I was."

I shook my head in wonder. For someone so damned smart, who'd always played it cool, he'd gotten hot headed and stupid. So many times one of the nuns or Jesuit priests would say, "pride goeth before a fall."

Maybe if Carter had gone to Catholic school, he'd have been able to restrain himself. The older I got, the more I thought what I'd learned in religion classes and cast aside the moment I'd had my diploma in hand hadn't been all bad.

"As your attorney I need to inform you of a few things," I started. I took a deep breath. It was all going to be bad news. It was time to rip off the Band-Aid.

"Go ahead," Carter said. Like always, he spoke for them both.

I laid my palms flat on the table.

"First, bail in federal court looks nothing like it does in Common Pleas."

Carter looked incensed. "What? Of course there's bail. I'll do whatever I need to."

"Not in federal court. Doesn't work at all the same. District court has something they call pre-trial release, but I'm going to bet that you two will not qualify. No judge is going to let you walk out of here with an ankle bracelet and a wave. A bail hearing for you will be an entire dog and pony show in and of itself.

"A magistrate or judge is going to want to know about your community ties, family ties, where the source of the bail money comes from. The seriousness of the crime. The threat to any victims. I could go on, but I won't. Not to say it can't happen. It'll be a bigger hurdle to jump than a five-minute hearing in the arraignment room."

"Doesn't matter," Carter said. "I can do a few days or weeks while you file the Contained papers. I did two and a half years."

Dion didn't say anything. For years, his whole job it seemed had been to be quiet, and he was still doing it.

"Second, there's no Contained," I said, dropping the other bigger, heavier shoe.

"What do you mean? I heard you explain it to us not once but twice." Carter must have been getting loud, because one of the deputies tapped on the door. I turned my face toward the slim square of wire-reinforced glass and nodded to let him know that everything was fine. I did not need to be rescued. "It's what you used to kneecap the prosecutor's case."

Glad I'd paid attention in law school, I started to explain.

"There's a thing called dual sovereignty. Ohio is one jurisdiction. The United States of America is another. Just because you were acquitted by the state—twice—doesn't mean that the U.S. Attorney's office can't go after you."

I didn't add that they probably wouldn't have if he hadn't provoked Tom Brody. Hindsight was perfect sight, though. The damage had already been done. There was no reason to rehash Carter's stupid, stupid move.

"Jesus fucking Christ." It was the first thing Fortune had said during the visit. The way he cut his eyes at his former boss told me it was unlikely they'd be tied together much longer.

"He's not going to help you in this case," I said. If prayers worked that way, none of my clients would be in the messes they were in. True contrition was not a get out jail free card.

"How much time are we looking at?" Carter asked.

"Twenty to life. That's on the sex trafficking alone. Twenty for holding someone against their will. The life is for the sex. This doesn't even include RICO which is another whole thing to account for."

Dion looked like he wanted to shit his pants. If I didn't represent both of them, I'd tell him to make the deal. There was no more prisoner's dilemma. It was every man for himself. Jarrod Carter had inadvertently fucked him over. The only way out was to fuck him back.

"What's next? How long before trial?" Carter asked.

"A hundred days at the most. They have thirty days to formally indict you. Seventy days after that until they have to bring you to trial."

"What's our defense? If you could beat the first two, let's go for broke." I was momentarily heartened by his faith in me to beat these charges a third time.

"Here's the last thing I have to tell you," I offered.

"What?" Carter asked.

"I can't represent you."

"Why not?"

"Federal court is not my specialty. Ethics rules say that attorneys should never practice outside of their competency." This was ninety-five percent true. I wasn't ready to bootstrap my much-needed education on federal criminal defense onto the backs of my clients. "I would do the two of you a disservice," I continued. "You'll need to find new counsel. And my advice to the both of you—" I looked between them, letting my gaze linger on Fortune for a few seconds longer than Carter. "—is get separate attorneys."

"Who—"

"I wish I could help, but you'll have to figure it out yourselves," I said. I did not want to be in the same situation I'd been in with Justin. Half in. Half out. Half monitoring how another lawyer would affect their cases. "You're pretty resourceful guys. I think you'll be okay."

I slipped on my coat. Lifted my bag and shook both their hands in my final goodbye. I knocked at the locked door and the deputy let me out. I strode down the hall back to the huge lobby.

Miles and his FBI sidekick were there. They didn't even have coffee cups in hand. They'd probably never left the building.

"So..." Miles prompted me to pause on my way out the doors.

"So? No deal today. Can't predict the future."

"Can we set up a meeting?" Miles asked. "We should have the formal indictment in a few days. We're going to push back against bail. Challenge the source of their money. Probably start a forfeiture action as well…"

"Maybe you can…set up a meeting. Not with me."

"Why not?" Miles asked. He looked around like more people were going to materialize from thin air. "Did they finally get separate counsel?"

"I'm not their counsel, so I can't say."

"You're not representing them?"

I was surprised to hear the same surprise in Miles' voice that I'd heard in Carter's. He'd been there when my first and last federal case had gone south before I'd even gotten out of the gate. My client had money forfeited. He'd had no receipts and I'd had no defense. Nearly twenty thousand in cash had disappeared like magic into federal coffers.

"You may recall that federal court isn't my forte. I'm not willing to practice on them. They need someone or some ones who can pull out all the stops." I was brutally honest.

"And that's not you?"

"Not today." I reached out and shook first Lou's hand, then Miles'. "Good luck. You finally got the big case. Hope it brings you whatever you're looking for."

I turned on my heel and walked out on Miles Siegel and Lou Valdespino. On Jarrod Carter. On Dion Fortune. On girls in containers. On Tom's secrets.

If I never had to see any of them again, it wouldn't be too long. I pulled my phone from my pocket. Slid up the screen. Texted first Ron, then Lulu. I needed to get my life back.

25

Tom
May 20, 2007

My father, and Andrew and Simon for that matter, had told me to stay away from the TV. For the most part, I'd heeded their warning that nothing good would come from watching the news coverage of my arrest.

Silence, though, nearly drove me crazy. I'd kept the television on and the volume low all day and night so I didn't feel so alone. Mostly tuned to movie channels.

I couldn't remember the last time I'd had hours and days to myself. I hadn't taken more than a few days' vacation in the ten years since law school. Dad had promised me my penance wouldn't last much longer. Someone in the legal community would give me a job. It was only a matter of patience.

I'd turned down my mother's invitation to move back home, at least temporarily. Battling my personal demons in

my apartment was far easier than suffering their near constant condemnation. That I saved for Sunday dinners which
were now mandatory.

I was standing in my kitchen deciding between Doritos
and Coke or Fritos and Arizona iced tea when something on
the tube caught my eye. It was someone in one of those
weird shadow things they did when a whistleblower was
hiding their identity. I fished between the couch cushions
for the remote and turned up the sound. Victoria Greenlee
was sitting on a news set I hadn't seen before.

"Today in this special report segment, I'm speaking with
Stephanie," she started. "We're withholding your last name
per your request. Thanks for joining me today."

"Thanks for having me."

My butt hit the couch before I knew my knees had given
out. I'd know that voice anywhere. It was Destiny. I looked
at the outline of her head and shoulders. I was ninety-nine
percent sure it was her. I turned the volume even higher.

"How do you feel about federal charges being brought
against this so-called Sledge Hammer?" Greenlee asked.

"It's good I guess." Stephanie's voice was shy, hesitant.
It had been nothing like that when she'd been with me. She
continued, "He probably needs to go to jail for what he did."

"You're not sure?" Greenlee asked. Her face was screwed
up in what I think was supposed to be incredulity.

"It's hard I guess," Stephanie said. "I feel like it's as much
my fault as his, but no one has come to arrest me even
though I committed crimes as much as he did."

The prosecuting attorney's office had made a big deal
about how they weren't going to prosecute the victims. Not
from the container case. Not a single editorial writer,
though, had pointed out how vice was still picking up working girls from Lorain Avenue on a nearly weekly basis.

The hypocrisy stood without comment. Lorraine Pope came out smelling like a rose. I was not so lucky. Something told me that I'd never grace the front of another publication as the most eligible bachelor in northeastern Ohio. Lorraine Pope, however, would ride her high horse to higher office.

I made a Herculean effort to put a stop to my thoughts and tuned back into the interview.

"Tell us how you came to work for Jarrod Carter," Greenlee asked.

"Dion Fortune was my boyfriend at first," Stephanie started. "At least that's what I thought."

"He wasn't?"

"Probably not. Except for a couple of times when he took me out to dinner, we didn't really have dates. I always went to his apartment. We watched movies. He made me drinks. I liked hanging out with him."

"Were these alcoholic drinks when you were underage?"

"I guess. Weren't my first. I sometimes drank a beer or two at home when my stepfather would…would…rape me. Helped me forget, you know. I liked the buzz."

My stomach churned. I knew what Stephanie was going to say next. I'd heard this story before. It was always the same.

A father or pastor or mother's boyfriend violated a girl. She ran away and got a job doing the one thing she knew how to do best. If the girl was lucky, her only addiction was alcohol. If she wasn't, it was crack cocaine or heroin. Then the drugs became a bigger crime than prostitution. Felony beat misdemeanor any day of the week. I pushed down on my stomach to keep it from betraying me. I turned up the volume even higher.

"Dion made me mudslides. They was sweet. Made me happy. He never tried anything, though. Thought he respected me. Now my counselors at New Day Sanctuary say he was doing something called grooming."

"Did you know about the prostitution?" Greenlee asked.

"I knew he hustled. He said it wasn't drugs. Could have been anything. Scrap metal. Car parts. People do lots of things in the hood."

"When did you find out?" Greenlee's voice was a whisper.

"The night he...initiated me. That's what my counselor calls it. If girls make it through that first night, they, the pimps, I mean, usually know that they can keep us."

"We will be back with more of container girl Stephanie's story right after this."

A commercial for a car dealership came on the screen. I hit a button on the DVR to pause it. My landline phone was ringing, probably had been for ten minutes. I pulled the cord from the wall. Silence filled the apartment. When I hit play again, Greenlee's overly made up face filled the screen. Her pause was dramatic. I held my breath.

"Do you remember Tom Brody?" the reporter asked.

My heart sped up. I wiped my hands on my sweats. I wanted to turn it off. Tune it out. But I couldn't do anything but watch.

"Yes," Destiny...Stephanie said. "He was one of the guys."

"How old were you the first time you met the prosecutor?" I don't know if it was my imagination, but Greenlee put a lot of emphasis on the word prosecutor.

"I didn't know nothing about his job," Stephanie said. "He didn't talk about that."

"Your age?" Greenlee pressed.

"I'm thinking I was seventeen or eighteen," Stephanie answered. I breathed a huge sigh of relief. Sledge had said one thing about her age. The truth had been another. I was never so relieved to be the victim of false advertising.

"So you weren't underage?" Greenlee pressed. The reporter was not great at masking her disappointment.

"Not then. I mean the first time, I was fourteen."

"But not with the prosecutor?"

"No, but with lots of others. Maybe hundreds."

"What kinds of things did Tom go for?" Greenlee was past crimes and now into salacious details.

"Tom Brody was the least of my problems," Stephanie said. Her undisguised voice was verging on angry. "When you came to New Day to talk to me, you said this interview was going to be about the...what you say...the exploitation of underage girls by hundreds of men in this city.

"But it's about that prosecutor, not me. Not all the other girls. It's about him. Maybe you need to talk to him, then. He can tell you why he came over to the other side of town to have sex with some poor black girl."

The camera switched to Greenlee as Stephanie abruptly stood, pulled off her microphone wire, and walked away from the cameras.

I turned off the set and went into my kitchen for a stiff shot of espresso. I had a job interview in an hour. Hopefully everyone at the firm was billing hours and not watching TV in the morning.

***

"Miriam Shively, nice to meet you. You and Ted Strohmeyer were in the same class at Cleveland State?" The older woman shook my hand. When I'd checked out her resume on the Morrell Gates website, I'd seen that she'd graduated law school about a decade before me.

Her smile was warm if not completely genuine. I didn't want to know what kind of short straw she'd drawn to get me on her morning agenda. I smiled big and played along. This wasn't an interview exactly. I'd skipped that step.

Simon had secured me a position at the firm. I took it knowing that I would not get to be picky about either the department or the assignments I worked on. I was to take what was given without complaint. As long as I billed my required hours, I'd get paid and my professional reputation would be saved.

"No, he was a year or two ahead, actually," I answered. "We were kids there together and now he's a partner here. So weird how everyone grows up."

Miriam nodded then turned. I followed her to an office that was neither first-year associate small nor senior partner big. It was a generic white box with pressed wood furniture and a long narrow window that overlooked Tower City. She sat in her chair, and I took that as a cue to do the same across from her desk. She turned to her monitor, typed something on the keyboard, then turned back toward me when she was done.

"I've been partner here for eleven years. You will be of counsel. Not an associate, but I still run the show."

Of counsel had been the title I'd been offered. The salary was better than the prosecuting attorney's office, though probably not as much as others from my class were making. I had signed the employment contract without complaint.

"Yes. Arthur wants me to work with you...for you," I stammered out. Firm hierarchy and politics were something I was going to have to figure out—fast.

"Do you know what I do?" Shively asked.

"He wasn't clear." I said. Arthur had been magnanimous in his favor. I hadn't asked questions.

"Toxic torts," she said. "I defend the indefensible to the best of my abilities. My clients are a stable three or four million of billings a year."

"Wow," popped out of my mouth. I was honestly surprised. The way Arthur had described Miriam, I'd thought she was on the bottom rungs of the hierarchy.

She shrugged it off.

"Peanuts compared to the insurance or financial industry. But that's rust belt Cleveland for you. Postindustrial means cleaning up the mess of the industries that are long gone."

"Sounds interesting," I said, because it sounded like the kind of thing I was supposed to say.

"It isn't," Shively said dismissively. "It's a job that pays for my mortgage, a nice car, and one vacation a year. It'll be your redemption job, I guess. Or what you're using to keep a low profile or whatever."

"I—"

"It doesn't matter either way." I was relieved that she wasn't going to probe into the charges against me. The misdemeanor I'd pled to or the bar discipline that had come in the form of a letter of censure. "Did someone go over billing and all that with you?"

"Yeah. It's new, watching the clock every quarter hour."

"You'll get used to it. Doesn't matter as much on this one as other cases."

"What are we working on?" I asked. I'd start formally in a week. I was hoping to take home some files and get my civil law legs up under me after years of being on the other side of the law.

Miriam stood, closed her office door. Sat down in the chair next to me. Her look had gone from friendly to serious.

"Look I'm only going to say this once. Don't fuck up. No in-firm sex scandals, please. I don't need the hassle. This means, for you, secretaries are off limits. Women associates are off limits. Partner's wives are off limits. Prostitutes are off limits. I never want to have this discussion again. And I never, ever want to hear about your sex life. Capiche?"

"You must not have watched the news coverage. No one here is my type." The black–white thing had played out on the news over and over again as if interracial sex were new to this country.

"Funny and not. You skated on that by the skin of your teeth. That girl, the one on TV, could have been underage."

My heart sank. My belief that no one had seen Greenlee's special report had been foolhardy.

"But she wasn't."

Miriam Shively shook her head. Closed her eyes for a long second. She leaned forward, obliterating any semblance of personal space. Her breath smelled like butterscotch. Her finger pointed at me.

"I already babysit Ted Strohmeyer. I can't look after you as well, okay? There aren't enough hours in the day to bill and babysit. I have no idea whether you can do this job or not. That I guess we'll figure out as we go along. But no fuckups.

"I need to keep my job here. I don't have a rich family to fall back on. Keep it in your pants. Don't talk to the clients without my permission. You have any questions, you ask me before you do anything. We clear?"

"Crystal."

"Welcome aboard."

26

Dion
May 25, 2007

"Jacob Schmidt." The attorney stuck out his hand. I shook it. We were in the jail's attorney room. This was the first time I'd been in here without Sledge.

"Thanks for meeting me," I said. I was grateful one of the city's top defenders had agreed to meet with me. I wasn't sure if anyone would want to represent someone whose case was nearly a sure loser. That was the answer my father had gotten when he'd interviewed Vernon Dinwiddie and a bunch of others. Before he went down the list any further, I told him to go straight to the top. Someone who'd done federal cases, RICO cases, infamous cases. That had landed me the guy in front of me.

"You have a hell of a case here," he said.

Before he launched into selling me on some kind of defense, I put my cards on the table.

"I want a deal."

"Talked to Miles Siegel, he's the prosecutor on this case. If you and Carter don't go to trial, then you get two hundred forty months—twenty years—straight time. You'll be out when you're fifty. Given the publicity on this one, it's not a bad offer."

"I don't want twenty years. I want less."

"The only way to do that is if you testify against Carter. Your cases have been joint all along. The state tried you together."

"It's time to sever. That's the term, right? Sever. I don't want to be tried with Sledge or make a deal alongside him. I'm my own person and don't want to do time for his crimes."

"What do you have?" He didn't need to ask any more. He was asking if I was a snitch. If I was willing to turn on Sledge. For the past ten years or so and up until now, the answer would have been no. With these federal charges, things had changed.

"I need immunity."

"It's possible," Schmidt said with confidence that slowed down my heart for the first time in days. "What do you have?"

"You know that tape of the prosecutor?" I asked.

"Tom Brody. At least the girl was of age. Saved him from being disbarred," Schmidt said, as if saving some white guy's reputation and job was the most important thing in this whole case. I didn't give a shit about Tom Brody. He had a family to save him. I didn't really have anyone.

"I don't care about that," I said. "What I'm saying is that it isn't the only tape. There are scores of tapes with other girls. In these, I promise the girls are underage. That prosecutor, the light-skinned guy, he would probably get promoted off this one."

"What else?" Schmidt prompted, as if having sex with underage girls wasn't enough.

"Murder. Maybe not that exactly, but a girl died her first time...during her...initiation," I stuttered out. I could hardly think of Dashanique without my stomach knotting up.

"That's on tape?" Schmidt looked skeptical "Why?"

"Sledge always called it insurance. If we was going down, he said, he'd take all the motherfuckers with him."

"Why now?" Schmidt asked.

"Because Sledge...Jarrod Carter got greedy. We got off. Case was closed. But he was mad at the prosecutor. That's why he released that Destiny tape. He was still mad over those three years he got, even if it was Derek Waters' fault. Even if it was outside the county. Even when he'd served them. He fucked up a good thing. I was going to move to Atlanta, where I went to college, start over."

"Where'd you go to school?" he asked, as if he'd never known a black man to go to college. I almost wanted to launch into one of my father's lectures on the creation of historically black colleges and universities post-civil war. But I didn't, because I was paying by the hour.

"Clark Atlanta. My father's alma mater." I'd thrown that last bit in so he didn't think I was no uneducated nigger from the streets.

"Why crime?" Why did people keep asking me this? I wasn't the first nor last person to run a shady business. I wonder if mafia guys got this many questions.

"Not a lot out there for a black man, okay? I ran a successful business. Wall Street wasn't exactly hiring."

"If you say so." I let that one go. I was sure I could count the number of black men in finance on my one hand. Lawyers too. But no one wanted to be called out on that shit. White people liked to believe in a meritocracy where black people never had any merit. "Where are these tapes?" he pressed.

"Lawyer's office."

"Casey Cort? Your former lawyer. Why are they there?"

"Safekeeping. Didn't want them to turn up if there were warrants. The rest are in the Sleepy Time motel. In the office. In the safe."

"I'll collect all of it," he promised.

Despite the fact that I know he didn't care, I started running off at the mouth with excuses.

"I wasn't the mastermind, you know. I was a deputy. I took orders. I let a couple of girls go when it was clear they couldn't take it anymore. I had a conscience. I want credit for that."

"If what you say about these tapes is true, I'm pretty sure I can get your time reduced. Maybe one hundred twenty months—ten years. But that's probably the best we can do. I think if these tapes are how you like, immunity is off the table. Regret isn't enough. If that was the case, the federal prisons would be empty."

It wasn't the answer I wanted. But I was starting to make peace with punishment.

"I need to be in a separate prison from Sledge," I said. I wanted to live all of those ten years so I could get out.

"That I can promise you," Schmidt said.

"It'll have to be enough, I guess." I shook my head. This was never how I saw any of this turning out.

"Crime doesn't pay," Schmidt said.

I stood and waited to get my cuffs back on, go back to my cell. I didn't challenge his damned cliché.

27

"I feel like you've been ignoring me," I said to my best friend, Lulu. It was a far cry from what I wanted to say. That I thought she needed to dump Sinclair. That he was taking over her life, and not in a good way. That if she didn't make a change she'd end up old and bitter when her married lover left *her* for a younger model.

"Ignoring you? Every time I looked up, I saw you on TV or in the *Plain Dealer*," Lulu said. "Didn't seem like a great time to hit you up." Her excuse was flimsy. I didn't challenge it. Now didn't feel like the right time.

I picked up my chopsticks, fiddled with them. Put them down in favor of a fork. We were in her office eating Chinese takeout, and I was proud of myself for eating fried vegetables over fried rice. It wasn't perfect, but it was one of the dietary improvements I'd made since I'd lost what I now thought of as my post-law school depression weight. The weight I'd put on when everything in my world had felt bleak.

"How are you?" I pressed. I needed proof that her life hadn't gone to hell in a hand basket since Carter had come back into my life.

"Good. Things with Sinclair are better."

"He seemed a little demanding." That was my diplomatic approach. I wanted to say *abusive*. I'd seen enough episodes of daytime talk shows to see red flags waving in the stiff Lake Erie breeze. I didn't want to alienate my best friend, though. In my gut, I knew she'd need me someday. And someday would probably come sooner rather than later.

"Living with someone is very different than having a college boyfriend, for sure," she said.

"Someone in my space would be a lot," I pointed out.

"Would they?" a familiar male voice asked. My head whipped around while my skin started to tingle and my stomach started to flutter. It was Ron. Mortification stole through my cheeks.

"I'm an only child…a single child," I stuttered. I'd been trying to convince Lulu that she might be better alone. I *had not* been ruling out marriage or cohabitation.

"Does that mean if I asked, you wouldn't live with me?" He winked. I dropped my fork. Thankfully had to bend to pluck the plastic utensil from the carpet. I hoped that in those few moments the blush had receded from my cheeks.

"For you, I'd reconsider." It was the boldest thing I'd ever allowed myself to say. I stared squarely at his…chest, hoping I hadn't scared him away.

"I thought it was your voice." His own was warm and full of affection. I wanted to banish Lulu from her own office, wrap my arms around him and see how far a kiss could go. I had to blink twice to comprehend his next words. "Want to see a movie with me? Maybe dinner?" he asked.

"Sure, that would be great." I was very proud of myself for getting out a fully intelligible English sentence. The nuns would have been proud.

He leaned down, kissed me like he meant it.

"Gotta bill some hours. I'll text you later, okay?" He gave a jaunty salute and was almost out of the door before I responded.

"Perfect," I said with a nod.

When the sound of his shoes had receded all the way down the hall, Lulu squinted at me. "Ron? Really?"

"I like him. He's…he's nice." I wanted to kill myself for that tiny stumble in speech. Lulu pounced on it like a zoo lion on meat.

"You sound hesitant."

"I just wish he were more…I don't know, present." That was the most honest I'd been with her or myself. Ron did all the right things. Said all the right words. But dating him was like trying to hold on tight to smoke.

"What do you mean? You keep saying that Sinclair is way too present."

"Ron is the opposite, then." I sighed. "Way too absent. He shows up only half the time. The other half he's late. He always says it's work, but I feel like if he really liked me, he'd be around more."

"What does he say?"

"He doesn't. I mean he does. That's the thing. He keeps saying that he likes me. That he wants to be with me. That he wants the same things, marriage and family. But he seems kind of distant, like I can't quite reach him."

"What about Justin?" she asked. In that question I saw a hint of the old Lulu in the waggle of her eyebrows, the innuendo in her voice.

"What about him?" I whispered, eyeing her open office door.

"You're sleeping with him," she said matter-of-factly. We hadn't exactly talked much, but I'd spilled that bit one night after too much wine.

"Shhh. I haven't exactly shared that with Ron."

I got up and shut her door.

"Would you date Justin?" Lulu cocked her head.

"Justin isn't dating material." I'd thought this through. It was the thing that had popped into my head between worrying about trial strategy and whether my clients and Tom were going to get into a courtroom fistfight. "He's got this whole life. He's got his job and apartment and dog. Justin very much isn't looking for anything."

"Then why?" The *was I sleeping with him* part went unsaid.

"I don't know. It's something about him. We just click. It's easy. If he wanted a relationship, maybe. No not maybe. I can't hitch my life to someone who's just like me."

My phone pinged. I put down my fork and fished it from my purse. I was traveling light today. No messenger bag full of files to churn.

"Speaking of." I turned the phone toward my friend so she could see the sender name: Justin McPhee.

"Gonna go see him?"

"He wants to meet in his office," I pointed out. "Not sex. Probably a referral. Money talks. Gotta go. It was good getting together, though. Don't be a stranger, okay?"

Lulu was her own thing. It was hard to leave her in her office with only Sinclair to go home to. I wanted to tell her to run while she still could. I loved my best friend. I truly did. But Sinclair was bad for her. I didn't think it would end well, but I didn't have any evidence either. Just a gut feeling was all. I waved goodbye without ever really getting into all that. Maybe another day when she was ready to hear it. When I was ready to put my real feelings out on the table.

I walked back across Public Square then through Justin's lobby and up to his office. The receptionist waved me back without so much as a second glance. I knocked and twisted the knob. Justin glanced up to see who it was then his face broke out in what I assumed was an unintended smile.

"You rang?" I asked before I took a seat on his couch.

"I actually texted."

"So." I shrugged off my coat and bag. Made myself more comfortable. Maybe I'd switch out my bookshelf for a couch...when I could afford it. I quickly decided against it. I'd probably take too many naps, and besides, I'd have to keep clients off it to ever feel comfortable napping. Nope. I nixed the couch in my mind. Too much work.

"I want to talk about something serious," Justin said, bringing me back to the present.

My stomach plummeted to my knees. Serious was not on my agenda for today—probably not something an adult would say. So I didn't say anything at all. I just lifted my open right palm toward him. Prompting him to do the talking.

"Have you ever thought of doing plaintiff's work?"

That was not on the list of things I'd bargained for. For a panicky second, I thought he'd wanted to talk about our sex life. Then I got more panicky when I thought he might want to discuss the ethics of the Waters referral. Plaintiff's work? I tried to wrap my head around it.

"You mean like personal injury?" I asked. My brain immediately went to those bus bench or late morning TV ads screaming about how much money someone could get for their injury...minus thirty-three percent.

"You say it like it's ambulance chasing."

"Well...sometimes it feels like it's only one step up from Worker's Comp." Legal specialties had their own hierarchy with white shoe law firm mergers and acquisitions on top and injured workers at the bottom.

"Ouch."

"I mean no disrespect," I backpedaled. "I mean I might have considered it. But I was never in the position to bankroll a case with no guaranteed win and hope for a payday down the road."

There *had* been the money. The other was that I was mortified that I'd come up against lawyers like Ron and Lulu, who were on the white shoe side of that equation.

"What if I bankrolled the case?" Justin asked.

"What are you talking about here?" I searched my brain wondering if we'd had some post-coital conversation about accident cases that I didn't remember. I couldn't fish one out of recent memory.

"I have a case that I can't do alone," he started. He spread his hands wide on his desk. "I know that you don't want to go back to criminal and domestic exclusively, so I thought of you."

"What are we talking about here?"

"Strohmeyer."

I leaned forward upon hearing the name of my law school nemesis. Like Voldemort, I tried not to speak his name. "What did you say?"

"Strohmeyer. I have a group of plaintiffs with various cancers and suppressed immune systems. I have a doctor on board who's prepared to testify that mycotoxin by-products from the brewery are responsible for a cluster of cancers, infertility problems, and immunosuppressive issues in Brighthill."

"Myco...wow. That's huge. You say that Strohmeyer is causing this? They've been brewing beer forever. Why hasn't anyone sued before?"

"Manufacturing has been the backbone of this city for over a hundred years. This family has singlehandedly brought back an NFL team. Who would be on board for suing them?"

"No one with half a brain, but somehow you thought of me."

"You have no love lost for Ted Strohmeyer."

"That's true."

"Plus Morrell Gates is on the other side."

My blink was slow. Morrell Gates had pulled my post-law school job right from under me when I'd crossed Strohmeyer. I no longer had dreams about that life lost. Life with me at a firm and Tom with the county prosecutor's office. Us married with kids. That fantasy had died the moment I'd seen Tom walk into that motel room. "I'm not still bitter, you know."

"You believe in justice, though, right? A family, a child's right to live their life free from being poisoned." Justin's voice was impassioned.

"Of course." Who didn't?

"There's a bonus to being on the right side of the law."

"What's that?" I asked. So far my only bonus had been the ability to sleep at night. It was small comfort in the face of law school debt.

"This case could make you a millionaire. Settlement is estimated at thirty million."

"That's ten million dollars." Like people did after buying a lottery ticket, my mind wondered at all that I could do with that much money. My face must have given my greed away.

"See, you have to be on this case, Casey. You'd be brilliant."

I preened at the compliment. I wasn't so full of myself to think I'd won Carter's case on my merits only. I'm sure the Brody family knowledge of the ruin Sledge could cause had maybe a tiny bit to do with the acquittal. The win, though, defeating Tom and Nicole at their own game, had felt amazing. I screwed up my eyes. Justin was generous in bed, but that didn't mean he wanted to split a multi-million-dollar payday with me for no good reason I could see.

"Why would you want to share?"

"Come here," Justin said. He stood. I followed him from his office, down the long corridor, past at least ten other offices, to a room at the end. It had no brass plaque announcing it was an office or conference room. He produced a key from his pocket, stuck it in the doorknob, and turned. He pushed open the door. I'm not sure if it was a storage room or an office or even a conference room. What it was, though, was filled floor to ceiling with bankers' boxes. Dozens or maybe even hundreds of them. Like jellybeans in a jar, I couldn't count that high.

"I'm about to take the Lord's name in vain," I said, heading off the curse words that were about to exit my mouth.

"Yeah." Justin turned to me. Nodded. "This is why I'm willing to share. I need someone smart and driven with a decent sense of morality to help me tackle this. Are you in?"

Was I in? I'd need some time to separate my feelings of revenge against Morrell Gates. What was the saying, the best revenge was success? Time to decide whether or not any of this, facing down the Strohmeyers, or being in the constant company of someone whom I couldn't keep my hands off of after a single glass of wine was a bright idea. I needed to unwind that ball of twine.

"Give me the weekend to think about it," I said to him.

He turned off the light, closed and locked the door on my possible future.

Justin leaned down and planted his lips on mine. "Fair enough, Casey. I'll give you time to think."

Even though my phone was buzzing in my pocket—probably with a text from Ron—I turned fully toward Justin and kissed him full on the mouth. I was going to need more than a weekend to figure all of this out.

ABOUT THE AUTHOR

Aime Austin is the author of the Casey Cort Legal Thriller Series. Casey is almost always in trouble. Aime's full time job? Rescuing her. Good thing Aime's got experience. She practiced family and criminal law in Cleveland, Ohio for several years—so she has the skills for the job. When Aime isn't rescuing Casey from herself, she's hosting her podcast, *A Time to Thrill*, raising her son, or traveling between Budapest and Los Angeles.

www.ingramcontent.com/pod-product-compliance
Lightning Source LLC
Chambersburg PA
CBHW020820260626
47169CB00003B/760